ROSE'S CHOICE

A MORGAN'S RUN ROMANCE

M. LEE PRESCOTT

Published by Mt. Hope Press

Copyright 2016, M. Lee Prescott

ISBN: 978-0-9912855-9-4

For my beloved family and friends, who make every day extraordinary

CHAPTER 1

Facedown, forehead on Gracie's cool granite counter, Sam Morgan groaned. *My life, or at least my career, is over, and there isn't a goddamn thing I can do about it.* The café owner emerged from the kitchen with his burger, curly fries, and iced tea and set the food in front of him. "What's this? Valley's famous architect havin' a bad day?"

He gave the tall, thin cook a crooked smile. As usual, there were flecks of food sprinkled in her frizzy salt-and-pepper hair. "Something like that. Thanks, Gracie. This looks great."

"What're you doin' in town, anyway? Your dad's always claiming you can't get outta Flagstaff."

"I'm out at Spark Foster's. My team's called so many times since construction began, I decided to come down for a few days."

"I hear it's a doozy."

"Gonna be cool. Spark's got great taste."

"And deep pockets."

Sam groaned as he bit into his burger. "God, this is good. Nothing like this in Flagstaff."

"Baloney," she said, a pleased grin on her face. "So, Foster's house is a castle, I hear."

He raised one eyebrow. "Would I design a castle and spoil the valley? It'll fit right in with the landscape, promise."

"Got it hugging a mountain, do ya?" Her gray eyes looked up as the café door swung open and Rose Dillon walked in. "Gotta get back to work, but here's someone to cheer you up." With a nod to the young woman, Gracie disappeared through swinging doors.

Sam turned and waved as Rose approached. Lovely as always, he thought, a pang of guilt washing over him as the lithe ash blonde neared the counter, her soft hazel eyes full of warmth. It had been almost a year since he'd seen her. In true Morgan style, he had flirted shamelessly with her at his sister's wedding. In fact, they had danced nearly every dance together. He knew she was interested, very interested, so what did he do? Hightailed it back to Flagstaff right after the wedding and hadn't called or written since. *What a shit you are, Sam Morgan.*

"Hi, Sam. This is a surprise." The Morgan boys were all gorgeous—*God's gift to women,* or so their reputation went—and Sam was no exception. His longish, dark brown hair fell over one eye, and his soft chestnut-brown eyes held a mischievous light, even today, when he looked a little down in the dumps.

Warning bells clanged as Rose slipped onto a stool beside him. *Poor guy looks like he's lost his best friend, but it's his problem, not yours. Stay away. Don't get involved! This is the second Morgan brother to break your heart.*

"Hey, Rose. How're you doing?" He pushed a lock of hair from his eyes, smearing some of Gracie's special burger sauce across his cheek. Rose resisted the impulse to reach forward and wipe it off, her senses on high alert with him so near.

"You've got a bit of sauce on your face," she said.

He flushed crimson and grabbed a napkin, dabbing his cheek. "Better?"

"Yes." Rose smiled, unable to look away from the dark eyes. A runner, Sam Morgan was thinner, lankier than his three brothers. "Are you here working on the Foster house?"

"Guilty as charged."

"I hear it's beautiful."

You are too. What kind of an idiot turns his back on a gorgeous, well-respected pediatric neurosurgeon? Although she was smiling, her hazel eyes regarded him warily. Hair loose, she wore a diaphanous, sleeveless top, a light blue linen skirt, and beige sandals, her only adornment a thin silver necklace inlaid with turquoise and matching earrings. He suddenly realized he had been staring for several moments, holding the dripping burger in one hand.

"It's gonna be pretty spectacular when it's completed. Not because I designed it. Spark Foster has incredible taste, and he doesn't do anything halfway. His plans for furnishing it sound amazing. So, what brings you to town?"

"I spent last night with my folks. My dad's been sick this week, and Mom needed a break." Her parents, Martha and Jaybo Dillon, owned and operated a successful Valley winery, and were close friends and neighbors of the Morgans.

"Nothing serious, I hope?" He realized he still had the stupid burger in his hand and plunked it back on his plate. *How could I have danced with her last year and not noticed the curve of her chin and those lips like delicate, perfect rose petals? The top of her lacy white bra was just visible under her blouse, and he found himself remembering the feel of her soft, round breasts against his chest. Cut it out, Morgan! You're hurting and cruising for comfort wherever you can find it, no matter who gets caught in the crossfire.*

"Just a cold, but my dad's never been a good patient."

"Will you join me? As you can see, I'm having a late, messy lunch."

"Thanks, but I just ate. I was stopping to get an iced tea for the road." Sam's face fell, and Rose resisted the urge to reach out and touch him. *There is something different about him. Where is the cocky hot-shot architect who turns heads wherever he goes? This man seems sad, vulnerable, not at all like a Morgan.*

"You're not heading back to Tucson, are you?" he asked.

"'Fraid so."

"Bummer. I was going to ask you to have dinner with me."

"Sorry, I have plans tonight."

He grinned, the gorgeous, wolfish grin the Morgan boys did so well. "A hot date?"

"As a matter of fact, yes."

"Double bummer," he said, and meant it. *This is what happens when you're a heartless cad, Sam Morgan. The beauties get away.* "Hope he treats you well."

"Yes, he does."

"Well, at least let me buy you an iced tea and keep me company while I eat like a pig." He waved to Maria, the waitress, who brought Rose a tea and refilled his glass.

"Thanks," Rose said, giving him a sweet, guarded smile. "How are things in Flagstaff?"

He blanched, pushing his plate away, burger half-eaten. "Couldn't be worse, if you want to know the truth."

"I'm sorry to hear that," she said, not wanting to pry. "I thought you were doing so well."

Sam had been home for four days and hadn't yet had the heart or stomach to confide in his family. Somehow, Rose, staring at him, her soft eyes full of concern, felt safe. He had to tell someone. "Have you got a few minutes?"

Rose nodded, surprised to see the seriousness of his gaze. "Of course."

"How about over there?" he asked, indicating an empty booth in the corner. She nodded, following him. "I'm all set, Maria," he called, grabbing his tea, but leaving the burger behind.

Rose sat, waiting for him to begin. His hands trembled. As she longed to reach over and take them in hers, she recalled the feel of his strong arms around her. She had loved Sam's older brother Ben from childhood, but that had been puppy love compared to the grown-up feelings she'd had for Sam, feelings she had believed he shared. So she had let down her guard, and another Morgan had broken her heart.

Now she was dating Dan—polite, respectful Dan. He might be a little full of himself, but he was steady and reliable. They both worked at the Heavers Clinic, where he was completing a neuro fellowship before seeking a permanent position. The relationship would probably peter out as had many of her previous relationships but she did enjoy his company. Dan was three years younger than she, and Mr. Sad and Gorgeous sitting across from her, a year younger. *What is it with me and younger men?*

"The truth is," he said, meeting her eyes, "I don't have to be here at this stage of Spark's building, but I had to get outta Dodge."

"Oh?"

"My firm is small. There were two senior partners and two junior people, myself and another guy who does mostly small commercial projects. We have a bunch of staffers, but we were struggling to meet the workload. A couple of our projects, including my brother's and sister's homes, have been featured in a bunch of trade and architectural journals."

"As well they should have. They're extraordinary."

"I was pleased with them, but what's truly extraordinary is their setting. The Valley makes them extraordinary."

"I think that's modesty talking," she said, smiling.

He shrugged, smiling. "Anyway, the PR brought in a ton of work. We were scrambling to cover jobs and the senior partners don't like to turn away work, especially jobs like Spark's, so they decided to expand and hire a couple of hot-shots. One's a junior partner like me and Roy, but they had to make the other one a senior partner 'cause she's already pretty major. Name's Meryl Wainwright. She's from San Diego, but was looking to relocate to the area cause her dad's in Sedona. She came in like gangbusters five months ago and has brought in a lot of clients. She's talented, aggressive and innovative.

"About six weeks ago, her boyfriend hightailed it back to California, and that's when the trouble started. She began flirting and coming on to me whenever we were alone. Then she started asking to have coffee, a drink after work, all ostensibly to go over work, but the conversations were all about her and her interest in knowing me better. She's at least ten years older than me and not my type. Besides, I make it a rule never to date people from work. I made it clear that I wasn't interested, but Meryl is used to getting what she wants.

"Last week she proposed dinner to go over plans for a joint project. I suspect she requested that I be assigned to the job, even though I'm swamped with several other things. Anyway, I consented to dinner, and we went to a restaurant in Flagstaff that has a few private rooms, one of which Meryl had booked. The waitress had barely closed the door after delivering our drinks and taking our orders when Meryl was all over me. I immediately extracted myself from her clutches and made it clear that nothing was going to happen.

"She backed off, but it was a very tense meal, all business. From my standpoint, it was a relief. She was clearly pissed, but we got the planning done and said good night. The next morning when I got to the office, the shit hit the fan—pardon my language. I walked in and Bob Rayburn, one of the senior partners, asked me to step into his office. The other senior, Alcera Davos, was already there. They didn't beat around the bush, but told me straight out that Meryl had spoken to Alcera and was bringing a charge of sexual harassment against me."

Rose gasped, "Oh, Sam, how dreadful. Did they back you up?"

"I'm pretty sure Bob doesn't believe a word of Meryl's story. I couldn't get a read on Alcera, but she recruited Meryl, so they're pretty tight. Doesn't matter. They still have to take it seriously and go through the process. So I left Friday afternoon and have been hiding out here since."

"What happens now?

"Attorneys. Every staffer will be interviewed."

"How awful. I'm so sorry."

"Me, too. Basically my career and my work at Davos and Rayburn is over."

"That doesn't seem right. Have you spoken to your dad and Spark? They seem to have lots of contacts."

He shook his head, and for an instant Rose thought he might cry. Forgetting her resolve to keep her distance, she reached across the table and took his hand. "You mean you've been home almost a week and haven't told your family?"

"Not yet. I'm gonna talk to Ben tonight," he said, referring to the oldest of the six Morgan siblings. "I can't hide out here forever."

"And I cannot believe your career is over. The truth will come out. Your colleague is clearly manipulative and nasty. She sounds a bit unbalanced."

"Maybe, but this is still the kiss of death for me. Who's going to want to hire a sexual predator?"

"Which you aren't."

"She's got one of the best attorneys on the West Coast representing her."

"Call me a cynic, but I'll bet she's done this before."

"That's what my colleague, Roy, said."

"He's probably right. Please tell your family and let them help."

"Thanks for listening Rosie," he said, squeezing her hand. "It was good to tell someone. I'm sorry if I've been a world-class shit to you. You didn't deserve last year."

"Don't think about that now." She gave him a sweet smile. "I know you're going to think I'm leaving because of what you just said, but I'm late. I've got to head out."

"He's a lucky man."

"Excuse me?"

"Your hot date."

"Dan. His name is Dan."

"Well, Dan is a lucky man. Will you be home again soon?"

His dark eyes pleaded, and Rose felt her treacherous feelings for him creeping back. *No, no, keep your distance. He's in crisis now, but once it's over, he'll be gone.* "Not sure. I have double shifts this week and next, but you take care. I'm sure things will be resolved in your favor. And in the meantime, you have Spark's magic kingdom to keep you busy."

He gave her a wan smile. "Unless they take it away from me. Apparently Meryl suggested that they turn it over to her."

"Never!"

"I'll fight it for sure, and I'm pretty certain Spark will too."

"Of course he will," she said, standing and grabbing her purse.

Before she knew what was happening, Sam stood and took her in his arms.

"Thanks, Rosie. It was *really* good to see you." Her sweet, peachy scent surrounded him, and he closed his eyes.

Her knees wobbled and Rose felt faint, his nearness and familiar scent overwhelming her for an instant. Finally, she broke away. Breathless, she sputtered, "You, too," practically running out of the diner lest he attempt to embrace her again.

His libido in overdrive, Sam watched her go, heart aching. *What a stupid idiot you are, Sam Morgan. You had your chance. Now she can't get away from you fast enough.* As he headed for the counter to pay his bill, he realized how much calmer and clearer he felt after talking with someone from home. It was time to tell the family. He needed them.

CHAPTER 2

Sam sat in his truck for half an hour, head resting on the steering wheel, as a pounding headache washed over him. He shared the tendency to suffer from migraines with his older sister, Beth, but none of their other siblings seemed to get the stress-induced malady. Of course, he'd forgotten his meds in Flagstaff. He decided to visit the walk-in clinic before heading to the ranch. An hour later, prescription in hand, he stepped into Valley Apothecary and dropped his slip with the pharmacist, a thin, bespectacled woman, all business.

As he browsed the magazine section, a voice called from behind. "Well, if it isn't Sam Morgan, my old chem lab partner!" He turned to find a short, curvaceous blonde in skin-tight capris and a cherry-red Band-Aid top. The top was at least two sizes too small, stretched to the breaking point across her ample breasts. She looked vaguely familiar. *Is it Sadie? Sally? Sarah?*

"Oh, boy, you don't recognize me, do you? Sookie Fisher? We graduated together?"

"Sookie, yes, of course, hi." He extended his hand, which she ignored, throwing herself into his arms.

"Oh, you Morgan boys, so above it all! Course you wouldn't remember a gal from the wrong side of the tracks."

"No, I do remember you. Sorry, it's been a rough few days and I'm kind of distracted."

"No problemo. It's great to see you. Are you livin' back in the Valley now?"

"No, just here for a visit."

"Well, don't be a stranger. I live two doors down, second floor. Work at Gabriela's part-time. I'm in nursing school."

"Yeah? That's great."

"Yup, U of A. Mostly online this semester. Blame it on our sophomore chemistry." She actually batted her eyes.

At that moment, the pharmacist called his name. Saved by the bell, he thought, giving Sookie a smile. "Gotta go. Nice seein' you again."

Without waiting for a reply, he turned away. After paying, he started for the door, only to find Sookie waiting in the aisle. "Here's my number. Love to have a drink or dinner sometime and catch up?" Before he could react, she reached forward and tucked the slip of paper in his breast pocket. "See ya, sugar."

"Absolutely," he said, almost running out of the shop, straight into Harley Langdon.

"Hey, Morgan, where's the fire?" The tall, handsome cowboy with deep green eyes, sandy hair, and a killer smile ran the stables at Morgan's Run. Harley was his brother Ben's best friend. Their youngest sister, Ruthie, had been madly in love with the wrangler since grade school. Harley claimed she was miles too young for him, but people who knew him well were pretty certain that he felt the same about her.

"Harley, hi. I was just heading your way. Where's your other half this afternoon?"

"If you mean your brother, he's at the house. Maggie wasn't feeling well, and he drove her home." Maggie Morgan, Harley's assistant and horse trainer, was pregnant with the couple's third child. At the moment, she was suffering from ferocious morning sickness that lasted all day.

The pharmacy door opened and Sookie strolled out. "Hey, Harls. How's tricks?"

"Hey, Sook."

She waggled a crimson-nailed finger at Sam. "And I'll expect to hear from you soon." With a wink at both men, she gave a backward wave and sashayed slowly down the sidewalk.

When she was out of earshot, Harley turned to him. "I'd steer clear of that one, buddy. She's a wild animal. Can strip a man's jeans off with her teeth."

"That firsthand experience talking?"

"No way, Jose. Common knowledge."

"Or Valley gossip?"

"You're on your own, my friend."

"Don't worry. I have no intention of stepping out with Sookie Fisher, although there were some memorable moments in high school copping a feel under her lab coat."

Harley laughed. "How's it going?"

"Been better. How 'bout you?"

"Just took Willow home. Her mom's actually having a good spell, so she wants to spend as much time as she can at home." Willow was Harley's teenage daughter, conceived in college, her existence unknown to him until her mom's recent cancer diagnosis.

"That's great. Ben told me she didn't have much time."

"We didn't think so, but she's defying medical science. Been to Mexico a bunch of times, trying all kinds of alternative therapies. Nothing's gonna cure her, but some of the treatments have bought her time."

"That's terrific."

"Yeah, Willow adores her mama. Hey, is something eating you, buddy? You really don't look so good."

Sam opened the bottle and swallowed two of the pills. "Migraine. Just got my magic pills, so I'll be drooling and in recovery mode within the hour."

"The Foster place giving you headaches?"

"Not at all. Spark's a great client. Just the usual office shit."

"You oughta think about comin' back here. No one stresses much in the Valley."

"Yeah, so I hear. I ran into Rose Dillon at Gracie's."

"Fine woman. Thought you two might've had a thing last year?"

"*Had* being the operative word. I blew that one."

"Too bad."

"You know her boyfriend?"

"Nope, haven't laid eyes on the woman for months. I get the impression she doesn't come home all that often."

"Well, see you around, Harl."

"Sooner than you think. We're all havin' dinner at the big house Friday night, I understand."

"That's right. See you then, if not before."

CHAPTER 3

Sam drove through the ranch gates and turned south on the long dirt road leading to his brother's home. As the house came into view, he couldn't help but smile. Despite all the shit going on in his life, here was his masterpiece, his favorite design and crowning achievement in his eight years as an architect. It wasn't his grandest project, but it was as close to perfect as anything he could imagine. In perfect harmony with the land, the modern, rambling farmhouse had the most spectacular views in the Valley. The two brothers had put their heads together and turned their grandparents' old homestead into a thing of beauty for generations to come.

As he hopped out of the truck, he spied Ben and Maggie on the porch. She was lying on the glider, a cloth over her eyes, her head in Ben's lap. Sam felt like an intruder stepping into a moment of such intimacy, but Ben waved him up. He stood, gently settling Maggie's head on three pillows, fingers to his lips. "She sleeps." After he covered her with a blanket, he led the way into the house.

"Is she okay?" Sam asked as they stood in the kitchen.

"Still feels shitty."

"Where are the kids?" he asked, referring to the couple's seven-year-old daughter, Emma, and eighteen-month-old toddler, Ben the third.

"With Mom and Dad."

"Both of 'em?"

"Carmela's there, and I think Ruthie was gonna take Emma up to the farm." Their sisters, Ruthie and Beth, ran the largest organic farm in the Southwest. An orographic effect had created this green, moist valley, surrounded by mountains and desert to the east and west. The rich soil and the ranch's innovative and environmentally responsive farming methods yielded a bounty unmatched by any of their competitors. Their meat and produce fed the Valley, but was also shipped to discerning customers throughout the Southwest and beyond.

"How's the farm doing? I've barely talked to Ruthie and have yet to lay eyes on Beth since I got home."

"Great, far as I know. Want something to drink?"

"Just coming down from a migraine, so water'd be great."

Ben poured two tall glasses of water, and the brothers headed for the back terrace. The afternoon sun was hot, so they sat under the shaded arbor. Mirror images except in build, the dark-haired, dark-eyed brothers gazed out at the valley and mountains in companionable silence.

Finally, Ben said, "So, how goes the Foster manse?"

"Gonna be cool."

"Spark's a keeper. Dad's like a pig in shit. Can't wait to have his old buddy here."

"Permanently, I hear."

Their father and Spark Foster had been college roommates at Stanford, and the friends had stayed close in the ensuing years. Now a widower, Spark had come to the Valley on an extended vacation a year earlier. By the end of it, he had bought land and decided to build.

Ben nodded. "He's putting the Portland house on the market. With Amy here, his heart's here, too."

"Not sure it'll be ready for the wedding, but we're sure trying," Sam said, referring to the upcoming marriage of Spark's only daughter Amy to Jeb Barnes, a wrangler on Morgan's Run. "Spark's already making noises about building their house after his is completed."

"I was surprised to hear you were home, bro. Sorry I haven't gotten up to the big house. Been crazy at the stables with the upcoming pack trip and all of us trying to cover for Maggie." He lowered his voice. "Don't tell her I said that! She pretty much runs the stables and it's not the same without her, but she just can't do it right now."

"No apologies necessary. I've been home five days and haven't even come to say hi to my niece and nephew."

"If you head to the big house after this, you'll run right into 'em. Mom, Dad and Carmela are keeping 'em till after dinner."

"Great."

"In your bedraggled state, I'd suggest a quick drive-by."

Sam smiled, taking a long drink.

Eyebrow raised, Ben studied him. "So, you gonna tell me what's eating you, or do we play twenty questions?"

"Basically, I'm fucked," Sam said, launching into the same description he had given Rose.

When he concluded, Ben whistled. "Sounds like a world-class bitch."

"She is, but she's a powerful world-class bitch."

"Even so, a good lawyer can get this tossed. Who have you got?"

"No one yet. It just happened. Bob and Alcera said the firm will be hiring someone."

"To represent *them*, not *you*. No, no, no, my naïve little brother. You need a shark. I have a couple of ideas, but you really should talk to Dad, and maybe Jaybo Dillon. They know every judge in the state, and most of the decent attorneys. Have you told Mom and Dad yet?"

"No."

"Tell 'em. There'll be the usual feathers flying from Mom, but then they'll muster the troops behind you."

"I feel like I've let them down."

"Bullshit. This woman's a barracuda. She needs to be hooked, scaled, and fried on a skewer."

Sam chuckled at the image of Meryl on a skewer. "Trouble is, she's a smart, well-connected barracuda."

"She's messing with a Morgan now, bro. Once she feels the full force of the family, she'll be sorry she messed with you."

"The cowboy Jedi strikes back?"

"Exactly! Have you told anyone else about this?"

"I talked to my colleague, Roy. You've met him a couple of times. And I told Rose. I bumped into her today and everything just kind of came out. Was actually really helpful to talk to her. She's a terrific listener and incredibly supportive."

"Rose is the best."

"Yes," Sam said, voice wistful.

"What's that long face about? I thought you two had a thing at Beth's wedding?"

"It was a thing, alright. A typical Morgan love 'em and leave 'em thing. I was a complete shit and now she's got a boyfriend. Do you know him?"

"Dan something, right? Mags and I had lunch with him and Rose a few weeks ago while Emma was at a therapy appointment. Nice guy."

"And?"

"And, what? We chatted for half an hour or so. He's a doc, same field as Rose. I think he's on some kind of residency."

"Did they seem serious?"

"Sammy boy, this is me, the clueless male, you're talkin' to. I wouldn't know serious if I fell over it."

"You can say that again," Maggie said, crossing the terrace and stepping behind her husband's chair, her slender arms circling his broad shoulders.

"Hey, Mag," Sam said. He rose to hug her. Dark circles under her blue eyes couldn't diminish his sister-in-law's beauty. She was gorgeous as ever, even if rail-thin and ghostly pale. "Feeling any better?"

"Much, thanks to Mr. Clueless here. Thanks, sweetie. I needed that nap. When are the kids comin' back?"

"Mom's keeping 'em for a few hours."

"But—"

"Relax. Carmela , Ruthie and Dad are with her. They'll feed 'em, bathe 'em, and have 'em back here by seven." Ben pulled his wife onto his lap and nuzzled her neck.

"Mmm, that's nice," she murmured, turning to kiss his cheek, smiling at Sam.

"He may be clueless, but he's a sweetheart. Sam, would you like to eat with us? Not sure I'll do much eating, but your brother's a great cook. He can whip something up. It'll probably be vegetarian, but tasty."

"Thanks, but I've got to head out. I have some work to do tonight. I have to stop at the job site on the way home, and it sounds like Mom and Dad can use another pair of hands."

As he started the truck, Sam thought of how much he wanted what Ben and Maggie had. What his sister and Lang Dillon, Rose's older brother, had. A deep, abiding love, like their parents'. *What's wrong with me?*

CHAPTER 4

The men were cleaning up for the day as Sam parked near the construction site. The huge house was framed and the slate roof had been laid, but the interior spaces were still open stud walls. One long section of south-facing roof held custom-designed solar panels, which blended perfectly with the slate. He had searched far and wide for a company that could make them and was pleased with the result. As he stepped from truck, he waved to Kevin Larrabee, the construction foreman. From Flagstaff, the forty-year-old Kevin was newly divorced. When Sam tapped him for the Foster job, Kevin had decided to get out of town and was renting an apartment in Saguaro. His crew was housed in mobile units near the site, and most commuted home on weekends.

Larrabee waved. "Hey, boss, ya just missed the big boss." The tall, broad-shouldered foreman removed his cap, sandy hair matted after a long day, a line of mud across his forehead.

"Yeah? What'd he think?"

"Happy as a clam. Wants to go over the kitchen plans with you to make a few adjustments."

"I'll catch up with him. Did he say if he's sticking around or heading back to Portland?"

"Said he'll be here at least till Saturday so he can be at Friday's dinner."

Sam laughed. He really liked Kevin and hired him whenever he could. He was an exceptional carpenter, had a highly skilled crew, and was a fair and honest boss. "Yeah, my dad said he'd asked you."

"Yup, I'm practically a regular at the big house. Must be movin' up in the world." Larrabee had overseen the construction of both Ben and Maggie's and Beth and Lang's houses, and Sam's kind and generous parents had welcomed him and his men with open arms on several occasions.

"I don't know about moving up, but my folks enjoy your company. They wanted to have the crew, but Spark says he's hosting you guys at the Lodge sometime soon?" The Morgan's Run Lodge, where Spark now resided when in town, was a luxurious facility, popular with the wealthy patrons who had discovered the valley and returned year after year for pack trips and spa vacations.

"Sometime next week. My guys all like to go home to Flagstaff over the weekend anyway."

"Any glitches today?"

"Nope, but you may want to take a look at the stairs. We roughed 'em in today."

"Thanks, Kev," he said, heading inside. Spark had requested an open floor plan with a two-story foyer and broad, winding staircase that branched to the right and left, taking one to the two distinct areas of the second floor. It was nearly a duplicate of the one in his grand Portland home, which he had flown Sam to Portland to view firsthand. At present the bones were in place. Kevin and his men had done a masterful job building the curved structure. Sam climbed to the second floor and walked through to a huge west-facing window, marveling as he always did at the spectacular view before him. This was Spark's bedroom and ran the length of the house so he could experience sunrise and sunset.

Sam gazed out, pleased and peaceful, headache almost gone. *Time to face the music, buddy,* he thought, turning away and heading down. His dad would be calm, his mom hysterical, but Ben was right. Once they knew, the Morgan juggernaut would rear up and be behind him two hundred percent.

"Looks great, Kev," he called as he walked to his truck. "See you tomorrow."

As he pointed the truck down the dirt road, his cell phone rang.

"Hey, Sam, glad I caught you," senior partner Bob Rayburn said. "How are things going down there?"

"Hi, Bob. Great, thanks."

"Listen, the firm's attorney, Sally Mercer, is trying to move things along with Meryl's complaint, and I wanted to see if you'd be available over the next few days or Friday to speak with her and sign some papers."

"Can we do it over the phone?"

"Not the best way, no. Sally has time at ten Friday morning or late tomorrow, whichever works best for you."

"I'm kind of tied up with the Foster house right now," he lied. *The last thing I want to do is run into the barracuda around the office.*

"This is important, Sam. For you and for the firm."

"Okay, I can get there tomorrow by four thirty. Would that work? Should I call Sally?"

"No, I'll let her know. She's happy to meet you at the office or hers."

"Hers, please. I know where it is."

"Would you'd like to discuss this with Alcera or me? I'm around tomorrow night. We could meet after you see Sally."

Sam agreed to meet his boss for a drink at six at a restaurant near Mercer's law office and rang off. *Just what I need, a four-hour drive to hell,* he thought as he drove through the ranch gates and straight up the hill to his parents' home.

CHAPTER 5

When Rose stepped out of the diner in the afternoon heat, she let out a huge sigh. Her legs still felt like wet noodles, and she knew with certainty that she was still in love with Sam Morgan. They had never made love and had exchanged only casual kisses, but she was more attracted to him than any man she'd ever known, including his oldest brother, Ben, who was now happily married to a woman Rose liked very much.

The Morgan brothers were a breed apart. In comparison, Dan seemed dull and insipid, even though he was good-looking and accomplished. Time to get home to Tucson and back to reality, she told herself, heading for her car.

Later, as she sat with Dan at one of their favorite restaurants, she found herself daydreaming about Sam Morgan's dark eyes, his chiseled jaw, the feel of his arms and his wiry strength as he held her.

"Hello? Earth to Rose," Dan said, reaching over to caress her cheek. "You okay, babe?"

Rose realized he had been speaking and she had no idea about what. "Oh! Yes, sorry."

"You don't seem like yourself tonight. Your parents okay?"

"Yes, Dad's much better."

"So? What going on that's pulled you away just now?"

"Sorry, an old friend from home is having some trouble."

"Is she okay?"

"It's a he, and I'm sure he will be."

"He, is it? Should I be jealous?"

"No," she replied, afraid to look him in the eye. Dan might be dull, but he was also quite perceptive.

"Do I know him?"

"No, but you've met some of his family. He's one of the Morgan brothers. Sam. He's an architect from Tucson."

"The one who designed those two showplaces for his sister and brother?"

She nodded.

"Now I *know* I should be jealous."

"He's a family friend. We grew up together. I bumped into him on my way out of town this afternoon, that's all."

"And?"

"And, he needed a friend to talk to."

"About?"

Suddenly weary, Rose looked up, meeting his eyes. "Can we please change the subject?"

"So, something did happen?"

"Nothing happened. Now, can we please order?"

"Then why won't you tell me?"

"Because he told me in confidence."

"This is bullshit, Rose."

It was the first time she had ever heard Dan swear. Rose averted her eyes and consulted her menu.

They shared a quiet, tense meal, and when he pulled up in front of her condo, Rose did not invite him in. "I've got to be at the clinic at four thirty in the morning," she said, reaching over to touch his jaw.

"I'm falling for you, Rose, but if this guy's going to get in the way, I'd like to know about it now."

"He's not, I promise." She kissed him lightly and hopped out before he could draw her closer.

And he will not get in the way, Rose Dillon! Whether you stay with Dan or not, you will not risk breaking your heart all over again with Sam Morgan!

CHAPTER 6

Squeals of laughter came from inside the house as Sam crossed the front porch. Inside, bedlam reigned. His niece Emma was chasing her brother, Ruthie Morgan in hot pursuit. Just as Sam stepped into the living room, his dad, Ben Senior, popped out from behind the sofa. The tall family patriarch smiled, his thick head of hair mussed and wild as he growled like a mountain lion and grabbed his grandson. "Gotcha!"

At that moment, Leonora Morgan swept in from the kitchen, her blond hair tied back with a bright green bandana. In capris, a printed top, and sandals, she looked lovely, as always, albeit a bit frazzled. "Alright, you two," she said, referring to her husband and daughter. "Enough! It's time to calm down for dinner. Oh, good, darling," she said, spying Sam. "You can bring some sanity to this mayhem." She came forward and hugged him. "You okay? You looked a little pale."

"Long day," he said, hugging her and winking at Emma, who was now creeping up behind her grandmother.

"Well, dinner's ten minutes away."

"Great. I'll run up and shower, then come to assist with the troops. Hey, Em, Bennie," he said, scooping up both children for a quick hug. "Be right back, promise."

By the time Sam came down, the children were settled at the table, Ben the third in a high chair next to Leonora and Emma beside her grandfather, whom she adored. Sam sat across from his red-haired sister, who lived with her parents. Occasionally, Ruthie made noises about getting an apartment in town, but the twenty-five-year-old baby of the Morgan clan was happy at home, and her parents loved having her with them.

"How go things at the farm today, sis?"

"Busy, as always. Beth and Raoul have added three new breeds of sheep, a couple of varieties of cattle and some awesome pigs, so cute. And don't even get me started on the chickens. They must have twenty varieties."

"Are Beth and Lang doing well?"

"Lovey-dovey, as usual. Everyone's lovey-dovey around here except for me."

"Your day will come, my darling," her mother said, waving her hand.

"Sure will, baby girl," her dad added, winking at Sam. "I know a certain cowboy who might even make a move someday."

"Humph, I'll be eighty before Harley Langdon makes a move. Anyway, I'm bringing a date Friday night, so too bad for him!"

Her mother frowned. "I hope it's not another one of those computer dates."

"As a matter of fact, Roger *is*. He's an engineer from Tucson. Real nice guy. You'll like him."

Leonora rolled her eyes and turned back to the baby, who was throwing his bits of hot dog all over the room. Ben Senior winked at Sam and smiled at his youngest child.

"So, how's my favorite niece?" Sam asked, grinning at Emma, who, as usual, exhibited perfect manners and was listening intently to the adults' conversation.

"Super, Uncle Sam. Wanta come down and see me ride?"

"Love to, sweetie."

"Mom hasn't been feeling well, so she can't ride with me."

"Well, I'd be happy to. Maybe this weekend?"

The child beamed, eating her last french fry, her plate clean as a whistle. At the opposite end of the table, her brother was wearing most of his dinner, what wasn't strewn on floor and walls. Leonora called for Carmela, who appeared with a wet cloth.

The sixtysomething housekeeper and cook had lived on the ranch for most of her life. She and her husband, Raoul, farm foreman, lived in the largest of the ranch cottages. A dark-skinned, raven-haired beauty, Carmela had never been blessed with children of her own, but she cared for Leonora and Ben's offspring—children and grandchildren—like her own and loved every one of them, as they did her.

"Carmela, Ruthie and I will clear. Do you think you could take the children to the back terrace?"

"Yes, ma'am," Carmela said, wiping the toddler, then extracting him from his high chair. "You going to help me, aren't you, Emma?"

"Yup!" The mirror image of her father, the tiny girl with dark curls and a smile that would melt an iceberg rose and followed the cook, her halting, funny gait the only remnant of her former paralysis.

When the door closed behind the trio, the four remaining adults breathed a sigh of relief. "I adore them," Leonora said, "but a few minutes of peace before bath time are most welcome. Now, how did your day go, Sammy dear?"

"Okay. I met Rose Dillon in town, at Gracie's."

"Oh?" his mother said, giving her husband a look.

"Surprised she'd even speak to you after you dumped her last year," Ruthie said, rolling her eyes and waving her fork at him.

"Don't be dramatic, Ruthie," Leonora said. "Sam did no such thing! Now either put that fork in your mouth or on your plate. We've had enough food flying around tonight."

"She's right, Mom. I treated Rose deplorably. Had it been the old West, someone might've strung me up."

Ben Senior chuckled. "Well, she's got a nice new fella now, so she's recovered, I expect."

"So I hear," Sam said, remembering the soft hazel eyes and Rose's hand on his.

"You snooze, you lose, big brother."

"Ruthie, hush!" Leonora said. "How is Rose, darling?"

"Great. Was really good to see her. I've been going through something I'd like to tell you about, and Rose and I got to talking and it all spilled out. She listened to my tale of woe and was incredibly supportive, making my telling you easier."

His father's sky-blue eyes gazed at him, full of concern. "I've known somethin's been eatin' you since you got home, but didn't want to pry. What's goin' on, son?"

"You didn't mention you noticed something to me," Leonora said, voice indignant.

"Now, Nora, let the boy speak."

"I wanted to talk with you sooner, but was afraid I'd disappoint you," Sam said softly.

"Darlin', nothing you could ever do would disappoint us," his mother said, eyes trained on her third-born.

Without preamble, Sam related the story of Meryl and the lawsuit for the third time. He concluded with, "So that's what's eating me. Sorry I didn't speak up sooner."

"What a witch," Ruthie said.

Sam nodded. "She's a nasty piece of work."

Ben Senior shook his head. "Well, the first thing we're gonna do is get you a lawyer, the best. Don't know the Mercer woman, but I'll make some calls tonight. Jaybo may know someone, too. He does a lot of business up north." Rose and Lang Dillon's family owned Saguaro Valley Winery. They also raised prized Angus cattle.

"Thanks, Dad. I've been kind of paralyzed, but I'll see what Sally Mercer says, then take it from there."

"I feel pretty certain that an attorney worth his or her salt will want to come along."

"I'll be fine, Dad."

Ben Senior sat up straighter. "We'll see. We also want to get a private investigator to look into this Wainwright woman. The whole thing sounds fishy to me. I'll just bet she's done this before."

"That's what several people have said." Sam remembered Rose's voice, and her soft eyes. *When will I see her again?*

After dinner, Sam and Ruthie volunteered to oversee bath time and then took Emma and Ben home. As Ruthie chatted with Maggie, his older brother took him aside. "How'd it go?"

"Fine. You know Mom and Dad. Any one of us could shoot someone right in front of them and it'd be the other guy's fault."

"But, this isn't your fault, bro. Let Dad put his feelers out. Jaybo, too. A good attorney should have this settled quickly."

"For a gazillion dollars and a tarnished reputation for me."

"I would guess the firm would want to keep this very quiet."

"Maybe, but no telling what the barracuda will do."

"Hang in there, buddy. Gotta help Mag with the kids. She's still feeling crappy."

"Thanks, big brother. Your support means a lot to me."

"Always," Ben said, hugging him. "And call Rosie. Ask her out, if you're interested. You never know. This Dan guy might be just a casual thing. They're not engaged or anything."

"Maybe."

"She's good people, Sammy."

He said good night and called to Ruthie. As they drove back, she turned to him. "So, I heard you talking about Rose. What's that about?"

"It was just good to see her again. She was really supportive today."

"I don't know her that well, but what I know, I like. I guess my only piece of advice, not that my brothers ever listen to me, would be not to lead her on. She's a sweetheart and it wouldn't be cool to hurt her."

Again, Sam thought. *Wouldn't be cool to hurt her again.*

After saying good night to his parents, he headed up to his old room. The mural on one wall depicting the desert and its wildlife still looked fresh as the day it had been completed by a local artist. His mother had replaced the bedspreads and curtains and modernized the bathroom in soft adobe hues. He threw his cell phone on the bed and started to undress when the phone vibrated. The number displayed was "unknown" and he almost didn't answer, but then picked it up. "Hello?"

"Sam?"

Her soft, familiar voice soothed nerves that had been building since dinner. "Rose?"

"Hi. I hope I'm not disturbing you?"

"No, never."

"Just wanted to check to see if you're okay."

"Doing better, thanks to you. I talked with Ben, then my parents. No surprise, everyone's behind me, and Dad'll be on the hotline in the morning."

"Please call my father. He'd be happy to help."

"Thanks. I'll see how far the cavalry gets me."

"I'm sure it'll all blow over soon."

"How was your hot date?" he asked, glad that she was home at such an early hour, alone.

"Fine, good," she lied.

"Lucky man."

"Well, just wanted to check in. It was good to see you today."

"You, too. Rose, I'm really sorry about last year. I was a jackass. I'd love to take you to dinner sometime, if that wouldn't ruffle feathers with Dan?"

"That would be nice," she said softly, ignoring the warning bells. Seeing him again had opened the floodgates, and there was no turning back. If he'd asked her to come to Saguaro, she would have jumped in her car that very minute. "Well, I'll let you go." *And I should let you go for good!*

"Would ask you tomorrow night, but I'm headed up to Flagstaff and won't be back until late."

"I'm busy anyway," she said. Better to be honest with herself and Sam.

"Something nice, I hope?"

"It's just a dinner party hosted by one of our colleagues. If I could beg off, I would, but I'm bringing the dessert."

"Our colleagues," she said. I presume that means Dan. "Oh, what are you making?"

She laughed. "I actually like to bake, but not tomorrow. I have to be in surgery at four thirty in the morning, so I've ordered pies from a great bakery."

"Wow, is that your usual routine?"

"No, but this is the only time we could gather the whole team."

"Well, I'd better let you go, then."

"Yes," she said quietly. *Even though I could listen to your voice all night.*

"Take care, Rose, and thanks again." *What wouldn't I give to hold you in my arms right now?*

"Night."

"Night."

CHAPTER 7

The drive to Flagstaff was interminable, the meeting with Sally Mercer looming in front of him. His father had retained "the best litigator in the state," Will Santiago, who agreed to meet Sam at Mercer's office. The entire drive he resisted the urge to phone Rose even though he longed to hear her voice. Ruthie's advice and his own emotional state won out, and he kept his phone in his pocket.

When he pulled into the parking lot behind Mercer's law offices, he spied a tall, lanky man who reminded him of Abraham Lincoln leaning against a beat-up truck. His face was craggy, his salt-and-pepper hair long and wild. He wore khakis and a blue dress shirt, his tie loosened round his long neck. "Mr. Morgan, I presume?" he called, grabbing a battered canvas briefcase from the truck and crossing the lot in long, easy strides.

"Sam, please."

"Will Santiago," he said, extending a long arm, handshake firm, a grin on his face. When he smiled, his homely features came into place, but even then the tall, gangly attorney would never have been called handsome.

"Thanks for coming on such short notice."

"For your dad, anything. I see the family resemblance."

"Strong genes."

"So, you've gotten yourself in a dust-up?"

"Disaster, more like it."

"I've got my guy on it. By tomorrow he'll have dug up every speck of dirt on Wainwright. We'll find something."

"Is that the only way?"

"No, there's your word against hers."

Sam groaned.

"Not to worry. People like Wainwright don't just suddenly become victims, especially of someone like you. Come on, let's go in. And not a word to Mercer unless I give the okay."

"But she's the firm's lawyer."

"Exactly."

"She's on my side."

"Out of the mouths of babes. Sally Mercer is *not* on your side. She's representing Rayburn and Davos, period."

The meeting was brief and to the point. Mercer asked a number of questions, most of which Will would not allow Sam to answer. She was sharp, but Santiago clearly intimidated her. Short with curly, dark hair, Sally wore a bright blue suit that hugged her compact figure, and metallic blue stiletto heels.

Finally, she threw up her hands. "Mr. Morgan, I'm here to help you, but I cannot if I don't know the whole story."

Before Sam could speak, Santiago said, "The whole story is this. Meryl Wainwright harassed my client repeatedly and when he finally rebuffed her, she became vindictive."

"And where is the proof?"

"I could say the same thing to you. What proof does Wainwright have?"

"She's very convincing."

"About what?" Sam asked. "Nothing happened! She just kept—"

"Whoa, boy, save it for Tuesday," Will said, laying a hand on Sam's wrist.

"I'm serious, Will," she said, sweat beading on her upper lip. "Meryl is the image of the helpless victim when she's telling her tale of woe."

Will laughed. "I'll just bet she is. We'll have what we need by next week."

"Well, I certainly hope so. Meryl has hired Lula Perry, and she seldom loses."

"Well, she will this time. When're we meeting with her?"

"At Rayburn and Davos, next Tuesday at eleven."

Will stood. "Always a pleasure, Sally. We'll keep in touch."

As they strolled across the parking lot, Sam checked his watch. It was quarter to six. "I'm meeting with my boss, Bob Rayburn, so I've gotta run."

"Want me to come with you?"

"No, it's fine. What'd you think of Sally Mercer?"

"Exactly what I told you. She's representing Rayburn and Davos, not you. Don't look so glum. It'll be fine."

"What do you know about Meryl's attorney?"

"Lula? She's a pit bull, but we'll muzzle her, don't worry. Give me a call after your meeting with Rayburn. Try to remember everything he says."

Sam extended his hand. "Thanks, Will."

"You betcha. Talk soon."

Sam watched the lanky man head to his truck, then turned away. *I can see why Dad likes him,* he thought, wondering how the two men had met.

CHAPTER 8

Bob Rayburn was already in a back booth at Fiona's when Sam walked in and waved. His boss held up two Dos Equis and motioned him over.

"Hey, buddy, I took the liberty of ordering. This okay?"

"Absolutely, thanks," he said, slipping into the booth. *The only time Bob calls me* buddy *is when he wants something, and wants it bad.*

"How'd things go with Sally?"

"As well as they could, I guess," Sam said, studying his boss's face. He was certain that the moment he and Will left the office, Sally had called Bob to debrief, Sam decided to play along.

Rayburn was a good-looking man. Balding, always tanned, he had the robust build of a rancher, not an architect who spent his days in the office at his computer. The past few years, he had turned over more and more of the work to his associates and had taken on the role of elder statesman, overseeing the work of others. Recently divorced, there were rumors of something between Bob and Alcera, his partner, but if there was something going on, they were discreet. *Too bad Meryl didn't set her sights on Bob.*

Sam took a sip of beer, then set the frosty mug on its cork coaster. "I've hired Will Santiago to represent me."

Rayburn shrugged. "Not necessary, but your choice, of course." There was a guardedness in his boss's manner that Sam had never seen.

"Everyone with whom I've spoken recommended that I retain my own attorney."

"We're trying to keep this quiet, Sam. For your sake and the firm's."

"I agree. I've spoken only to family and one close friend. They are the soul of discretion."

"Let's hope so. I'm hoping the whole thing can go away next Tuesday."

"Me, too."

"Have you got a plan for Tuesday?"

"Excuse me?"

"What you'll say, I mean."

"I'll tell the truth. Nothing happened on my side. Meryl flirted and came on to me, and I said no. She got pissed at being rejected and brought a phony charge against me."

"That's probably not gonna fly."

"Well, it's the truth, Bob. You believe me, don't you?"

"Course I do, but Meryl's convincing, son."

"What are you saying?"

"Maybe there's some way you can apologize, we'll settle up, and this will all disappear."

"That's bullshit, and you know it. I'm not apologizing for something I didn't do. If you want me to say I'm sorry I wasn't interested in her, fine, but other than that, I have nothing to say except she was harassing me."

"Meryl Wainwright's a big land for us. She's been involved in some major projects in this part of the country."

Involved in, *being the operative phrase.* Sam had looked into Meryl's work shortly before her arrival. She was always a member of a team of architects working on the major projects, not the lead person. "That doesn't make this right, sir. She's a liar, and I'm not going to fall on my sword here."

"No one's asking you to. Just compromise, show the two of you can work together, and ideally this will go away."

Sam could feel his temper rising, and he willed his voice to calmness. "You can't be serious. Work together? After the woman accuses me of something I didn't do and brings a huge lawsuit against me?"

"Now, now, Sam. I know you're upset, but this is the reality in cases like this. By the way, Meryl's in Saguaro today to meet with Spark Foster. She'll be taking the lead on that project from now on."

For a second Sam thought he might vomit. "You're kidding, right?"

"No, she asked for this and indicated that it might persuade her to drop the suit. We thought it was a great idea. Help you and help her branch out, get to know that part of the state."

"I'm sorry, but this is bullshit, Bob. Spark and I have been collaborating for over a year. I designed that house from the bottom up."

"Yes, and you are a junior partner at Rayburn and Davos. Meryl, as a senior partner, has the right to step into any project she wants. She chose this one. Thought it needed a fresh pair of eyes. She ran her ideas past by Alcera and me, and we agreed."

Sam took several breaths, then stood up and threw ten dollars on the table for the beer. "You'll have my resignation on your desk as soon as I can write it." With those words, he turned and walked out of Fiona's. *If I thought my career was over before, now it's a certainty.*

He swung by his condo and grabbed two suitcases of clothes and a few other things, made himself a peanut butter sandwich, and started the long drive back home. Several times he grabbed his phone, wanting to hear Rose's voice, but then remembered she was out with Dan.

When he arrived home, everyone was asleep except his father, who sat in the study, reading. "Hey, Sammy," he called as the door opened.

Sam looked at the clock. It was almost eleven thirty. "Hey, Dad. What're you doing up so late?"

"How'd things go? Was Will helpful?"

"He was great," Sam said, flopping onto the leather chair opposite his father's, running his fingers through his hair.

"And?"

"And, I've quit my job. This lawsuit'll probably drain me of every last dollar. Probably never work as an architect again."

"Glad about the first. Doubt the last two. We do have a situation, though. That's actually why I waited up."

"I know, Bob Rathburn told me. The barracuda's taking over the Foster job."

"Well, she thinks she is, but she doesn't know Spark Foster. He was bowled over when she came barreling in today. He didn't know the back story, so he just listened. She brought a bunch of documents for him to sign, but he said he'd need to consult with you and his attorney before signing."

"Good ole Spark. I'm not sure what recourse we have. The project was contracted by Rayburn and Davos."

"But it's all your work."

"Technically, but—"

"First thing to do is talk with Will. Then we'll see."

"Dad, I can't ask Spark to get into a lawsuit, too."

"Let's sleep on it and we'll see in the morning. He's expecting you at the Lodge at nine."

The two men rose and hugged each other. "Thanks, Dad," he said wearily. "This is all you need."

"Son, no one hurts my family in this valley and gets away with it."

While he knew his father spoke the truth, Sam wanted to crawl into a hole and never come out.

CHAPTER 9

Rose's time with Dan on Thursday evening had been brief and a bit frosty. They met at the colleague's home, and she managed to stay in conversation groups until the end of the evening. As she said her goodbyes, Dan caught her in the hall. "We still on for Saturday, Rose?"

She hesitated, then replied, "Yes, of course." She owed him an explanation in person, not a "Dear John" letter or email. While nothing might come of her nonrelationship with Sam Morgan, Rose was beginning to feel that her relationship with Dan had run its course for a number of reasons.

"So, I'll pick you up around five thirty?"

"Perfect." They were going to dinner and an open air concert at the university.

"My shift changed tomorrow, so I'm free. Want to catch dinner and a movie?"

"It's been a long week. Let's just stick with Saturday," she replied, not telling him that she had taken the day off to go home. Martha Dillon had called to say that the Morgans had invited all the Dillons to dinner Friday, and her mother begged her to come home for it.

"You busy then?" he said, challenge in his tone.

"Goodnight, Dan. See you Saturday," she said, taking the arm of a female colleague. She walked out with Celia and her husband, forestalling any further conversation. Rose said goodnight to her friends and quickly jumped into her car.

After faxing his letter of resignation to Bob Rayburn, Sam met Spark on the Lodge terrace at nine on Friday morning. His father's college friend was enjoying coffee and the newspapers, the staff tending to him as if he were royalty. Spark was a billionaire. His Portland-based engineering firm was a leader in solar, wind, and hydroelectric power. Tall, robust, and balding, he had sometimes been mistaken for the actor Fred Thompson, to whom he bore a remarkable resemblance. "Here's my main man," he said, rising to shake Sam's hand. "Have you had breakfast?"

"Thanks, I have."

"Sit, please. Coffee?"

Sam nodded, and the waiter brought him a mug and glass of ice water. "Anything else, Mr. Morgan?"

"Thanks, I'm good, Neil," he said, smiling up at Neil Robertson, who'd been with the ranch for several years.

"Don't know what you're missing," Spark said. "I've gained ten pounds with these scones," he said, indicating a half-empty basket. "Amy's threatening to put me on a diet." Amy, his daughter, a physical therapist, was living on the ranch now with her fiancée, Jeb Barnes, and their foster child, Toby. She had taken a part-time job in Tucson until they decided where they wanted to live.

Sam smiled. "Spark, I'm sorry about all this."

"Your dad phoned this morning. We cardinals rise at dawn, early bird and all," he said, referring to the mascot at Stanford, his and Ben Senior's alma mater.

Sam's brother Ben had also gone to Stanford, but Sam had chosen Pomona and enjoyed every minute of his time as an undergraduate in the vibrant Claremont area. He had considered living there permanently, but after his last year at the UCLA School of the Arts and Architecture, he had interned at Rayburn and Davos. The partners recognized talent when they saw it and did not want to lose their young star, so they made him a very generous offer. He had loved his life in Flagstaff and would miss it.

"I figured Dad would call you," Sam said.

"It's your job, son. Whatever we have to do, we'll do it."

"She's a shark, Spark."

"Wasn't impressed. Not my type. Didn't want to be rude till I spoke to you. She made it seem like you sent her."

Sam laughed. "I'll bet she did. She knows what she's doing. She wouldn't have made this play if she didn't think she could win, or cost us a fortune to get rid of her."

Spark waved his hand. "I've got two of my guys flyin' in from Portland. They can talk with the Santiago kid. They'll have this fixed before the weekend's out."

"I quit the firm."

"Your dad told me. Smart move."

"But you hired the firm."

"Mickey and Clay'll straighten things out. You comin' out to the house today?"

"Do you need me?"

"Not unless young Larrabee does. Nice fella. Does good work."

"Yeah, Kevin's the best. There's another mess. Technically, he and his crew were contracted through the firm."

"And where do you think his loyalties lie? Told me yesterday that your jobs are the only ones he takes from that rinky-dink outfit. Looked like he'd eaten bad chili after five minutes listening to that Werewolf woman."

Sam laughed again, picturing Kevin's face. "It's Wainwright."

"Wainwright, Werewolf, Weasel, what's the difference? We'll get her straightened out. I'm goin' off with your dad all day to steer clear of her and her forms."

"Too late for that," Sam said, shocked to see Meryl step onto the terrace.

"Hello, good morning. You men are up early," she said, smiling from one to the other as if the past nightmarish week had never happened. "May I?" Not waiting for an invitation, she sat beside Spark, patting his forearm. "How you doing, Spence?" she asked, batting eyelashes at the older man.

Sam had never heard anyone call Spark by his given name, Spencer, let alone Spence. He watched his father's friend turn on the charm. "Ms. Wainwright, lovely to see you. Are you staying at the Lodge?"

"No, I'm at the Lemon Drop in town, but I see I made a mistake. What a place! Sam, you never told me how spectacular your family's ranch is." She smiled at him briefly, then quickly turned back to her prey. "Have you gotten to the papers I left with you, Spence?" More eyelash batting as she moved close enough to slide onto Spark's lap. She wore a sleeveless summer dress in bold black-and-white zebra stripes and five-inch heels. The dress's neckline plunged, revealing ample cleavage, which was now pressed against Spark's chest.

Spark moved aside, and she nearly fell out of her chair. "Thanks for checking in, but I've got my attorneys flyin' in today. They'll take a look and get back to you."

Her face fell, and Meryl's eyes clouded over. She was angry, but trying very hard to conceal it. Sam had no doubt she had checked into Spencer "Spark" Foster and knew he was one of the wealthiest men in Portland. *She's clearly after him for more than this job,* Sam thought with disgust.

Straightening up, she recovered herself. "Shall I book a few more nights in the Valley? I could move here, if they have any rooms." She winked at Spark, leaning in again.

"They don't," Sam said, finally finding his voice. "We're booked for the season." *And so will the Lemon Drop be if my parents give them a call.*

Unruffled, she smiled at them both. "No problem. I'll just speak to—"

"No need for you to stay around, Ms. Wainwright. When I've talked with my people, we'll be in touch. You can toddle on back to Flagstaff. Sam has been doing outstanding work. If there are any documents to forward, we'll fly 'em up by messenger. Now, if you'll excuse me, I've got a busy day."

As Meryl and Sam stared openmouthed, Spark Foster stood, donned his Stetson, gave it a slight tip and strode off into the Lodge.

"Well, that was interesting," she said, staring after him.

"Is that all you have to say?" Sam asked, willing his voice to stay calm.

"Now, now, Sam, dear. I hope you're not going to be difficult about this. Spencer and I will get on just fine. Now that you've quit the firm, you have no standing here."

"Listen, you bitch," he said, voice low. "You can fool everyone else, but I know what you are."

"Oh, dear, I tried so hard to reach a compromise in our sticky situation, but I see my efforts are in vain."

"Yeah, sure. You took one look at Spark Foster's business profile and you elbowed your way in to get close to your next victim."

"How dare you?"

"How dare you," Sam said, rising. "And if I were you, I'd get out of Saguaro as soon as you can."

"Is that a threat?"

"No, just some friendly advice."

"Go to hell, Sam."

"You first," he said, stalking off the terrace. *One more minute and I'd have punched her in the nose.*

Chapter 10

When Sam walked onto the terrace at six that evening, he headed straight for the bar, where Raoul, the farm foreman, and Lang Dillon were mixing margaritas and serving drinks. So far, it was just Morgans and Lang, who was now a part of the family. As usual, Ruthie and her dad were playing on the grass with the ranch dogs and Emma and baby Ben. Shrieks of laughter echoed in the still night, not a breath of wind. "Just look at him," Leonora said, waving at her husband. "Sammy, please make him slow down."

"It's good for him," Beth Morgan-Dillon said quietly, winking at Sam. "Hey, brother, good to see you." The siblings hugged, and she leaned back. "It looked like you were making a beeline to the bar. Mind if I tag along?"

As they set off arm in arm, he said, "Hey, Beth, sorry I haven't been up to the farm to visit. How's the house? Settling in okay?"

"We couldn't be happier."

"I thought our baby sister was bringing a date tonight."

"He cancelled this afternoon. I wouldn't bring it up if I were you. How you holding up?"

"Dad told you?"

"You know Mom and Dad. When they're worried, they blurt. Can Lang and I help?"

"Not at the moment, except to be here."

"Always, and if the folks start driving you crazy, as you know, Lang and I have plenty of room. You're welcome to stay as long as you want."

"Thanks, Bethie," he said. "That means a lot."

"Hey, Sam," Lang said as they reached the bar. "I know my beautiful wife wants a margarita, but hers will be minus the tequila. I'm assuming yours should be high test?"

"Please," Sam said, looking at Beth. "Since when are you…? Oh, my God, you're… Do people know?"

She smiled, finger to lips. "We're gonna tell everyone tonight."

Sam hugged them both, and as Lang handed him his drink, he whispered, "So happy for you, man."

"We're keyed," his brother-in-law said, beaming at his wife. "Hey, if you're in town for a while, let's get in a few long runs." Blond like his sister, Lang had the lean body of the long-distance runner he was. Co-owner of a successful Boston-based online sports equipment company, Lang had opened a West Coast branch of Rambler Sports after his marriage to Beth. At the end of its first year of operation, the company was doing very well.

"Absolutely. I'd love that. Haven't run in nearly a week. My body needs it."

"Well, I go out most mornings around five thirty, so let me know." Lang patted Sam's shoulder, but his eyes were gazing toward the house. "Here comes the family. My sister already looks frazzled, and she's been home less than an hour. You don't know how lucky you are with your dad." He gave Beth a peck on the cheek and headed across the terrace.

Lang's sister! Sam spun around. There she was, dressed casually in a pretty beaded tee shirt and beige capris. She did, indeed, look frazzled. Lovely, but frazzled. A scowling Jaybo Dillon was leaning on both his wife's and daughter's arms. As Sam watched, Lang came to the rescue and relieved his mother, who kissed him gratefully, then went to greet Leonora Morgan.

Brother and sister exchanged looks as they led their dad to a seat in the shade. Once he was settled, they hugged. "Hi, sweetie," Lang said, leading her away.

"Before you start, he's fine," Rose said, eyeing her brother. "Nothing to drink. He should last through dinner. Please, Lang, for Mom's sake."

Father and son did not get along, and Jaybo's alcoholism and declining health were a constant source of tension and stress for all of them. Martha Dillon took the brunt of it, but her children tried to relieve her as much as they could.

As she patted her brother's arm, trying to calm him down, Rose peered over his shoulder and caught Sam's eye. She smiled and he returned the smile, waving. *I couldn't stay away. Now my knees have turned to jelly, just catching sight of you.*

Sam wanted nothing more than to sprint across the terrace and draw her into his arms, but Ben and Maggie appeared, blocking his view. "Hi, Sam," she said, hugging him. "Better today?"

He smiled at his sister-in-law. "Define 'better.'"

One arm around his wife, Ben patted his shoulder. "Heard about the dust-up at the Lodge. Can't believe the bitch had the nerve to show her face."

"Shh!" Maggie said, poking him. "The kids'll hear you."

"Yeah, right. Look at 'em," he said, gazing at their children. "Do they look like they're hanging on my every word?"

Maggie rolled her eyes. "Get me a lemonade, please." Ben kissed her temple, then headed for the bar.

"How're you feeling?" Sam asked, regarding his sister-in-law.

"A little better, thanks. My mother hen husband is using this as an excuse to keep me from working. I adore my children, but I go a little stir crazy if I'm housebound too long."

Sam grinned the Morgan grin, and Maggie marveled as she always did at the brothers' resemblance.

"Need any hands at the stables? I'm out of a job, in case you hadn't heard."

She reached over and patted his arm. "I'm so sorry you're having to go through this, Sam. It's so unfair."

"Thanks, Mags. I'm sure it will all work out."

"Oh, and look, Rose is home! I'm sure her mom is thrilled."

"What's the story with Jaybo, anyway?"

"He's never been an easy person, but since his heart attack, he's been very difficult. They hired a manager for the vineyard, so that's covered, but he's bored, still drinks too much, and can be quite a handful for poor Martha. Lang has no patience with him, so Rose has been coming back and forth a lot."

"Too bad for all of them. Hey, there's your dad," he said, spying Ned Williams strolling round from the front yard. "He looks well."

"He is," she said, waving. Her father blew her a kiss, stopped to say hello to Leonora, and then joined his fellow grandfather on the lawn. "The kids keep him young."

"He still sits for them?"

"Emma's in school now, but he takes Ben two days a week. Leonora and Ben Senior have him two days, or I should say, Carmela has him. I'm working only four days. We hired a new guy, Nick Parker. Have you met him?"

"No, but I hear he's good."

"Exceptional. He's as near a horse whisperer as we've ever had, and he's a hunk to boot. Been a godsend with Jeb starting school and me under the weather. He's supposed to be coming tonight."

CHAPTER 11

As if on cue, Amy Foster and her dad appeared with two young men—Jeb Barnes, Maggie's assistant, and a stranger, brown hair, medium height, brown eyes. "Speak of the devil," Maggie laughed, waving them over.

Spark split from the group to greet his hostess, then headed out to the lawn to join his buddy as Jeb, Amy, and Nick headed their way. Maggie introduced the men, and Sam shook Parker's hand. He had a firm grip, and his wiry frame exuded strength. "Great to meet another Morgan brother. Haven't met Kyle, but you other three look like clones."

Sam laughed. "So we've heard. Maggie's just been singing your praises."

"Don't know about that, but it's great to be here. Everyone's been terrific."

Maggie and Amy wandered off, and Jeb went to the bar, leaving Sam and Parker together. Parker's eyes scanned the terrace. "You guys are sure lucky. This is an amazing place, and your parents are terrific."

"Yes, we are, and yes, it is," Sam said. "I know Robbie recruited you, but did you grow up in Sedona?"

"Yuma. In fact, my younger sister went to school with Stacy Winchester, Jeb's old girl," Parker said, referring to Jeb Barnes's former girlfriend, who had died in car crash the previous year.

"Small state sometimes, isn't it? Yeah, Stacy's death was really rough for everyone in the Valley. She was a sweetheart."

"So's Amy. Jeb's a lucky guy."

"They both are. Where's Toby tonight?"

"He's up north with Jeb's parents for a few weeks while his school's out," Parker said, nudging him. "Who is that babe?"

Sam followed his companion's gaze to find he was ogling Rose. "Rose Dillon," he said drily. "She's a close family friend, and she has a boyfriend."

"Too bad. She's gorgeous. Outta my league, of course, me bein' the hired help and all, but wow."

Wow indeed, Sam thought morosely, watching as Rose circulated, saying hello to everyone while keeping one eye on her dad.

The two men were startled as Harley Langdon, Nick's boss, came up from behind them. "Evenin', men. How's it goin'?"

"Hey, Harl. Wanta a beer? Parker asked.

"Sure do. Thanks, buddy."

As Nick headed off, Sam noticed he veered slightly in order to introduce himself to Rose, who took his hand, looking vaguely startled. "He's a player, our new hand," Harley said, chuckling. "Knows how to work a room of ladies, that's for sure. Better watch out he doesn't try to horn in on your girl."

"Rose is not my girl," Sam said.

"Yeah, and I'm the Easter Bunny."

"She has a boyfriend."

"Then you'd better make your move while you still can."

At that moment, Leonora Morgan clapped her hands. "Dinner is ready, everyone! Come get it while it's hot!"

The buffet was set up at the north edge of the terrace with two long tables displaying Leonora's beautiful collection of pottery and linens. Guests were free to grab a plate and sit at a table or on the grass. Carmela brought a picnic basket out for the children and laid a blanket on the lawn at the edge of the terrace. Maggie and Ben got their food and headed out to sit with them, and Ned Williams joined them.

As always, Carmela had outdone herself. The table groaned with food. Raoul had grilled skewers of beef, chicken, and fish, which were piled high on platters. There were bowls of citrus queso salad, green chili cheese quinoa, green salads, squash blossom quesadillas, and sweet and savory empanadas with queso fresco. On a separate table she had laid apple and quince tarts with cacique queso fresco filling, and when the time came, her homemade ice cream would appear with the tarts for dessert.

After making sure that everyone had what they needed, Leonora and Ben Senior presided over the largest table, joined by the Dillons, Lang and Beth, and Spark Foster. Amy and Jeb sat at another table, soon joined by Harley and Nick Parker. Sam was tempted to join the crowd on the lawn, but was hanging back to see where Rose landed. As she turned away from the buffet with a full plate, Ruthie called to her, "Join us over here, Rose!" So she sat down at the table with Harley and all.

As Sam filled his plate, he noticed an empty seat beside Rose and hurried over. When he approached and asked, "Is this seat taken?" Ruthie said, "No, join us, Sammy. Have you met Nick?" she added, leaning toward Parker, who sat on her right, Rose to her left.

"Yes, I have," Sam said, nodding to Parker, then sitting beside Rose, remembering to breathe. "Hey, Rose," he said softly, gazing into her hazel eyes.

"Hi, Sam," she said, shyly, their interchange not lost on the others. Her hand trembled as she raised a forkful of Carmela's to-die-for quinoa to her lips. "How're you doing?"

"Okay. I'm jobless and soon-to-be homeless, but I'm hanging in," he said quietly. "But let's not ruin the evening by dwelling on my troubles."

"Absolutely right," Ruthie said, waving a slice of quesadilla at him. "The Morgan-Foster army has been mobilized! So, tell us what's new at the stables," she said, batting her eyelashes at Nick. Nick and Jeb launched into a discussion of the past week's happenings as the others listened.

Ruthie's flirting with Nick was entirely for Harley's benefit. As she continued playing up to Parker, the wrangler watched, a grin on his face, but green eyes not quite concealing his irritation. *He's as in love with my sister as she is with him,* Sam thought, watching the normally laconic cowboy.

"How's work?" Rose asked Amy. She had helped Spark's daughter find a position as a physical therapist at one of the university clinics in Tucson, and the women often met for lunch in the city.

"Great, but I'd still love to be closer. The evening commute isn't all that fun for Toby or me."

Toby Hooper, Amy and Jeb's five-year-old foster child, was wheelchair-bound after a childhood accident damaged his spine. While the authorities were never certain, they suspected his mother's boyfriend had thrown him down a flight of stairs when he was barely two. Jeb and Amy met Toby, and each other, the previous summer, when Amy was serving as resident physical therapist at the ranch's summer camp Emma's Dream where Toby was a camper.

As the couple fell in love with each other, they also fell in love with the tiny boy, half the size of most children his age. When Jeb proposed, they decided to make Toby a part of their new family. At the moment, they were his foster parents, but the adoption papers were in the works, and they were hoping to celebrate Toby's adoption at the same time as their marriage.

Rose smiled at Amy as she felt Sam's hand touch hers, shivers running through her. "I know what you mean. I've been back and forth a lot, and it's a pain. How's Toby's school working out?"

"Great. And he's over with us for therapy four days a week, so I see him most days." Toby's school was adjacent to the clinic where Amy worked, a perfect arrangement, which Rose had also helped to arrange.

"Why not move to the Valley?" Parker said to Rose, oblivious to the interplay between her and Sam.

"My work is in Tucson," Rose said, surprised.

"What do you do?" he asked, drawing a frown from Ruthie.

"I work at a clinic."

Not to be ignored, Ruthie waved her fork at him. "Rose is a brilliant surgeon. She's the reason our niece is running around now and not confined to a wheelchair."

"Wow, that's cool," Parker said, nodding to Rose.

Sam reached down and took the hand Rose had rested in her lap. Her warmth suffused him, and for the first time since they parted at Gracie's, he felt calm. They continued to hold hands throughout dinner, Sam gently caressing hers, feeling himself grow hard with her nearness. Except for Amy, who noticed that right-handed Sam ate the remainder of his dinner left-handed, their tablemates were oblivious. Ruthie continued to flirt with Nick, Jeb and Harley talked work, and Amy listened to her fiancé while quietly observing Sam and Rose.

As everyone finished dessert and coffee was served, Beth and Lang rose to tell everyone their news. Rose watched her formerly commitment-phobic older brother as he gazed at his wife, their love for each other palpable. He had confided in her earlier in the evening that Beth was two months pregnant, so she was not surprised by the announcement. *When will I have that?* she thought as Lang spoke and everyone cheered.

Soon after dessert, Ben and his family departed, as did Spark and Ned Williams. Rose had driven her parents' car, but Lang and Beth offered to see them home. Lang drove his mother's car, and Beth followed in his Land Rover. Harley and Nick were headed into town to have a few drinks. They asked the others to join them, but everyone declined except Ruthie, who, after a sharp look from her older sister and a reminder of the early day they had tomorrow, begged off as well. Jeb and Amy had walked from their cabin, a half-mile away on the ranch's east ridge. They said their goodnights and walked arm and arm into the night.

Rose and Sam helped Raoul and Carmela clean up and failed to notice the others' departure until it was too late. She suddenly realized she had no ride home and decided the others had conspired to throw them together. Then Sam disappeared into the house. Blushing, she turned to her hosts. "I wonder if I could ask someone to drive me home? My brother seems to have forgotten me."

"Of course," Leonora said, waving to her housekeeper. "Carm, where's Raoul? Rose needs a ride home."

"Sam can take her, Nora," Ben Senior said, stepping forward, arm circling his wife's shoulders as he winked at Rose. "Can't you, Sammy?" he added as his son stepped back on the porch.

"Can't I what?"

"Drive our Rose home."

"Of course, happy to."

Chapter 12

Rose thanked her hosts, and they walked around the house to Sam's truck. "Kind of grungy in here. We could take my mother's car," he said.

"This is fine," she said, smiling at him, eyes twinkling in the moonlight.

"You look so beautiful."

"Thank you," she said, blushing as she ducked her head round to hop into the truck.

"I've missed you," he said, sliding in beside her. "I know I don't have the right to say that, but I have missed you the past few days."

I've missed you too. I've missed you, Sam Morgan, for much longer than a few days. Now you're in crisis and suddenly saying the words I longed to hear last year. "What's caused this change, do you think?" she asked.

"I guess I deserved that. Are you tired?"

"Not especially."

"Got time for me to show you my favorite place on the ranch?"

"Okay," she said softly.

"It's not far," he said. At the end of the drive, he turned right, onto the dirt road that led to Ben and Maggie's. At first, Rose imagined he meant to go to his brother's since the farmhouse was widely acknowledged to have the best views in the valley. Several hundred yards later, he turned right into a small clearing. "It's a short hike. You game?"

She nodded, and Sam grabbed a flashlight from the glove compartment. "The path's a little overgrown. You warm enough? I've got a sweatshirt in the back."

"I'm fine," she said, stepping out, snakes and mountain lions on her mind as he took her hand and led her into the thicket. As they progressed slowly, the ground rose and they began climbing up a gradual rise. Several times they heard rustling in the bushes nearby, but nothing disturbed them as they continued. Branches brushed against her, snagging her hair, bits and pieces of twigs and leaves clinging to her. She was about to suggest they turn back when they reached a clearing, the valley stretching before them to the shadowy mountains beyond.

"Here we are. Cool, huh?" he said, turning back to her. Even in the darkness he could see twigs and leaves entwined in her hair, and he smiled. "You okay?"

"Yes, but I'm glad we're here. It's beautiful."

"It's my secret," he said, squeezing her hand. "I've never brought anyone here. If I ever come back to the valley, this is where I'll pitch my tent."

"I wish I could see it in daylight."

You will, my darling Rose, if I have anything to say about it. He pointed to the right. "There's a stream over that way. It runs the length of the ranch. On the rare winters when we had a freeze, we used to skate on it, which is how I discovered this place. There's also a pond that way, and the land below is on an alluvial plain, so the soil is really rich."

"Amazing."

"So are you," he said, turning to cup her cheek. "Rose, I'm sorry about last year. I'm a world-class jerk."

The brightness of the full moon outlined every feature of his handsome face, a lock of hair falling over one eye. Rose didn't know what to say, so she kept silent, eyes gazing into his.

"Would you be offended if I kissed you?" he asked softly.

In answer, she placed her hand over his and stepped closer. Sam drew her into his arms and captured her luscious lips, his tongue tickling, probing, twining round hers. Rose sighed, a deep sigh of longing, and gave herself to him. As her arms circled his neck, Sam moved his hands down to cup her small, round breasts, teasing the nipples to hardness through the thin fabric of her tee shirt.

He groaned. "Rose, tell me to stop or I'm not sure I can."

"Don't stop," she whispered as she ran her fingers through his hair, returning his kisses as their bodies pressed against each other.

"You warm enough, baby?" he asked as his hand reached under her tee shirt to unhook her bra and release her small, perfect breasts.

She nodded, one hand caressing his chest, then moving down to rub against his erection as it pressed against her tummy. *I love you, Sam Morgan. I could never be cold when you're holding me.*

Arms round her waist, Sam lifted her, wrapping her legs round him as he moved to a nearby ledge. "That's better," he said, smiling, as his hands gently slid her capris to the ground, her panties following. Before she knew what was happening, his fingers moved between her legs to her moist wetness. She was ready for him. More than ready, and he nearly lost it as she caressed him, fingers moving to unbutton his jeans and release his penis. Before his jeans fell, he grabbed them, pulling out his wallet, in which he kept a condom.

"It's been a while," he whispered. "So let's hope this is still intact."

All coherent thought left her as Rose arched her back, legs gripping his waist, drawing him closer. "Please, Sam, please," she begged as he plunged into her soft depths, depths that massaged and enveloped him. Never had a woman fit him like this, and Sam feared he'd lose all control as she squeezed him deep inside her.

"Oh, God, Rose."

Their bodies grew slick as they matched each other thrust for thrust. In the midst of their passion, she opened her eyes and gazed into his. *There you are, the man I love,* she thought, as Sam Morgan took her to heights she'd never climbed before.

In the moonlight, Sam's eyes never left hers as they reached a blinding climax, each crying out into the stillness. *Rose, Rose, Rose, where have you been all my life?* he thought as their breathing slowed and they melted into each other's arms. The sharp, jagged rocks dug into his back, but Sam barely noticed them as he held her, legs shaking now in the aftermath of their lovemaking. "Are you okay?" he whispered, kissing and then sucking her tiny ear lobe.

"More than okay." She rested her head against his neck. The cool night air sent goosebumps up and down her spine, so she held tighter, absorbing his warmth.

"You're cold."

"I don't mind," she whispered, never wanting to let go of this wonderful dream.

"Well, I do, darling," he said, withdrawing from her moist, nurturing depths with a groan. "Let's get you dressed."

They fumbled around in the dark, locating clothes and dressing each other playfully. Fully dressed, they stood facing each other, her hand caressing his jaw, Sam's hands around her waist. "You're still cold, aren't you?" he said. "Come here."

He drew her close and kissed her. Rose returned the kiss as his tongue delved deeper. After several minutes, he pulled back slightly, gazing down at her. "Much as I'd like to take this further, you're shivering, so we'd better head back."

Rose took his hand, and he led her back to the path. Descending was easier, and they were soon standing by the truck.

"You want my sweatshirt, sweetie?" he asked, pulling her to him.

"I'm fine."

"Have I taken advantage of you?"

She shook her head. "In case you didn't notice, I was a willing participant."

"I did notice," he said, kissing the tip of her nose. "But I'm not a complete ignoramus. I knew how you felt about me last year."

"You did?"

He nodded. "I knew and I walked away."

"Yes, you did," she said softly.

"Can you ever forgive me?"

"Well, I guess I have. Either that, or I've fallen under your charms and will soon have my heart broken again."

"What about Dan?"

"Yes, there's Dan," she said, not wanting to discuss her conflicted feelings about him with Sam.

"And?"

"I don't know. We're seeing each other tomorrow night."

"And?"

Her hand touched his cheek, fingers running lightly along his chiseled jawline. "I'd better get home, Sam. There are no words to describe how I feel right now. It was incredible, but it's not like me at all. I'm the steady, sensible one. I can't. We can't."

"Is this because I mentioned Dan?"

"Yes. No. I don't know." She looked away, unable to meet his eyes.

"I wish I could spend the night holding you in my arms."

Me, too, she thought, but simply said, "It's getting really late, Sam."

They rode back in silence. After Sam parked in the Dillons' circular drive, he hopped out and came round to open Rose's door.

"What time do you leave tomorrow?" he asked.

"Early."

"No time for breakfast?"

"'Fraid not."

"When will you be back?"

"Hard to say. Next week is crazy busy." Rose longed to throw herself into his strong arms, but she held back, confused and wary. No man had ever made love to her like that, but he'd also broken her heart and was perfectly capable of doing it again once his crisis passed.

"Can I call you?"

She nodded. "Of course."

"Can I kiss you goodnight?"

Rose moved closer and her arms circled his shoulders, fingers caressing his neck. He bent to kiss her, softly at first, then harder, more desperately as his tongue thrust deeper. She found herself weak-kneed as she gave herself to him. Rose was certain that if he'd asked to take her into the barn and make love again, she would have agreed in a heartbeat. Finally, a warning voice sounded in her head, and she pulled away.

"Goodnight, Sam."

"Goodnight, my sweet Rose."

His hair was mussed, eyes sad. Rose softened, and she reached out to brush a lock of hair from his forehead. "Good luck with everything this week. It sounds like you've got a great attorney. Between you, your lawyer, your dad, and Spark, I'm certain they'll settle this quickly. And don't hesitate to get in touch with Dad as well. He may be difficult with us, but he's got lots of connections, and he'd love to help. Give him something to do."

Reality, Sam thought as she spoke. *Back to reality now.* He kissed her lightly on the forehead, then smiled. "This was an amazing night." *A magical night.*

"For me, too," she said, turning away and walking up the steps and into the house. At the open door, she waved.

As she disappeared, closing the door behind her, Sam's heart ached. *What a fool you were, Sam Morgan. What a stupid, stupid fool.*

CHAPTER 13

The next morning, Sam's cell rang at six. *Who would be calling at such an ungodly hour?* His hand groped around the night table, finally grabbing it. "Yup?"

"Good morning, Mr. Morgan?"

Sam sat up. The voice was familiar through the fog, but he couldn't place it. "Yes?"

"Will Santiago here. Didn't wake you, did I?"

"Hey, Will. What's up?"

"I've got good news and mediocre news."

"Oh?" Sam rubbed his eyes, pulling on sweat pants.

"Our little Ms. Wainwright has gag orders in place at her last three places of employment. My guy will ferret them out Monday, but that usually means someone's left under a cloud. We'll have the particulars soon. Even if we can't use 'em in court, it'll give us lots of leverage."

"What's the mediocre news?"

"Once she and your bosses—"

"Former bosses."

"Yeah. Once she and your former bosses got wind that you'd hired me, she changed tactics. She wants the Foster project bad, and so do Rayburn and Davos. Turns out it's the biggest thing they've got going now. Ms. Rainmaker is not pullin' in as much business as she promised, and now that their up-and-coming star has quit, they're in panic mode."

"That's because neither senior does much work, and my colleague Roy is strictly small commercial."

"Don't know the reason. Don't care. All I know is they want the Foster money and Wainwright wants the man himself. Once she learned he was a widower, she had her secretary digging into his net worth all over the place. I'll bet my bottom dollar that she's aimin' to be the next Mrs. Foster."

"How do you know all this?"

Santiago chuckled. "I have my sources. Turns out Ms. Meryl isn't well-liked at the firm. Big surprise there.

"So where's this leave us?"

"My guess is we'll be able to settle the harassment Tuesday. I've got a couple of aces in my pocket there."

"What are they?"

"Better if you don't know. Just show up and do as I say, which will mostly be to remain silent."

"What about Spark?"

"I've spoken to the two guys he flew down. They'll get him out of the contract. May cost a bit."

"No, I don't want him to pay for my mistakes."

"Out of your hands, Sam, my boy. And if I hear you talkin' about your mistakes again, I'll bring a muzzle Tuesday. You have made *no* mistakes, comprende?"

"What a mess," Sam mumbled.

"Meryl's mess, not yours. Remember that. Gotta go. Have a great weekend."

Will clicked off, leaving Sam shaking his head. Since he was up, he decided a long run would do him good. Lang had said to call early, so he dialed his brother-in-law's cell.

"Just heading out. Meet you at the crossroads. We can run along the Gila. Riverbed's dry now," Lang said. "See you in fifteen."

The two men ran eight miles along the dry riverbed until the path began to loop and circle back toward Morgan's Run. "Got enough left to run the ranch loop?" Sam asked. "Thought I'd stop in at the stables to see my brother."

"Sure," Lang said, "but I'll bet he's over at the camp. They open in less than four weeks." He referred to the summer camp for handicapped children, Emma's Dream, the brainchild of Maggie Morgan. She and Ben ran it, along with help from many others. The ranch loop circled round the far edge of the camp and then right by the stables.

"Let's give it a try," Sam said as they headed down the path leading to the well-worn trail.

When they reached the camp grounds, no one was about, so they continued on through the woods and thicket and emerged a short distance from the stables. As they neared the corrals, it was clear no one was in yet as no vehicles were parked alongside the barn. "Saturday," Lang said as the sounds of horses nickering came from within.

"I think I'll hang here for a bit," Sam said. "Someone's bound to come soon. Want a water?"

They grabbed two water bottles from the office fridge and sat in the shade overlooking the corrals. They had spent most of the run talking sports, work, and the latest Rambler Sports line of products. Lang Dillon was a few years older and had left the Valley for college. He had not returned until the visit when he fell in love with Beth, so Sam didn't know him very well. He made his sister happy. That was all he needed to know. They sat in silence, staring out at the beautiful day unfolding before them.

Finally, Lang broke the silence. "How are things going? Don't mean to pry if you'd rather not talk about it."

"Well, let's see. I quit my job, I'm the subject of a lawsuit, and the project I took almost a year planning is about to be snatched away from me unless Spark pays through the nose."

"Which he can."

"Yeah, but I won't let him."

Lang chuckled. "Good luck stopping him."

"I've got a good lawyer and Spark's got people working on it, so who knows. Everyone here is behind me, which means a lot."

"Always, buddy."

"Your sister's been great."

"Rosie? Yeah, she's pretty terrific."

"Yes," Sam said, voice trailing off.

"Thought you two might be getting together last year."

Sam stared at the other's steely blue eyes. "Yeah, and I blew it."

"Thought as much. My sister doesn't say much, but she was hurting last year after our wedding."

"I'm sorry about that. I was a world-class shit." *How many times have I said that in the past week?*

"Rose is a big girl. She knew what she was getting into, especially with a Morgan."

"Yeah, I guess so."

"Thing is, I wouldn't want to see her messed about with again. You're hurting and looking for solace, and she's a kind, generous soul."

"I know, but it's different now. She has a boyfriend."

"He's an ass."

"Excuse me?"

"Dan the Man, he's a self-important prick."

"I heard he was a nice guy."

"Maybe, but I've spent some time with him and am not impressed. Falls all over Rose when everyone's around, but he's manipulative as hell. Part of me thinks he's dating her only to get ahead in his residency, but don't tell anyone I said that. Our mom likes him. He sucks up to her big time whenever he's here. Dad too."

Sam wanted to ask more, but at that moment the barn door swung open, and Harley and his brother appeared. "Hey, guys," Ben said. "What brings you two over here so early? Applying for a job?"

"End of a run," Sam said, drinking the last of his water. "Got a few minutes, brother?"

"Only if you wanta come down and talk at the camp."

Lang stood. "I've got to head out. Harley, Ben, see you around. Sam, thanks for the run."

"Want a lift?" Harley asked. "I'm running into town in five and can drop you."

"Thanks, but one more mile won't kill me," Lang said, heading round the side of the barn to the loop trail.

As the brothers walked to Ben's truck, Jeb and Nick Parker drove in. During the short drive to the camp, Sam said, "Cocky one, that Parker."

"He's a good guy. Hard worker, and we really need him right now. He's going on the next pack trip with Harley cause I don't want to leave Maggie."

"I'd say I'd help out down there, me being out of a job and all, but I'm not sure how much help I'd be."

Ben laughed. "I'll keep that in mind in case there's a call for a tenderfoot. So, did I sense a bit of a freeze back there?"

Sam looked over at his brother, who was now grinning from ear to ear. "I've been warned off."

"Yeah, he's pretty protective of Rosie."

"I really like her."

"Yeah, well, go slow. That's my advice. She's got that boyfriend, and you're going through a rough patch. Let things settle, why don't you?"

"The rough patch is what I wanted to talk to you about. How can I prevent Spark from paying off the vultures from Rayburn and Davos?"

"You can't, and if I know Spark, by the time he gets through with them, they'll be paying him. He's a teddy bear with us, but make no mistake. In business, he's fair and honest, but don't cross him. Those guys he's brought down make your barracuda look like a guppy."

Sam smiled as they hopped out of the truck near the camp office. "Let's hope so. Now, tell me about Emma's Dream. What's in store for this year's campers?"

CHAPTER 14

Dan had chosen the restaurant. Rose did not particularly like Parson's. It was a stuffy place, and the food was mediocre and overpriced, but it was a favorite of some of the clinic physicians, and Dan was always looking to network. As she sipped the excellent cabernet he had ordered, she consulted her menu, not sure how to begin what would certainly be a very uncomfortable conversation.

As the waiter bowed and disappeared with their dinner orders, she took another sip of wine. Before she could speak, Dan said, "You're very quiet. I mean, you're always quiet, but more so tonight. What'd you do last night?"

"I went home."

"Oh? Why didn't you say anything?"

"Mother called and begged me to come for the night."

"Why? Is something wrong?"

"Just same old, same old. We were invited to Morgan's Run for dinner, and she wanted me to come with them."

"I see." His eyes flashed fire, but Dan forced a smile. "Fun?"

She gulped. "Yes, actually. It's always comforting to be with old friends."

"Instead of me? It's not comforting with me?"

"That's not what I meant. It meant a lot to Mother, so I went."

"And clearly didn't want me along. Was *he* there?"

"If you mean Sam Morgan, yes, he was."

"Of course he was, hence your running back to Saguaro after your very tiring week."

Rose sighed, wishing she were a million miles away. "I didn't run back to Saguaro. My mother called and I went. That's all."

Dan drank his wine in one gulp and refilled his glass. "Do you love him?"

"He's an old friend, that's all," she lied, unable to meet his gaze.

"Tonight was supposed to be a celebration."

"Oh?" she looked up and met his brown eyes, which were softer now.

"I've been offered a permanent position in Pittsburgh. A combination of teaching and surgery."

"That's wonderful! Congratulations!" she reached over and grasped his hand, genuinely pleased for him.

"I was hoping you might consider coming with me."

Shocked, she stared at him. "But we've only known each other a short time. Besides, my work is here. I helped Dr. Heavers set up the clinic."

"Yes, but it's a well-oiled machine now with many people to carry on the work."

"Dan, I can't just up and leave. I have no position back east."

"Marry me, Rose. Marry me and come to Pittsburgh. I can support us both, and you can look for a position after we're settled." He was right about that. A trust fund baby, Dan had millions and had financed his entire medical education without a single loan.

"This is very sudden. Why, we've never even—"

"Made love," he whispered. "We can change that tonight. Please say yes, Rose."

At that moment, the waiter appeared with their meals, serving them with a flourish. When he departed, she said, "I'm sorry, but I can't."

"Can't what?"

"Move to Pittsburgh, marry you, any of it right now. I'm sorry, but it's too soon."

"I love you, Rose," he said, reaching for her hand, which she withdrew and placed in her lap.

She liked Dan and enjoyed his company, but Rose couldn't help thinking that all this was because he was jealous of Sam. Dan had never professed love or any strong feelings for her. Proposing marriage and asking her to pull up stakes and move across the country now, all of a sudden, seemed forced and precipitous.

"I'm honored by your proposal, but I cannot give you the answer you want right now. I'm sorry. Maybe it's best if we leave it for now."

"Of course, my darling," he said, turning his attention to the enormous slab of red meat on his plate.

Rose picked at her salmon, which was dry, and ate some of the overcooked vegetable medley served with the fish. They talked a little about work and what was ahead for the coming week. When she asked about the Pittsburgh job and when he would begin, he was evasive and changed the subject. Both declined dessert, and Dan insisted upon paying.

When they reached the car, he came around to open her door. As they stood together, he kissed her softly, his lips dry, breath heavy with wine. He had consumed nearly a bottle and a half by himself as she nursed her first and only glass. She reached up and touched his cheek as she pulled back. "Would you mind awfully if we skipped the concert?"

"Is that an invitation?" he asked, speech somewhat slurred.

"No, it's just that I'm a bit tired and feel a headache brewing."

"Whatever my lady wants." He opened the door with a slight bow.

It was only a short distance to her condo, but he had clearly overindulged. "Would you like me to drive?"

"I'm fine," he said, shutting the door.

As they started off, his driving seemed fine and Rose breathed a sigh of relief, leaning back, praying the night would end soon. He pulled up in front of her condo and parked, hopping out to open her door.

"Thanks, Dan. I'm sorry about the concert and the rest," she said as they stood side by side at the curb.

"Aren't you going to ask me in?"

"As I said, I'm tired."

"And you have a headache. Gotcha. I can at least walk you to the door and make sure you're safely inside."

"Of course, thank you," she said, taking his arm.

She lived in a two-story townhouse, a short walkway leading to the front door. As she pulled her keys from her bag and unlocked the door, Dan hovered.

Rose turned around and looked up at him. "Well, goodnight. Thank you for dinner and everything."

"Is this the brush-off?"

"Dan, it's late."

"No, it isn't. It's barely dark, and I'm sick of your teasing. Bet you wouldn't send Sam Morgan packing at eight thirty!"

Before she knew what was happening, Dan had his arms round her, kissing her roughly as he forced his way in and slammed the door shut with his foot. His hands were everywhere as he groped with her clothes, ripping her skirt off. Grasping claw fingers tore her linen blouse, casting it aside along with her bra as he held her in an iron grip. Rose screamed and lashed out at him, but he held fast, tearing her panties off as he fumbled with his jeans. As they struggled, he moved them toward the sofa, teeth sinking into her neck.

"Dan, let me go!"

"Not on your life, my darling," he growled, flinging her downward, his body on top of her. As he spread her legs, Rose struck out again, finally sinking her teeth into his shoulder. "Why, you little bitch," he snarled, rearing back and slapping her hard across her cheek.

Dazed, Rose came to her senses as he forced himself on her, thrusting into her with a savagery that took her breath away. As he rammed into her again and again, she struggled, then went limp, tears streaming down her face. Over in minutes, it seemed like days. As he stood, zipping up his pants and collecting his clothes, Rose curled into a fetal position, turning away from the sight of him, afraid she might pass out or vomit.

"That's how a real man does it, honey," he said, stalking out and slamming the door.

Bruised and battered, she sobbed, pulling a blanket around herself, then crawling to her purse to retrieve her phone. She punched the number, praying her brother would answer. When he did, the sound of his voice brought fresh sobs, and she was unable to speak for several seconds.

"Who is this?" Lang said, voice startled.

"It's me," she finally said. "I…I need you, Lang."

"Where are you, Rosie?"

"My house. He, Dan, he attacked me and I need to go to the hospital."

"Jesus Christ, sweetheart. Hold on. I'll be there as soon as I can. I'm gonna call an ambulance."

"No, I'll call them. I'm going to ask to be taken to University Medical, okay?"

"Of course, sweetie. I'm leaving now."

Rose gathered the blanket around her shoulders, unlocked the front door, then collapsed onto a nearby rocker to wait for the paramedics. She closed her eyes.

Chapter 15

Lang and Beth arrived at the hospital ten minutes after the ambulance. Beth had insisted on coming, gripping the seat the entire ride as her husband broke every speed limit. The only time she dared look, the speedometer read a hundred and ten.

They found her in a trauma room, alone, waiting for a doctor. One look at her bruised face and Lang went ballistic. "I'll kill him!"

Beth put her hand on his arm and he calmed a bit, hugging Rose gently.

"Hey, sweetie," he said. "How're you doing?"

She gave him a crooked smile. "I've been better. They're really busy tonight. There was a shooting in the south end."

"That's no excuse. Where's the doctor?"

"They've already collected the rape kit. I'm fine. The physician's assistant thinks this needs stitches," Rose said, pointing to the cut on her forehead.

Lang looked at his wife. "Stay with her. I'm going to find someone."

When he disappeared, Beth took the chair beside her. "Rose, I'm so sorry. Does it hurt much?"

"Only in here," she replied, hand over her chest. "He asked me to marry him."

Beth face registered shock, and she took her sister-in-law's hand.

"He asked you to marry him and then did this?"

"I'm pretty sure his proposal was spur-of-the-moment, brought on by jealousy."

"Of who? What?"

"Last week, I told him I'd seen Sam and he was going through a rough time. I told him he was an old family friend, but I wouldn't tell Dan what was going on, and that made him angry and jealous."

"He's more than a friend, isn't he?"

"Yes," Rose said softly. "But I'm trying to ignore it."

Beth nodded. "I am well acquainted with my brother's 'love 'em and leave 'em' behavior, and I'm sorry if Sam hurt you last year."

"My fault, I guess. Falling too fast. I fear Dan saw something when we talked. Something that made him jealous and possessive. When I told him I'd gone home for the dinner last night, he was furious."

"Oh, dear."

"Yes. I intended to break up with Dan tonight. I had my speech all prepared when he proposed, and the evening spiraled down from there."

"Were you breaking up with him because of Sam?"

"Maybe. I don't know. But Dan and I weren't going anywhere. We're too different. He's gotten a position in Pittsburgh and wanted me to go with him. Even if I loved him, I'm not sure I'd have gone, but I didn't love him, and he knew it. We had never done more than kiss each other goodnight before this."

Rose began to sob, and Beth stood and put her arms round her. "Don't think about it anymore. We'll get you home as soon as we can."

"No, I can't go home! I never want to see the condo again, or at least not tonight."

"Then come home to Saguaro. Lang and I have plenty of room, if you'd rather not stay at your folks'."

Rose nodded. "Can I ask you a favor?"

"Of course, anything," Beth said, taking her hand again.

"I—he ripped—I mean, I don't have any clothes. They brought me in wrapped in a blanket. Could you possibly go to the condo, pack a suitcase for me, and grab something for me to wear out of here? I'm determined to leave as soon as they stitch me up, and I'd rather not walk out of here in a johnny."

Beth waited while Rose made a list and explained where things were. Then she went to find Lang, who was pacing up and down the hall. She took his car keys, explained where she was going and headed out with, "Darling, please stay calm for Rose's sake."

Several hours later, they had her settled in their newly furnished guest room. "Our very first guest," Beth said, smiling. "You okay? You need anything?"

"No, this is lovely, Beth. Thank you. And thank my big brother."

"I'm sure he'll be up to say goodnight."

"Yes, I will," her husband said, peeking his head in the door. "You ladies doing okay?"

Rose gave him a tired smile. "Thank you, big brother." She reached out her hand and he came forward to take it, eyes rimmed with tears.

"Glad we could be there," he said. "You got everything you need?"

She nodded.

"You want me to call Mom in the morning?"

"Let me sleep on it first, okay? I'm not sure what I want to do."

"You got it."

He hesitated, staring at her for a minute or two. "I didn't call the police, but I'm going to, first thing. I'm assuming that's what you want?"

"Let me think on that, too. I know I can't work with him, so something will have to be done. Let's talk tomorrow, okay?"

They closed the door and Rose drifted off into a restless, troubled sleep.

CHAPTER 16

At Ben's request, Sam agreed to help out at the stables Sunday morning. Harley was called away, Maggie was ill, and Ben and Jeb were back and forth between camp and stables, completing a long list of jobs. They needed Sam to help with routine chores so that Nick could devote most of his day to their two newest acquisitions. A week ago, Maggie had received an emergency call from a breeder in Prescott, asking if they'd be interested in taking on two Friesians. Light draft horses, graceful and nimble for their size, the pair had been abused and neglected by a rancher near Prescott. Jim Santos, the local breeder, had brought charges and successfully impounded the two.

"Mag's really excited about 'em," Ben said when he called. "They're young, only five or six. Poor things are in pretty rough shape. We've got Ned comin' to check 'em out." Maggie's Dad, Ned Williams, had completed three years in veterinary school before dropping out for financial reasons. He often served as vet for local livestock unless surgery was needed, as the nearest vet was in Tucson.

When Sam arrived, the two black stallions were in separate corrals behind the barn, Nick with one. Both horses' ribs were visible, their coats dull and blotchy. Their manes had been combed but were scraggly. When Nick spied Sam, he nodded, his movements slow as he spoke softly to the horse, feeding him small handfuls of oats.

"Poor guy," Sam said, watching Parker's gentle hands as he stroked the scared, neglected creature.

"Asshole should be shot," Nick said quietly as he led the horse to the fence. "Meet Thor. That's his buddy Raffles," he said, indicating the other horse.

"Are they related?" Sam asked, looking from one to the other.

"No one knows. They couldn't get any documentation on 'em. Must've been registered sometime, though. Maggie's looking in to it."

"Has she seen them?"

"No, says she'll be over later today."

"I'll bet they were beauties once."

"And they will be again, if we can save 'em. They're in pretty rough shape. Hope Ned has good news for us."

"Me, too. Have you seen my brother?"

Nick nodded. "He and Jeb left for the camp a while ago. I think they're plannin' to be there most of the day. Maggie had a lesson, but she's rescheduled it."

"Well, I'll get started inside," Sam said.

As Sam and Nick mucked stalls, Ned Williams spent several hours looking over the new arrivals. Afterward, he sought them out. "Poor fellas."

"Just what I said," Sam said, leaning on his pitchfork.

"They both have some skin infections and, from the looks of it, some kind of digestive issues. Give this to my daughter. Feed 'em pellets in small quantities at first. I'll write up a plan. She can get the meds and supplements on there from Ferris Feed." he said, handing Nick a paper. "Where is she, anyway? Thought she planned to be here for this?"

"Hey, Dad," they heard, turning to spy Maggie with the two kids in tow. Ben the third was in an umbrella stroller, his sister pushing him. "So, how are they?"

Ned kissed his daughter, then bent to kiss Emma and the baby. "With lots of love, they should pull through. Raffles is worse than Thor. Look like he's been whipped and beaten. Owner should be hung. Parker here has all my recommendations. No saddles, no ridin' till they're stronger."

Nick handed her the list as they walked out to the back corrals. Emma climbed the fence and reached out to pet Thor, who had trotted right up to her. "Hey, honey," she said softly, hand gently rubbing his nose.

"Their teeth are pretty good," Ned said, "so watch out, Emmie."

"He's not gonna bite me," she whispered, resting her face against the horse's neck. Like her mother and grandfather, Emma had an innate connection to horses. She had absolutely no fear of them, except her mother's enormous draft horse, Tabasco, another rescue, who now lived in their barn along with Sunny, her pony.

Thor stood quietly, basking in the attention as the others observed. Sam had taken a break and now stood beside his sister-in-law. "How're you feeling?"

"Better than earlier, but I still feel like crap. Wanted to come see these guys, and I've got to find Ben. Beth called and really needs to speak with him, and he's not answering his cell. I don't know why he even has the thing. Never has it on him!"

"Everything okay?"

"Something about Rose, but the baby was screaming so I had to hang up. Dad, could you possibly watch the kids here while I run down to the camp?"

"Course, honey. Scoot," Ned said, patting baby Ben's head.

Heart pounding, Sam said, "Want me to drive you?"

"Not necessary, but thanks," she said. "You carry on here. The stalls are looking great, by the way. Thanks."

Before he could protest, Maggie disappeared into the barn with a backward wave.

CHAPTER 17

Rose woke, every inch of her body sore. When she looked in the bathroom mirror, she found she had two black eyes and her forehead was swollen an angry purple and blue around the seven stitches. Idly, she wondered if she would need plastic surgery. Clearly she was not going back to work looking like this. She called Sadie, her assistant, at home and asked her to cancel and reschedule all her appointments for the next two weeks.

"Are you okay?" Sadie asked, concern in her voice.

Rose trusted her assistant implicitly, but wanted to talk to the other members of her team and the acting clinic director, Richard Pruit, before relating last night's incident to anyone else. "Getting there, Sade, thanks. I promise I'll call and tell you more later. I want to speak with Richard first. I'll ask him to find coverage for my surgical schedule, which is relatively light for the next few weeks."

"Of course," Sadie said, ringing off.

The conversation with Richard Pruit was long and difficult. Rose related the entire story, ending with, "I cannot work with him, Rich."

"Of course you can't, but it may take some time. Let me see what I can do. Dan's a bit of an ass, but he's reasonable and a very talented surgeon. Maybe he'd agree to go now and Pittsburgh would welcome an earlier start."

"I've asked my brother to contact the police."

"As is your right, of course. We'd like to keep things as quiet as possible, though. I hope you understand."

"Yes."

"And Rose, I will support you any way I can. You are his superior, so it may be tricky. Everyone knows you've been dating. In fact, last week people were speculating whether or not you'd be leaving us for Pittsburgh."

"Well, I'm not and never was. In fact, he just told me about the job last night."

Pruit sighed. "Not to worry. I'll alert the surgical team and get coverage. Take your time and let me know when you're ready. I believe I will ask Dan to take a few days' leave until we sort this out."

"Thanks, Rich," Rose said, hanging up and leaning back against the pillow. *What a nightmare. Once this gets out, how will I ever face my team?* She thought of Sam and their tender lovemaking. *Just two nights ago, but it seems a lifetime away.* She curled up her legs, wondering if she would ever again want a man to touch her.

***

By noon, the stalls were all clean with fresh bedding raked smooth. The horses were fed and exercised, and Nick was back out with the Friesians. Ned had taken the kids on a walk up the eastern slope, so the barn and environs were quiet. Sam grabbed a water and a granola bar from the office and came to sit in the shade of the barn, observing Parker. As the young trainer walked Thor around the corral, Sam marveled at how good he was with him.

Finally, impatient and restless, he chugged the water, ate half the bar, and threw the rest away. Then he headed back into the barn and saddled Royal, his dad's horse. He might not have been a horseman, but he could handle the gentle morgan on the short ride to Emma's Dream. Royal nickered softly as Sam tightened the saddle and slipped on the halter. Horse in tow, Sam walked out of the barn and called to Nick, "Won't be long. Just riding down to the camp."

Parker waved and turned back to Thor as Sam led Royal around the barn, then mounted easily. The camp was an easy half-mile ride, and they made their way slowly, Royal in no particular hurry and Sam loath to encourage him lest he break into a full gallop. As they neared the end of the dirt road and the camp grounds opened up before them, he marveled again at the amazing facility Maggie and Ben had created. He had helped design the buildings, but the vision had been all theirs. Now, as they readied for their third season, plantings had matured, the grass was green and lush, and the huge pool glistened, ready for the eager campers coming soon.

Ben's Rover was parked by the office, so Sam headed Royal that way and tied him to a post nearby. As he massaged the horse's flank, he spied his brother and Maggie sitting in the shade of the dining hall porch. As they looked up and saw him, Maggie headed toward the office and Ben waved. "Hey, Sammy. Mornin', or is it afternoon?"

"Just about," Sam said, coming to sit beside him.

Ben's face grave, he forced a smile. "Thanks for all your help this morning, bro. Mag said the stalls looked terrific. Wish we could keep you, but after Parker gets the newbies settled in, we should be fine. College kids start next week. Wouldn't want to damage those fancy architect hands."

"Which may never work again."

"Bull."

"Camp looks terrific."

"Yeah, we're pretty pleased with it. Can't wait for the new crew. What brings you down here?"

"Something's happened, hasn't it?" Sam could see in his brother's face that something had, indeed, happened.

"What d'you mean?"

"Rose. Something's happened to her, hasn't it?"

His brother stared straight ahead, unable to meet his eyes. "Beth called."

"And?"

"Now, look, Sammy, I'm not sure. It's not my—"

"Ben, please tell me. Is she okay?"

"She's fine, just shaken up."

"From what? Please."

"That boyfriend of hers attacked her last night. Lang and Beth went to Tucson and brought her home. She's at their house. They haven't told her folks yet, or they hadn't when Beth called."

"What do you mean, attacked?"

"She was raped," he said quietly. "Pretty roughly from the sound of it."

"I've got to see her," Sam said, standing, pacing back and forth.

"She doesn't want to see anybody."

"What are they doing about the guy? Has he been arrested?"

"From what Beth said, bastard's in the wind. They can't find him."

"I've gotta go."

"Leave her be, Sammy. You've got enough on your plate right now, and I'm pretty certain Rose wouldn't want you to see her in her condition."

"Thanks. I've gotta get Royal back. Call if you need any more help."

Ben watched his brother stalk off, knowing full well he would ignore his advice. *He'll find a way to sneak over there before sundown. He's crazy in love with Rose Dillon, even if he'd never admit it in a million years.*

CHAPTER 18

As he nudged Royal on in the direction of the stables, Sam's thoughts were with Rose. His troubles now seemed trivial and inconsequential. *I've got to see her. All they can do is turn me away.*

As he reached the top of the camp road, instead of turning north to the stables, he reined Royal to the left, turning south and cantering through the ranch gates and along the shoulder of the road leading to the winery. Beth and Lang had built their dream house at the northwestern corner of the Dillon property. Like Ben and Maggie's, it sat on a rise facing west. Their views were westward over the valley to the mountains and southward overlooking the vineyards and grazing pastures dotted with the Dillons' prize Angus cattle.

Sam could have taken the ranch loop, which eventually wound around to the house, but then he would have had to pass the Morgan's Run stables, and he had no wish to stop and chat. At the first opportunity, he veered off the shoulder and guided Royal along a dry creek bed, which he was reasonably sure hooked up with the ranch loop trail in a mile or so. Royal hesitated, whinnying softly, and Sam wondered if he might be leading them astray. As they proceeded slowly, familiar rock formations appeared, and horse and man relaxed. Ten minutes later, the creek bed intersected with the ranch loop just south of Ben and Maggie's.

He turned south again, and in five minutes, horse and rider pulled alongside Turtle Rock, which meant the house was around the next bend. As Sam made his way down the winding trail, the house appeared on the rise. Lang's fondness for Cape Cod beach houses had led him and Sam to design the beautiful house with shingled siding. Unusual for the southwest, the house had been featured in several architectural journals the past year. When asked about it, Sam always credited Lang, but Beth and Lang disagreed, and were quick to say that what made the house livable and spectacular was all her brother's doing.

Beth's truck and Lang's Rover were both gone, so he tied Royal to the fence in a shady spot, fetched a bucket from the terrace, and filled it from the outside faucet. After setting it near the horse, he headed up the front steps and opened the unlocked door.

"Hello, anyone here?"

Rose was upstairs, indulging herself with lunch in bed. She was reading a novel she'd found on one of the bookshelves. She had just taken the last bite of her avocado and sprouts sandwich and was sipping iced tea when she heard him call. She jumped, nearly upsetting her drink. *What is he doing here?* She considered not answering, but felt foolish hiding in her room.

"Hi, I'm up here. No one else is home."

"Can I come up?" he called, already at the bottom of the stairs.

"Give me five minutes and I'll come down," she said. Rose gazed in the mirror, and tears sprang to her eyes. *Do I really want him to see me like this?*

She pulled a thin sweater over her tank top to hide the marks Dan had left on her upper arms. She wore jeans and socks, and her hair was tied back in a haphazard ponytail. She removed the tie and ran a brush through her hair. *Not a pretty sight, but it will have to do.* As she descended, she called, "I have to warn you, I've looked better."

"I'll close my eyes if you like," he said, but his eyes were wide open when she stepped into the living room. Had he not known it was Rose, he might not have recognized her. Her lovely face was bruised and battered.

"Oh, my God, what did he do to you?"

Unbidden tears sprung to her eyes. As she stood staring at him, she began to tremble, and Sam rushed to envelop her in a gentle hug. "I'm here, sweetie. I'm so sorry." She went limp in his arms and he lifted her, carrying her to the sofa and setting her down gently.

She reached over and grabbed a tissue, wiping her eyes, then sat up straight, moving away from him. "Pretty scary-looking, huh?"

"No, of course not."

"Want something to drink? There are lots of things in the fridge. Beth made some delicious iced tea this morning, and there's—"

He gently placed two fingers over her lips. "Let me get you something. What would *you* like?"

"I'm fine. Just had a tea." Dusty from the ride, a line of dirt across his brow, he still looked gorgeous in jeans and an olive-green ranch tee shirt. Despite his nearness, Rose felt nothing. It was as if all her senses had numbed, and she was an empty shell staring vacantly at the man she once loved. "You didn't have to come."

"I had to see you. How are you holding up?"

"Been better, but they're taking good care of me here."

"Please, Rose, what can I do?"

"Nothing. You've got troubles of your own."

"Have they charged the bastard?"

"I'm not sure what's happened. Lang reported it this morning. The clinic knows, too."

"Should we form a posse?"

"Let's not talk about it, okay?"

"Of course, sorry." He reached across to take her hand, but she shrank from his touch.

The thought of being touched repulsed her, and Rose feared she might vomit. "Sam, I'm sorry. I'm not very good company right now."

"You have nothing to be sorry about. I shouldn't have barged in."

"It's okay."

"I was worried."

"Thank you."

"Do your folks know?"

"Not yet. Lang was going over to tell them today."

"Are you going to stay here for a while?"

"I've taken a two-week leave. We'll see how I feel. I can always go back sooner, but it's been a while since I took any time off, so it might do me good."

"I'm sure it will." Sam smiled warmly but did not attempt to touch her again.

"What about you? Are you heading back to Flagstaff soon?"

"There's a meeting Tuesday, but after that, I don't know. I quit my job."

"Why?"

"Too much crap going on. Meryl is still trying to take over Spark's job, so that's another nightmare."

"Which Spark will handle, I'm sure."

"Yeah, but he shouldn't have to."

"Can you seriously see him allowing another architect to take over while kicking his best friend's son to the curb? I don't think Meryl has thought things through."

Suddenly weary of talking about his mess, he gazed over at her, wanting so badly to hold her, but staying put. "I have to head north tomorrow. I'm staying the night at my place cause Tuesday's meeting is now scheduled at seven thirty in the morning, supposedly the only time Meryl is free."

Rose felt sad hearing the bitterness in his voice. *At least he can say her name. I cannot bring myself to say Dan's name aloud.* "I hope it goes well for you," she said. "Will Santiago is the best."

"So everyone tells me. Can I come by tomorrow before I go?"

Surprised by the question, she smiled at him. "I'm sure you have lots to do."

"I want to see you, please. Just for a few minutes."

She stared into the intense brown eyes for a minute or so, then said, "I can't guarantee what state I'll be in, but that would be fine. The way I look and feel, I don't expect I'll be venturing out much for a few days."

"Would two be okay?"

"Yes," she said, reaching out to touch his cheek, finger tracing along his strong jaw, the muscles tensing under her touch.

He placed his hand over hers. "I wish I could take away last night."

"Me too," she said, gently withdrawing her hand.

At that moment, they heard a car door slam and Martha Dillon's voice. Rose's mother hurried up the front walk, her son at her side. Sam stood, giving her a soft smile. "I'd better get Royal back."

"You rode here?" she asked, incredulous.

"Yup."

"A horse?"

He laughed. "I did grow up on a ranch, you know. Hey, Mrs. Dillon," he said, turning from Rose to her mother.

"Oh, my darling," Martha Dillon said, nodding to Sam as she rushed to hug her daughter.

"Surprised to see you here," Lang said, looking at Sam.

"Just came by to see how she was. Short visit."

Rose winced in pain. Aghast, her mother released her. "Oh, honey, I'm sorry. Your daddy would have come, but he's too upset. We'll see him when we get you settled at home."

Rose looked up at Lang, eyes pleading.

"Well, about that. Beth and I have Rosie all settled here. We have plenty of room, and you have your hands full with Dad. Why don't we let her rest a few days and then see?"

"Nonsense. She belongs at home."

Taking a deep breath, Rose sat up. "I think I will stay here for now, Mama."

Disappointment registered on her mother's face, but she recovered and said, "Of course, darling. Whatever you want. Beth and Lang are busy, though, so I'll have Jon make up some meals and bring them to you." She referred to their full-time chef, Jon Wilson.

"Thanks, Mama. That sounds perfect."

Sam waved at her from the doorway and said his goodbyes. Lang walked him out. "I'm impressed. Didn't know you rode much."

"I don't, but Royal's a good ole guy. Point him in the right direction and he'll get you there safely."

"I'll remember. Fortunately, my wife is the Morgan with the least interest in horses."

"Yeah, after her fall, Beth was more afraid of 'em than I was." Sam hopped up into the saddle and took hold of the reins.

"Shortest way back is the loop. That the way you came?" Lang asked.

"Sort of. Lang, please let me know if there's anything I can do. Is he locked up yet?"

"They can't find the bastard. He's vanished." Rimmed with tears, Lang's eyes flashed anger. "Just as well. If I saw him now, I'd beat him to death."

"I'm sorry, man," Sam said. "If this happened to one of my sisters, I'd be going crazy, too."

"She's strong. She'll be okay," Lang said without much conviction. "Thanks for stopping by, and good luck with your shit this week."

Sam nodded and nudged Royal. "Heading to Flagstaff tomorrow, but told Rose I'd stop in around two, if that's okay?"

"Fine by me. I'm guessing my mother will be moved in here by then." With a wave, he turned back toward the house.

CHAPTER 19

When he rode up to the barn, Sam was surprised to see Beth's truck parked beside their brother's Rover. Nick appeared to be just leaving, but he said, "Here, I'll take old Roy," and walked the horse toward his stall to be groomed and fed.

Sam found his siblings sitting behind the barn.

"Hey, Sammy," Ben said, handing him a beer.

"Hey, guys. What's up?" Sam asked.

Beth looked up at him. "Just talking about Rose. You heard, right?"

"Just came from your house."

She gave him a quizzical look. "Oh? How was she?"

"Okay, if you ignore what the bastard did to her. Martha showed up just as I was leaving."

"Was she insisting Rose come home?"

"Yes, but Rose put her foot down. Says she's staying put."

"Good for her. That means my mother-in-law will be camped at our house for the foreseeable future."

"How was it last night?" Sam asked, voice low.

"Horrible. He ripped her clothes off her." Beth gazed at her brother, surprised to see tears in his eyes. "She'll be okay. Have you guys got something going?"

"Not really," he lied. "I blew it with Rose last year."

"Well, she can use a friend right now," Beth said. "So let's all try to support her."

Ben stood up. "I gotta go, but you'll let Mag and me know if there's anything you need or Rose needs, right? Food, whatever."

"Thanks," his sister said, rising herself. "My guess is that Martha's already arranging round-the-clock catering."

Sam nodded. "That's what she said."

Sam said goodbye to his siblings, thanked Nick for taking care of Royal, and walked out to his truck. He was thinking about Friday night and their lovemaking, wondering if Rose would ever let him touch her again.

When Sam got home, he grabbed a beer and joined his parents and Ruthie on the terrace. "Hi, Sammy," Leonora said, patting the chair beside her.

"Beth just called," his father said. "We're all so sorry about Rose. What a terrible thing. I understand that they can't locate the bastard."

Ruthie and Sam stared at their father openmouthed. While Ben Senior might throw a few cuss words around on the trail with the guys, he never swore in front of his wife or daughters. Sam nodded. "The coward hightailed it. Cleaned out his apartment and left. Family is loaded, so I'm sure he can disappear without a trace if he chooses."

Leonora waved her hand. "Good riddance, I say! Save poor Rose the agony of a trial, not to mention having to work with that despicable creature. I never liked him."

"Yes, you did," Ruthie said. "You said he reminded you of a young Robert Redford."

"Hush, Ruthie. This is not the time for levity." Leonora held out her wineglass. "Please take this in and pour me half a glass, and while you're there, check with Carmela about dinner."

When Ruthie disappeared, Ben Senior turned to Sam. "How are you holding up, son?"

"Just when you think life can't get any worse. You should see her," he said, tears filling his eyes.

His father's kind eyes regarded him with understanding. "Hard to see those we love hurting, but she's a strong gal. She'll get through it. You will too."

Confused, Leonora gazed from husband to son. "You mean you and Rose? When did this start?"

"Nothing's started, not really," Sam said. "I blew things last year, and she's like a scared rabbit around me now."

"Give her time," his father said, patting his knee. "Time's a great healer."

Leonora stared at her husband. "You mean you knew about this and said nothing?"

"Knew about what?" Ruthie asked, stepping onto the terrace and handing Leonora her wine.

"Nothin', darlin'."

Ruthie opened her mouth, ready to argue, but stopped when she looked at her brother, who looked ready to burst into tears. "Carm says dinner's ready and wants to know if she should serve it out here or inside."

"Table's already set inside. Let's not fuss tonight," their father said, offering his wife a hand up, then kissing her forehead.

Leonora brushed by him, still miffed, and the others followed. Polar opposites, the elder Morgans' love deepened with each passing year. Leonora was the doer and her husband the listener. He picked up on the nuances of his children and friends while she bustled about, making sure everyone was taken care of. The past few years, she had turned most of her attention to her beloved spouse, whose heart was slowly failing. Ben Senior continued to look the picture of health, as robust and strong as ever, but the doctors had warned them that it was only a matter of time before he would begin to slow down.

Later, when Sam got to his room, he pulled out his cell and saw several missed calls from Bob Rayburn and one from Meryl Wainwright. "Fuck you," he muttered and switched it off.

***

Rose lay in her bed, thinking of Sam. Needing to hear his voice, she dialed his cell, but it went straight to voice mail. She listened to his warm, friendly voice apologizing for being unavailable, then hung up, closing her eyes.

Before she drifted off to sleep, Beth knocked on the bedroom door and peeked round. "Hi, I'm off to bed. You need anything?"

"Thanks, Beth, for everything. I'm fine and so glad to be here."

"We're glad to have you for as long as you like."

Rose's eyes filled with tears. "I can't stop thinking about it, you know?"

Her sister-in-law came to sit in a chair next to the bed and took her hand. "Give yourself time."

"I just feel numb, like I'll never be able to feel anything again. Never be able to have a man touch me or hold me."

"Have you considered seeing someone? I have a woman in town, Haley Alvarez. You might have met her? She came to our wedding?"

"Ethereal, waist-length silver hair?"

"That's Haley. She saved my life. Maggie recommended her. I'll leave her number on the kitchen table before I head to work in the morning, just in case."

"Thanks, Beth."

"Want me to stay a while till you nod off?"

"Absolutely not! You have to get up at dawn. Now scoot, and tell my brother I'm asleep, okay?"

Beth smiled. "Will do. Night."

"Night."

CHAPTER 20

When Sam came down to breakfast, Spark Foster was chatting with his parents. All three turned to say good morning.

"Hey, Spark, you're up early."

"Always. How's my architect doin' on this fine valley morning?"

"Don't know about the 'your architect' part. Maybe 'former' is more accurate?" Sam filled a plate with eggs, hash browns, and bacon and sat, nodding to Carmela as she poured his coffee.

"Not if these ole geezers have anything to say about it," his father said, grinning at Spark.

"Dad, no. I refuse to have you get into this."

"Too late," Leonora said. "Now hush and eat your breakfast. Have you lost weight? You look as skinny as a fence rail."

"Leave the boy be, Nora," her husband said, winking at Sam. "I want to help, son. You know I can't stand by when one of you is in trouble."

"Listen guys, I appreciate it, I really do, but this is my fight, not yours."

Spark sat up, elbows on the table. "I beg to differ, my boy. No one tells me who I can and can't hire as an architect. When Ms. Wainwright pushed her way into our job, it became just as much my fight as yours. I hired you, and it's you I want. Not some scheming two-bit you-know-what." Sam started to speak, and Spark raised his hand. "Not another word, son. This is business and I'll handle it. You get things settled in Flagstaff. If I know my team, this'll be gone by the time you get home."

Yeah, right, and a herd of pigs'll be flying over at sunset, Sam thought. "Thanks, Spark. I owe you big time."

Spark stood up, all six-foot-four of him. "Nonsense. Gotta git goin'. Thanks for breakfast, Nora. Sam, I'll see you when you get back. And buddy," he added, turning to his friend. "We still on fer that late afternoon ride?"

"You betcha. I'll meet you at the stables at five," the elder Morgan replied. Bracing himself for his wife's response, he waved his friend out, and Spark beat a hasty retreat.

"Now, Papa, you promised," Lenora said.

"I did nothing of the sort. We're takin' Royal and Dandy. Can't get into too much trouble with those two. Harley's standin' by, so we'll be perfectly safe."

"What does standing by mean?" she asked, eyes blazing.

"Never you mind, darlin'. What's your mornin' like, Sammy?"

"I've got some work to do, and then I'm heading north," Sam said. Since he had to go home, he intended to phone his real estate agent and see if he could meet him at the condo. *No sense delaying the inevitable.* With no job and stiff legal fees looming, he'd have to sell. It had been an excellent investment, and he was reasonably certain that it would sell quickly for nearly double what he'd paid for it.

"What time, sweetheart?" Leonora asked.

"Maybe around noon." This was earlier than he had told Rose, but he hoped it would be okay.

"I'll have Carmela pack you a lunch. What would you like?"

"Anything's fine, but I'll go back and ask her in a sec. Thanks, Mom."

His father regarded him with kind eyes. "Too bad Maggie's unwell, cause I'm sure your brother'd go with you, son."

"I'm a big boy. Besides, Will'll protect me."

"He'd better," Leonora said.

Sam looked from one parent to the other. "I don't suppose there's any way I can persuade you and Spark to stay out of this?"

His father shook his head. "What else have we got to do? You and your brothers and sisters are our whole world."

Sam teared up, and excused himself, giving each of them a hug. As he headed for the kitchen, Leonora grabbed hold of his hand. "It's going to be fine, Sammy."

"Thanks, Mom." *Wish I could share your enthusiasm.*

Sam asked Carmela to fix two lunches, then went upstairs to phone Rose. He was hoping she'd agree to have lunch with him as he headed out of town. He switched on his cell, spying many missed calls, including one from Rose, but before he could dial, the phone rang. Not looking at caller ID, he clicked on. "Hello."

"Sam, I really think we should talk before tomorrow, don't you?" Meryl's voice was syrupy sweet. She wanted something and wanted it badly enough to muddy up tomorrow's hearing.

Several years earlier, Sam had added an "instant record" app to his phone in order to keep a record of client conversations. Then, later, as he went to work, he could review details as he began drafting. He switched it on and said, "Hello, Meryl. I doubt we have much to say to each other."

"Oh, but I think we do."

"I'm listening."

"I don't want to mess you up, Sam dear."

"Too late for that. Your lies have cost me my job and a lot more."

"Well, what if the lawsuit simply went away?"

"Excuse me?"

"I never wanted your body, honey. This was business."

"You've lost me." *What the hell are you up to?*

"You agree to step back from the Foster project completely and I'll drop the lawsuit."

"You've got to be kidding."

"Honey, I never kid about business. I want that project, and given the circumstances, it's probably best that you step away and I bring in my team. Might be awkward for us to work together."

Sam didn't know whether to laugh or slam down the phone. Then he remembered the recorder. "So this is what the lies were about? That whole seduction scene and coming on to me were all fake?"

"Sweetcakes, you're not my type. Too wholesome."

Yeah, right, Spark Foster and his billions are much more your type. "I'm not sure what you're saying?"

"This is business, and the Foster project is tailor-made for my expertise. You're in way over your head, Sam."

"Spark and I have spent over a year collaborating on the design of his house."

"I understand that, which is why I'm eager to jump in now to prevent further mistakes."

"Mistakes?"

"That's getting into details you don't need to worry about, honey."

Sam thought his head might explode, but he took deep breaths, keeping his voice calm. "This isn't what Spark wants, as I'm sure you're aware."

"That's where you come in, honey. You can persuade him with the right incentive."

"Which would be?"

"I drop the harassment charges. Rayburn and Davos keep you, their up-and-coming star, and Spark gets the dream team working on his house."

Sam thought back to the past six months and how often Meryl had popped in, feigning interest about all of his projects, but always slipping in a few questions about Spark's. She had claimed to be interested in more single residential projects as she had spent most of her career designing commercial and high-end multidwelling projects. *What had she said—such projects lacked the personal touch?* Sam knew damn well what personal touch Meryl was after. Her hands on Spark's millions.

"So, it *was* all a setup?"

"Honey, it is business, and I always get what I want."

"Even if you have to lie to do it?"

"What's a little white lie? You're a handsome guy. Your family has millions."

"What if I had responded to your advances?"

"Then I would have brought you along as my assistant. You'd have learned a lot, and we'd have had a bit of fun."

That should do it. "I don't know what to say."

"Just say yes. I can have my attorney draw up the papers."

"Let me think about it. I'll let you know tomorrow."

"Be better to do it now."

"This has come out of the blue, Meryl. Sorry, this is the best I can do."

"Fine, of course. Please think about it. I know Spark is very eager to get on with things."

You have no idea. "Gotta go, Meryl. I'll see you tomorrow."

Sam hung up before she could utter another word. He immediately phoned Will Santiago, who assured him they didn't need the recording and it would not be admissible should they go to court. However, as he rang off, Will was whistling. Sam then called Rose and asked if he could bring lunch. She agreed, warning him that she would probably be poor company.

When he stopped in the kitchen to pick up lunch and bid his mother goodbye, Leonora eyed him. "What's happened to you? You look like the cat who's swallowed the canary."

"Gotta go, Mom."

"Must be the prospect of two for lunch," she said winking at Carmela as her son headed off. "Take care, sweetie, and phone the second you get out of the meeting tomorrow."

CHAPTER 21

Feeling less battered and bruised, Rose had spent a productive morning consulting with the physicians who were covering for her for the next several weeks. She also phoned Haley Alvarez, Beth's therapist, who had had a cancellation for four in the afternoon. Swallowing hard, Rose had said she would be there and rang off. She had been surprised to hear from Sam so early, but looked forward to their lunch. She changed out of her sweats and into jeans and a pale pink top she knew flattered her figure. She might not have the cleavage of Maggie Morgan, but the shirt's V-neck gave a peek at her breasts, and the fabric hugged her slender frame in all the right places.

She regarded herself in the mirror and was pleased until she got to her face, still black and blue, the angry stitch lines not quite hidden by her hair no matter how she styled it. She thought about borrowing Beth's makeup, what little she had, but then gave up. *He saw me yesterday and is still coming back today, so why pretend?*

Shortly after twelve, she heard his knock and then his call as he stepped inside. "Anyone home?"

"Hey, Sam," she said, emerging from the kitchen, barefoot and looking as lovely as he'd ever seen her.

The bruises did nothing to diminish her fragile beauty and that jersey she was wearing. *Whoa, baby!* "You're looking better," he said, setting down the basket and approaching her. "Okay if I hug you?"

Her eyes registered fear, but Rose nodded, so he took her gently in his arms. Immediately she stiffened, so he didn't linger but stepped back, his eyes warm as he smiled at her. "What do you think? A picnic, or would you rather eat inside?"

"Why don't we sit on the terrace. It's nice out there, and shady."

She led the way, and Sam found himself following every move of her perfect rounded bottom, the jeans hugging her as he longed to do. *Only a few nights ago,* he thought, remembering her softness as she opened herself to him.

Rose sat at one of several wrought iron tables shaded by a large umbrella, and he set the picnic basket in the center.

"Let's see what Carm has for us."

"Something delicious, I'm sure." She smiled, glad to be out of the bedroom and in the company of this kind, gentle man she loved so much.

"We've got turkey, avocado, and sprouts or her special portabella mushroom baguettes. She makes these for my vegetarian brother, but I love 'em too."

"Oh, that's a tough choice."

"Let's split 'em, then." He placed a half of each kind of sandwich on the two plates. As usual, there was enough food for ten. He also brought out potato salad, coleslaw, iced tea, and cookies, most of which she declined.

They ate in silence for several minutes before she asked, "How are you doing? Are you ready for tomorrow?"

He grinned and told her about his conversation with Meryl as well as his breakfast conversation with Spark and his dad. "I'm still out of a job, and I suspect I'll be repaying my parents and Spark for the rest of my life, but if I had to guess, the lawsuit will most likely be thrown out tomorrow."

"How could she be so careless?"

"Ego. She's also so eager to get her hands on Spark's billions. Apparently she didn't even consider the possibility that he is immune to her type. You know Spark. I'm sure he was oozing charm when they met. That's who he is. But in business he doesn't fool around. I doubt Meryl's the first person who's set her sights on him since Patsy died."

"Oh, Sam, I'm so happy for you."

"It isn't over yet."

"Still, let's celebrate," she said, raising her iced tea.

Her crooked smile went straight to his heart. "I don't know how I'd have gotten through this without you, Rose."

"I'm glad I was here," she said, resting her hand on his, drinking in his warmth. Electricity coursed through her, and she longed to fling herself into his arms. *Oh, Sam, if you only knew how much I love you and want you.*

His thumb softly caressed her fingers, and Sam was relieved that she didn't pull away. "Enough about me. How are *you* doing?"

"Okay. Beth gave me the name of her therapist. I'm seeing her this afternoon. Maybe that will help."

"I'm sure it will. You still planning to stay here a while?"

"For at least two weeks. Maybe more if I need it. We have very generous medical leave policies, and I have about two months of vacation time I could take. I've been working since I graduated without more than a day's break once or twice a year."

He reached over and brushed an errant lock of hair from her face. "Does it hurt much?"

"Only when I smile," she said, grinning.

"Rose, would you have dinner with me when I get back? We could go to the Red Mesa Inn?"

"I haven't been there for years. Dad used to take us on birthdays, but we stopped that tradition when Lang left for college."

"How about this Wednesday?"

"Okay," she said shyly.

"Great. I hate to eat and run, but I've got an appointment at four, so I'd better get moving."

"Of course. Thanks so much for lunch, and please thank Carmela."

"Will do."

Sam gathered up the lunch things and placed most of it in the basket. Rose walked him to the truck. After throwing the basket in the cab, he turned back to her. "I'll miss you."

"We'll see each other soon." *I'll miss you too, my love.*

He held out his arms. "Can I?" She nodded, and he gently enveloped her. Rose's arms hung limp at her sides, but for an instant she rested her head on his shoulder, drawing strength from his warmth. "Oh, God, Rose, I'm so sorry about everything. I promise, it *will* get better."

As she nodded and stepped away, he spied tears in her lovely hazel eyes. "Take care, Sam, and good luck."

"You, too." He bent and lightly kissed the tip of her nose, glad to see her smiling as he pulled away.

'

CHAPTER 22

After meeting with his real estate agent, Sam spent a quiet evening in his condo, packing, sorting, and mentally preparing himself for the morning. Bob and Alcera had given him his start as an architect. Bob in particular had been an invaluable mentor and friend. Facing them would be difficult. Quitting had been his idea, but they had clearly taken Meryl's side to protect the firm. He couldn't blame them. After all, it wasn't only him but the entire staff and all his colleagues who would suffer. They were meeting at Rayburn and Davos, so he grabbed a couple of empty boxes. If there was time, he would pack up his office after the meeting.

The next morning at six thirty, he headed out to meet Will Santiago for breakfast. As he stepped into the cool recesses of the Coffee Connection, a café two blocks from Rayburn and Davos, the tall, lanky attorney waved from a back booth. "Hey, Sam. How're holdin' up?"

"Pretty good. Here, you better have this, just in case." He slid his cell across the table. "It's turned off, but all set. You just select the app with the green R. It's the first recording."

Santiago slipped it into his breast pocket. "Thanks. As I said, we probably won't need it, but if things get ugly, it might come in handy."

The waitress took their orders and poured coffee, then disappeared. "So, what's our plan?" Sam asked, watching as Will shuffled papers. In a dark suit and red string tie, he looked even more like Abe Lincoln this morning.

"Our plan is that I talk. You say nothing unless I ask you to speak."

"Won't they be asking me questions?"

"Not if I can help it. My man has dug up some interesting background on Ms. Machiavelli. No surprise, there's a pattern going back to her college days at Pepperdine. Undergraduate. Didn't find anything during her graduate years, but that doesn't mean it didn't happen. She's left every firm under a cloud, usually with a big financial settlement to keep things quiet."

"How does she get away with it?"

"She's smart and a bit of a sociopath. Home life as a kid was pretty horrible."

"Then why would she talk so freely to me the other night?"

"She's desperate and thus careless, or maybe reckless. Spark Foster's the biggest mark she's ever set her sights on. She's well aware that a powerful man like him has the resources to fight almost anything. The only way she could possibly win was to get you on her side before today. This will dampen her spirits a bit, I'm afraid," he said, holding up a thick manila envelope.

"What's that?"

"Paperwork from Spark's people. He's prepared to make a big payoff to get rid of her and Rayburn and Davos, but with your tape, that may not be necessary. It's probably inadmissible, but you could testify to the bribe if it got that far. Either way, she'll never get within ten miles of Spark Foster again. His team has made sure of that."

They ate in silence, Sam unable to force down more than a piece of toast. When they arrived at Rayburn and Davos, everyone waited in the conference room. Sally Mercer, dressed in fire-engine-red suit and a paisley scarf round her neck, sat at the head of the table, Lula Perry and Meryl to her left, two empty seats to her right. Alcera and Bob sat together at the opposite end of the table, a short distance from the others.

"Hey, Will, Sam, good morning," Sally said, waving her hand to indicate the empty seats. "There's coffee and Danish."

"Thanks, Sal," Will said. "Just ate." He sat adjacent to Sally and Sam took the chair beside him.

Sally waited several minutes while Will arranged a series of files in front of him, took out his reading glasses, a pen, and a legal pad, and gave her a nod. "Well, we're all here. This is an informal meeting to see where we are. The hope is that through compromise and discussion, we may be able to settle this without going to court. We will hear from Meryl and Lula first, then proceed from there. Lula?"

Lula was what would have once been called a blonde bombshell. On the far side of forty, her platinum hair was pulled back in a severe chignon. The neck of her white sleeveless Spandex dress plunged to reveal startling cleavage, her breasts most likely manmade. Jeweled reading glasses pitched on the end of her nose seemed to be her only concession to age. "My client is under the impression that Mr. Morgan may have a compromise in mind? Before we get to that, let me say that the harassment charge is a serious one and could result in jail time. I understand Mr. Morgan has quit his job at Rayburn and Davos, but should my client prevail, his employment would most likely have been terminated anyway."

Will listened quietly, his expression impassive. Meryl seemed distracted, her eyes darting from her colleagues to her attorney. She wore a conservative beige linen suit, no cleavage in sight thanks to a cream-colored shell underneath the jacket.

Finally Perry paused and asked, "Shall we review the harassment allegation, or would Mr. Morgan like to speak?"

Will cleared his throat and stared hard at Meryl, then turned his steely gray eyes on her attorney. "My client will not be speaking today, unless you ask him a direct question."

Perry threw up her hands. "Okay, if that's the way you want to play it. I had understood from Ms. Wainwright that your client and she had a friendly conversation yesterday and that they might be able to reach an amicable solution, but if—"

"Oh, we'll get to that conversation," Will said, pulling Sam's phone from his jacket and placing it on the table. "But first, let me go through the allegations. Your client has accused Mr. Morgan of sexual harassment. Has this kind of thing happened before?"

Lula feigned surprise. "Excuse me? What is the relevance? Ms. Wainwright is a successful, attractive woman. Unfortunately, women like her often fall prey to sexual predators."

"Oh, I see, so now you are calling my client a sexual predator?" he said, making notes on the legal pad.

"If the shoe fits," Lula said, glaring at him.

"Exactly. I have here a thick dossier cataloging Ms. Wainwright's litigious actions in this regard. It would appear that she cannot leave the house without someone harassing her."

"As I said, if the—"

Will waved his hand. "Shoe fits, yeah, I heard you. Only trouble is, the shoe is a stiletto, not a boot. In every case, Ms. Wainwright walked away with a huge settlement. Hush money."

"That's ridiculous! Where's the proof?"

Will slapped a thick file in the middle of the table and slid a second toward the senior partners. "Be my guest. These are your copies. I've read 'em. Despicable doesn't even begin to describe it."

Meryl turned ashen and sputtered, "Those are sealed!"

"Were sealed. Not anymore."

Lula glanced through the top few sheets, then looked up at him over her glasses. "Of course, I'll need time to study these, as you are well aware."

"Study all you want, but what they show is a pattern, and with pattern there is intent, and with intent there is fraud, and so on."

"Pattern or not," Lula said, closing the file, "this is still not germane to this matter."

"I see. So you are intending to persist with this frivolous suit?"

"Unless your client has a compromise as per yesterday's discussion with Ms. Wainwright?"

"Ah, yes, that," Will said, grabbing the phone. "You mean this one?" He hit the play button, and the group listened, transfixed until the very end. At one point, Meryl said, "Turn it off," but Will paid her no heed, his eyes on Lula the entire time. Sam stole a glance at his former bosses, whose mouths hung open. Bob shook his head at one point, mopping his brow.

When the tape clicked off, Lula shook her head. "You know damn well that's not admissible should this go to court."

"Perhaps not, but I doubt this nonsense will see the inside of a courtroom."

He slid files from Spark's attorneys to Lula as well as the senior partners. "As you can see, Ms. Wainwright, Spark Foster is willing to pay whatever it takes to see the back of you and this firm. His attorneys have drawn up restraining orders that will see that you don't come within a mile of him or any of his properties. When your attorney has a chance to review all of the files, she'll be well-acquainted with the term 'grifter,' which is often used to describe you and your so-called ex-boyfriend. My sources say he's still calling the shots."

"Oh, my God," Bob Rayburn said. "How could this have happened? Sam, I'm so sorry."

"Mr. Morgan does not want your sympathy, Mr. Rayburn. He desires, as does Mr. Foster, your signatures on this document releasing your firm's claim on the Foster project. He was prepared to pay a sizable sum to ensure your signatures, but in light of Ms. Wainwright's helpful phone call yesterday, I would guess that no money need change hands?"

Sally Mercer, who had sat mute and astonished throughout, suddenly found her voice. "If you will excuse us, I would like to speak to Bob and Alcera in the hall. Bob, bring the files, please."

"I believe I will do the same with my client," Lula said. She stood and gazed down at Meryl. "Your office, now."

CHAPTER 23

When they were alone, Sam said, "Can I speak now?"

Will grinned. "Be my guest."

"So she had a partner in all this?"

"Yup. My guys didn't get that far, but Spark's team did. His pockets are deeper and his reach is a hell of a lot longer."

"I can't believe it." Sam shook his head, thinking about the past week.

"My guess is they'll be kissin' our feet in a minute or two."

Sam's phone buzzed, and he saw his brother's name on caller ID. He shot a quick text back saying he would call soon. Will poured them both water, and they stood by the window, looking over the city that had been Sam's home for the past eight years. "Pretty town, isn't it?" Will said, and Sam nodded.

Sam thought about leaving and where he'd go. *Wherever I go, it has to be near Rose Dillon.* As he sipped his water, he realized he loved her. *For the first time in my life, I love someone, and she can't stand my touch.*

"Here they come, Morgan. Back to the table," Will said, patting his shoulder. Both groups entered at the same time, taking their original seats.

When all were seated, Sally waved the file folders, then slapped them on the table. "Why don't you begin, Lula. What does your client say in light of all this?"

"Ms. Wainwright is prepared to drop the harassment charges against Mr.

Morgan and Rayburn and Davos. She also feels it is in her best interest to terminate her employment with this firm, effective immediately. To this end, she asks for a strong reference, a draft of which I will provide by the end of today. Of course, this means that she will also relinquish any claim to the Foster project."

Will grinned, looking from Lula to Sally. *He's actually enjoying this,* Sam thought, watching his lawyer, who now reminded him of Wile E. Coyote from the cartoon.

Sally cleared her throat. "Is that all?"

"Yes, I believe so," Lula said. "Of course, we will ask as part of the settlement that these documents and proceedings be sealed and kept confidential."

"I see," Sally said. "Well, now, let me tell you Rayburn and Davos's position. Ms. Wainwright's employment with this firm is hereby terminated, effective immediately. There will be no reference, and the documentation contained in the Foster files will be submitted to the State Board of Technical Registration. As we speak, our security people are packing Ms. Wainwright's office. We expect her to vacate the premises immediately. If these instructions are not followed to the letter, we will bring counter suit for false and malicious behavior in the case of Mr. Morgan as well as fraudulent resume and background documentation submitted at the time of her hiring. Furthermore, this firm would like to offer Mr. Morgan his job back with a salary increase and a promise of promotion to senior partner within five years."

Lula looked over at Meryl, who nodded. "My client accepts these terms, but you will be hearing from me by the end of today with a restraining order preventing the documents from being passed on to other parties, including the state board."

"Good luck with that," Will said, turning to Sam. "You have anything to say, Mr. Morgan?"

"Only a thank-you to my attorney. Bob and Alcera, I'm appreciative of the offer, but I respectfully decline. I cannot work for people who would sell me down the river like you did."

Will supplied documents for the dismissal of the lawsuit, which Meryl signed. After which she and Lula beat a hasty retreat. Sally Mercer stood and addressed her clients. "Bob, Alcera, I'll be in Bob's office." She stepped out and closed the door.

Bob Rayburn stood and approached Sam and Will. "Sam, I am truly sorry. I wish you'd reconsider, but understand if you don't."

Alcera echoed his words, then left the three men together.

"I've been happy here, Bob, and I really appreciate all you've taught me. I just need time to think about my next steps. I suspect they will not involve living and working in Flagstaff, but if something changes, I'll be in touch." He reached out his hand to his boss.

"I hope you will," Bob said. "You're one of the brightest, most talented architects I've seen come along in years. Good luck with the Foster project. He's damn lucky to have you."

"Thanks."

Sam waited outside while Will talked with Sally Mercer. Finally, he spied his attorney exiting the building, his lanky stride unmistakable. The two men talked for a few minutes. Then Sam said, "You'll send me your bill, then?"

Will grinned. "That's all taken care of."

"Yes, I know my father and Spark, but this is my mess."

"Nothin' to do with those gray foxes, although they were ready and willing. Nope, Rayburn and Davos are footin' this bill, and you can bet I charged them top dollar."

Sam laughed, shaking his hand. "Thanks again. I hope we'll meet again, though not when I'm in the hot seat."

"Take care of yourself, Morgan. You'll land on your feet, once you and your sweetheart get together." Sam gazed at him openmouthed. "You lovesick cowboys wear it all over yer faces, man. Don't know who she is, but you'd better grab her up, or someone else will." He turned, giving Sam a backward wave as he headed for his truck.

CHAPTER 24

From the moment Rose stepped into Haley Alvarez's warm, inviting space, she felt at home. The therapist was a big woman, her waist-length silver hair tied back in a long braid. She wore a flowing caftan and sandals, her every movement welcoming. "Come in, dear. So good to see you."

"Thank you," Rose said shyly, shaking her hand. "We met briefly at Beth's wedding, I believe? My sister-in-law and Maggie think the world of you."

"And I them. Sit, please. Would you like tea?"

When the session ended, Rose felt calmer and at peace. Haley had listened to all of it. To her heartbreak of last year, Dan's attack, and her fears about growing close to Sam again. Before she left, Rose made two more appointments, and the therapist had given her suggestions for the next few days. They hugged and said goodbye, Rose with tears of gratitude in her eyes.

***

After saying goodbye to Will, Sam grabbed a quick lunch at his favorite café, then headed south. He called his parents, who were overjoyed but not surprised at the outcome. He then phoned Spark, who chuckled and said, "Atta boy!" They arranged to meet at the job site later in the afternoon.

Finally, his mind clear, he called Rose. She answered after one ring. "Hi, Sam."

"It's over."

"I'm so glad. How was it?"

"Will handled the whole thing. I barely spoke. And Spark's guys did their homework. All costs fell on the firm and the plaintiff."

"Oh, Sam, I'm so happy for you!"

"We still on for tomorrow night?"

"Yes, I'm looking forward to it."

"Me, too. Wish it was tonight, but I'm swamped."

"Me, too. Lang's hired a lawyer and an investigator, and I'm going to sit down with him tonight."

Sam wanted to ask, but decided it wasn't his place. "I miss you, Rose. I can't tell you how much."

"Me, too," she said softly, thinking back to her conversation with Haley. When Rose asked her point blank if she thought a relationship with Sam was a mistake, Haley had said, "You'll never know if you turn your back. There are worse things than a bruised heart."

Rose and Sam talked for over an hour. Neither was certain what the next step would be career-wise. They said goodbye just as Sam drove the truck through the ranch gates. Maggie, Ben, and the kids were at the big house for dinner when he arrived, so he was immediately caught up in the family celebration. His dad was waiting on the porch when he drove in, and came down to greet him with a huge bear hug.

"Hey, Sammy, good to have you back."

"Thanks, Dad, and thanks for everything. Will was terrific."

"He's a good man. Now come on in and join the crew. Your mom's got poor Carmela rushing from here to there, fixin' all your favorite foods."

"Poor Carm."

"She loves it," Ben Senior said, a twinkle in his eye. "Only woman I know who can keep her sanity workin' with your mother. Don't ever tell her I said that."

"Hey, buddy," his brother said, Ben the third wriggling to get free of his grasp. "Congratulations."

"Feels good. Now let me have my nephew," he said, grabbing the toddler and flying him over his head. He found Maggie and Emma on the terrace with his mother. Leonora jumped up to hug him, and Maggie followed.

"So happy for you, Sam," his sister-in-law said.

"Thanks, Mag. You look terrific. Are you feeling better?"

"Much. These last two days, I'm finally feeling like myself again."

"So, lots to celebrate!"

***

Rose, Lang, and Beth found their parents on the porch when they drove into the winery and headed up to the house. Not quite as grand as their dear friends Leonora and Ben Morgan's place, Martha and Jaybo Dillon's house was still impressive. Two stories with a red tile roof and four chimneys, the house rambled north and south, its white adobe walls freshly painted, grounds immaculately groomed. Their mother looked lovely as always, in a lime-green summer dress and matching flats, her short, snow-white hair perfectly coiffed. "Hello, hello," she called, rising and coming down the steps to greet them.

Her husband waved but stayed seated. Lang hugged his mother. "Hey, Ma, our desert flower, looking amazing as always."

"Pish tush," she said, shooing him away to hug Beth and Rose. "How you doing, baby?" she asked, blue eyes full of concern as she gazed at her youngest.

"Better, Mama, much better. "You do look pretty. New dress?"

"Yes, my incredible daughter-in-law here has introduced me and Nora to Gabriela's," she said, winking at Beth. "I swear that woman scours the world to find enticing items that us easy touches can't resist. I never get out of that shop without spending a small fortune. Come on up and Neecy'll get you something.

Such a nice night that Papa and I decided to enjoy it out here."

Lang frowned when he spied the large goblet of red wine in his father's hand. Watching him, Rose prayed for a peaceful dinner. Father and son had a tenuous relationship in the best of times, mostly related to Jaybo's alcoholism. Their father had suffered several heart attacks and was no longer the robust rancher who had traveled the country promoting their beef and the Saguaro Valley wine labels. Several years old than his wife, he was overweight, complexion florid, hands and gait shaky. In the wake of his second heart attack, they had hired a ranch manager, a decision to which Jaybo had agreed, but which did not sit easy. He adored his wife, but had abused her verbally and physically over the years, which further fueled his son's anger. Martha refused to leave him, so Lang remained civil for her sake as well as Rose's, but it was an uneasy truce.

Rose bent to kiss her dad. "Hi, Dad. How are you feeling?"

Jaybo gazed up at her. "Never mind me, baby. How're you doin'?"

"I'm okay," Rose said, taking the chair beside him. "Hi, Neecy," she said as her parents' housekeeper, Neecy Roderiquez, appeared on the porch to take their drink orders.

"Good to see you," Neecy said, coming to hug her friend and childhood playmate. Smooth, flawless skin and brown as a berry, Neecy was just this side of plump. She had grown up on the ranch with Lang and Rose. Besides Neecy, the Dillons had a chef, Jon Wilson, who had come to the Valley from Laguna Beach, California. A chef, not a cook, and an attractive fortysomething man, Jon had a dream to live and work at a winery. He had a boyfriend in Tucson, but seemed quite content living above the garage, in the lovely apartment Martha had decorated for him. The Dillons were very generous to their help. Neecy lived in one of the property's guesthouses with her husband, Manual, who was the assistant manager of the winery.

"You, too, Neece," Rose said.

"What am I, chopped liver?" her brother said, hugging the housekeeper. Beth said hello and took a seat beside Martha. She liked Neecy but always felt a little intimidated in her presence. Although she and Manuel were happily married, it was clear his former playmate still had a crush on her gorgeous husband.

"What can I get you?" Neecy asked her.

"Seltzer and lime would be great, Neecy, thanks."

"I heard about the baby. Congratulations!" She disappeared, and the five talked about the ranch, the weather, and various other topics, avoiding the one on everyone's mind.

It wasn't until dinner that Rose decided it was up to her to speak. She waited until Neecy had served everyone Jon's savory grilled summer squash and chicken, then set down her fork. "I know that my situation has been on everyone's mind, and I am enormously grateful to Beth and Lang for taking me in and to all of you for nurturing me so lovingly. I've thought a lot about what happened and what I'd like to do, and I'd like to tell you all together.

"As you know, Lang has hired an attorney, and his investigator has already learned a bit about Dan Partridge, his whereabouts, and so forth. He is apparently in France at present. His family has the means to keep him abroad forever, if he so chooses."

"And we can initiate criminal charges, which will trigger extradition orders," her brother said.

"Yes, we could," she said, smiling at Lang, her champion and protector. "But I don't want that."

"The bastard should pay," her father said, words already slurred.

"He will never work in the Heavers network again," she said. "That's punishment enough for me. His reputation has been tarnished both because of the incident, which has been documented, and by his skipping out on his duties as resident. No reputable clinic will touch him."

"Rosie, this is craziness talking," Lang said, blue eyes pleading with her. "You're still recovering. Let me get things started, and you don't have to be involved until—"

Rose raised her hand. "No, sweetheart, I appreciate all you've done and I am beyond grateful, but this is my decision. I want to move on and put this behind me. I don't want to find myself in a courtroom six months from now facing Dan Partridge. Date rape is extremely difficult to prove. Maybe there is a part of me that led him on."

"That's bullshit!" her brother said. Beth reached over, hand on his wrist.

Before he could say more, Rose nodded her head. "Yes, it is bullshit—excuse me, Mama—but it's what I want. I know what he did was despicable and wrong. I also know that none of it was my fault and by keeping this quiet, there is the very real danger that he will do it to someone else.

"I'm still mulling over what I want to do when I return to work, but at least he won't be there. I have wonderful colleagues. Dr. Heavers wrote yesterday, and we've scheduled a call tomorrow morning. I'll talk things through with him."

Martha looked at her daughter, eyes full of love. "Are you thinking of taking more time off, darling?"

"Not necessarily, but maybe."

Where does my brother fit into all this? Beth thought, watching the interplay between her in-laws and husband.

<h1 style="text-align:center">CHAPTER 25</h1>

The house was quiet Wednesday morning. Beth left for the farm before dawn, and her brother had gone to his office space in town, corporate headquarters of Rambler Sports West. He had two employees and thus had outgrown his home office. As she nibbled at the fresh strawberries Beth had left out, Rose thought about the evening ahead. She had taken a survey of the clothes she had from home and decided a visit to Gabriela's dress shop might be in order.

Her cell phone rang just as she was heading out. "Hello, Rose, is that you?" a familiar voice asked, the connection spotty.

She stepped onto the porch and sat down. "Dr. Heavers, is that you?"

"I've just gotten off the phone with Rich. My dear, I am so sorry."

"Thanks. I'm doing okay."

"If Rich didn't make it clear, Dan Partridge will never hold a position in the clinic or our network again, no matter what punishment the legal system metes out. I understand your family has hired an attorney? I'm glad."

"It's kind of a sore subject right now," she said.

"Oh?"

"I've asked my brother to drop it. Richard did tell the attorney that Dan would be barred from employment. That's enough for me. I would like to be done with it and get on with my life.."

"I completely understand, my dear. The pediatric neurosurgery world is small. Word will get around, and he'll be hard-pressed to find a position anywhere."

"How are you doing?"

"Good days and bad days. They're trying an experimental treatment right now, which seems to be helping."

"Oh, I'm glad. How is your family?"

He chuckled. "Wild and crazy as ever." Christopher Heavers, her mentor and founder of the Heavers Clinic in Tucson, had moved back east after a cancer diagnosis to be near his family. The initial prognosis had been grim, but the stalwart, much-loved physician had defied all odds and was still practicing medicine at the Heavers East Children's Center in Annapolis. "Actually, my dear, I was planning to call you this week on a different matter. My assistant back here, Jerry Downing, is headed to Mayo Children's in Minnesota. We're running a search for his replacement, and I thought of you."

"I don't know what to say," Rose said. A position at Jerry's level was a huge leap for her. He was an up-and-comer and one of the top young pediatric neurosurgeons in the world. "I'm not sure I'm ready to fill Jerry's shoes."

"Nonsense. You're ready. You're a very gifted surgeon and one of the best physicians with whom I've ever worked. I should know. I trained you."

"Chris, I really don't know how to respond. I'm sure you have a number of highly qualified candidates."

"Yes, we do, but I'm asking you to join them. Interviews will be starting as soon as we can review all the applications."

"So soon?"

"The deadline for applications is tomorrow. I have most of what I'd need for you, but you'll need to write a formal letter of interest."

"Can I think about it?"

"Absolutely. You've got twenty-four hours. I'll have my secretary, Sandra Haskell, send you everything you need. You can send her your letter and any documentation you'd like. Please think about it, my dear. I would love to have you here."

"I will. Thank you."

Rose's head was still reeling when she stepped into the dress shop. Gabriela, the owner, was sitting at the counter, eating a sandwich. One woman was trying on hats, but otherwise the shop was empty.

"Welcome," Gabriela said, slipping off her stool and coming to greet her. The shopkeeper wore white skinny jeans and a navy embroidered tunic, her waist-length auburn hair tied back in a ponytail. Dozens of silver bracelets jangled on both wrists, and enormous silver hoops dangled from her ears. "You're Martha's daughter, right?"

"Yes, Rose. Hello," she said, extending her hand. "We met at my brother's wedding."

"That we did. How are you?"

"I've been better," she said, pointing to her forehead. "Stitches come out Thursday. I'm looking for an outfit that will draw attention away from my face, if you know what I mean."

Gabriela laughed, waving at the hat woman, who was at the door. "No luck?"

The woman ignored her and disappeared. "Touristas," she said, rolling her eyes. "Now, let's see what we can do for you, sweetie. You're a size four, correct?"

Surprised, Rose nodded. She bought most of her clothes online.

"What's the occasion?"

"Dinner at the Red Mesa."

"Hmm, romantic. Is it romantic?"

Rose smiled. "I hope so."

"Well, then, let's see what we can do."

Within minutes, Gabriela had a handful of outfits, dresses, skirts, and gauzy blouses draped over her arm. She ushered Rose into a dressing room and hung everything inside. "Now the fun begins. I want to see everything!"

The first few outfits were pretty, but not quite what she wanted. Rose dutifully tried each and came out to twirl in the three-way mirror.

Gabriela regarded her as she turned in a dark navy sheath and shook her head. "With your flawless skin, dark colors don't suit. Try the white one with the flouncy skirt."

When Rose emerged, the shopkeeper whistled. "Now, that's more like it!"

The bodice of the strapless, asymmetrical sheath fit her like a glove, the flouncy folds of the skirt coming just above her knees. Rose gasped when she saw herself. "Oh, this doesn't look like me!"

"But it is, honey. You wear that dress and he'll be drooling before you even say hello. Hold on a sec. What's your shoe size?"

"Eight."

Gabriela disappeared, returning with two shoeboxes. "Try these," she said, handing Rose a pair of three-inch strappy sandals, off-white with just a hint of bling. They fit perfectly and complemented the dress beautifully. "Wow, you look sensational, hon. What d'ya think?"

"That I'll probably fall flat on my face. I never wear heels."

"Well, you should with those legs. If they're too high, I have a lower heel in the same style."

Rose turned round and round in disbelief. "Don't I look a little overdressed?"

"For the Red Mesa, no way."

"Let me try on the rest."

After an hour of playing dress-up, Gabriela had convinced her that she needed the strapless dress, two summer sheaths—one in light green, the other sky blue—three pairs of shoes, two pairs of very sexy jeans, and several new tops. Rose loved every item and even chose several pieces of one-of-a-kind jewelry to accessorize. She particularly loved the delicate silver pearl drop necklace Gabriela had paired with the strapless dress, and knew her own pearl earrings would match perfectly. When the shopkeeper totaled everything and handed her the slip, she almost fainted, but then decided, *why not?*

By the time she got home, she was having second thoughts, so she called over to her parents' to see if anyone was home. Martha Dillon answered, "Hi, darlin', of course I'd love to see your new duds! Come on over and give Neecy and me a fashion show." They heartily approved of every purchase and declared the strapless dress perfect for the evening ahead. As Martha watched her shy, lovely child twirl to Neecy's applause, worry and concern knitted her brow. *Sam Morgan had better appreciate my beautiful, amazing daughter, or I'll horse whip him!*

***

Sam spent the day making calls and thinking about his future. He spent most of the afternoon out at Spark's conferring with Kevin and his men. On his way back, he stopped by the stables and found Ben and Harley sitting in the shade, drinking beers. "Hey, brother," Ben said. "What brings you down with us dirty folk?"

"Just checking in. Where're Jeb and Nick?"

"Let 'em go early. We've got a monster day tomorrow, and my stubborn wife insists she's comin' back to work."

"She looks much better," Sam said, pulling a water from the cooler.

"What, not drinkin'?" Ben said, regarding him.

Harley grinned. "Probably has a hot date."

Ben pushed his hat back off his forehead. "With Rosie?"

"Yup."

"Where're you guys goin'?"

"Red Mesa."

"Whoa, this is serious," Ben said. "Good luck, buddy."

At that moment, Ruthie Morgan appeared, riding Jadie, her multicolored pinto. "Hey, who let you off work, pipsqueak?" Ben said as their sister hopped off Jadie and led the horse toward them.

"Slow day. Beth had to go into town, and we're gearing up for the slaughter Friday, so we both took off early. What's new, Sam?" she asked, ignoring Harley completely. She had decided to take a new tack with him.

"Not much. Wanta hang out with us?"

"Not especially," she said, turning her nose up at Harley. "And, besides, aren't you supposed to be getting ready for your dinner with Rose?"

"Yup. Do you need a ride back to the house?"

"I can take her after she cools Jadie down," Harley said, leaning back, grinning.

"Thanks, but I'd rather walk!" she said, huffing as she led Jadie into the barn.

Sam stood, gazing down at his brother's best friend. "When are you ever gonna put our sister out of her misery?"

"She's too young for me."

"Bullshit," Ben said, elbowing him.

"Gotta go, guys. See ya," Sam said.

He walked through the barn to say goodbye to Ruthie.

Sam patted her shoulder. "See you later, sis."

CHAPTER 26

Sam pulled into his sister's driveway a little before six. His truck was filthy with construction dust, so he was driving Leonora's Volvo. As he hopped out, Beth came out on the porch and whistled. "Hey, you clean up pretty well, brother."

"Thanks. I'm a little early. She ready?"

"Almost. Come sit a minute. Lang's not home yet, but I cut out early."

"So I understand from Ruthie, the hothead."

"Harley?"

He nodded.

"It's kicked up again, I'm 'fraid. Her last Internet date crapped out on her, so she's between men, never a good place for Ruthie. Still thinks Harley's hiding women all over the place."

"Is he?"

"How should I know?" his sister said, throwing up her hands. "The only one who knows Harley's business is our big brother, and his lips are sealed."

"He's probably just busy with Willow, right?" Sam said, referring to Harley's fourteen-year-old daughter. "How's her mom's health these days? Harley seemed to indicate that she's doing better."

"Last time I asked Ben about her, he said she's been having a little rally. Prognosis still sucks and the cancer's progressing, but if she has a little plateau of good days, that's great."

"You look amazing, by the way," he said, gazing at his slender, lovely sister. "The pregnancy glow?"

She smiled, her brown eyes misting. "Maybe, or it could be happiness. Lang makes me happy."

"I know," he said, patting her hand. "He's a lucky guy."

"We both are, and speaking of lucky, I'm glad you and Rose are seeing each other."

"Me, too."

"You're not just messing with her, are you?"

He stared at Beth, then shook his head. "No, but the way my life's going, I'm not in a position to make any promises."

"You know if you mess with her Lang'll kill you."

"I was a jerk last year."

"Maybe, but what's changed now?"

"I don't know, Bethie, but I do care for her."

Footsteps approached, and they turned as Rose pushed open the door. Sam's mouth dropped open as she stepped out. Her hair was pulled back with silvery combs, and the dress, *oh, my God, the dress*, hugged her like a second skin, the skirt swishing softly as she took a step toward him.

As his sister smiled, gazing from one to the other, Sam finally found his voice. "Rose, you look so beautiful."

"Thank you," she said, smiling shyly. "You don't look so bad yourself." In fact, he looked good enough to eat in his linen suit the color of the desert, white dress shirt, and a ranch tie in greens and golds. The way his brown eyes gazed at her, Rose knew she had made the right choice of outfit. *Thank you, Gabby!*

"Have fun, you two," Beth called, and they headed off. Sam's hand rested lightly on the small of Rose's back as they rounded the car. His touch sent shivers of pleasure through her, and for an instant, she feared her legs might buckle.

"I have to warn you," she said as he opened the door, "I'm not used to heels and I might fall into you unexpectedly, so be ready to catch me."

"You can fall into me right now and I'll never let you go," he whispered, lips grazing her ear. He felt himself growing hard as she slipped her gorgeous legs in, arranging the folds of her dress around her. *Oh, Lordy, Sam Morgan, how are you ever gonna make it through dinner?*

When they arrived at the Red Mesa, Rose was surprised as Oscar, the maitre d', ushered them to a private terrace with one table, located inside the inn's walled garden. Flowers bloomed everywhere—in beds, climbing the stone walls, and in colorful ceramic pots. "Oh, my goodness," she said, peering around. "I never knew this existed."

"Blame your brother. He suggested it," Sam said as Oscar seated them.

The maitre d' bowed. "I will send Robert out to take your drink orders," he said, handing them each a menu and disappearing.

"It's perfect, Sam. Thank you."

"My pleasure. My only problem is figuring out how I'll make it through dinner without wanting to relieve you of that amazing dress."

Rose's face fell, fear registering in her soft green eyes. Too late, he realized what he'd done. "Oh, God, Rose, I'm sorry. That was incredibly insensitive of me."

"No, it's okay," she said, gazing up as Robert the waiter appeared.

But it's not okay, Sam thought, watching her. Recovering himself, he said, "We could order a nice bottle of wine. You're the expert there. What do you like?"

"Well, it's going to sound really boring, but I'm very partial to Saguaro Valley's sauvignon blanc."

"That's an excellent choice," Robert said. "One of our most popular wines."

"A bottle of that, please," Sam said, smiling at the young, dark-haired man. His black uniform, just slightly too large, hung on his slender frame.

Robert told them about the specials, then disappeared. When the door closed behind him, Sam reached across the table. "Rose, I'm so sorry for my thoughtlessness. That was a stupid, idiotic thing to say after all you've been through."

"No, it wasn't," she said, smiling at him. There was nothing she wanted more than Sam Morgan's arms around her, hands all over her, and him inside her, suffusing her with his warmth and strength. "I actually talked to Haley, the therapist, about this, us, the physical part of our relationship."

"Oh?" Sam sat, afraid to breathe lest he spook her.

Rose nodded. "She suggested taking it slow."

"I can do slow," he said, wondering if that was true. He had never wanted a woman as much as he wanted her, now, at this moment.

"And this is the tricky part," she said, her alabaster cheeks turning bright red. "She thinks it's really important that I initiate things."

He smiled, resisting the urge to reach across and take her hand. "That's a great idea."

"I might not be very good at it."

"We'll learn together, then. You willing to try?"

In answer, she leaned across and kissed him lightly. "Thank you for understanding."

"Always," he whispered as the terrace door swung open and Robert appeared with the wine. *I don't know how you're gonna do it, buddy, but she's sure worth it.*

They both ordered the halibut special and an appetizer sampler to share. She asked about his day, and she described her trip to the dress shop.

"If she picked out that dress, I love Gabriela."

Rose laughed for the first time in four days.

She asked about his plans, and Sam took a sip of wine, meeting her eyes. "I've been thinking about next steps. I've got savings, and Spark's job'll keep me busy another few months. My condo should sell quickly, too."

"You're selling your home?"

"I don't want to stay in Flagstaff. Where I'll go, I'm not sure. I could set up an office here and work out of the valley, but I'm not sure my reputation's strong enough to make a living here. I'm going start researching firms in the Southwest and see what comes up."

"I'm sure any firm would jump at the chance to hire you."

"Maybe. What about you? Still planning to go back to work?"

She nodded.

Robert appeared with their appetizers. He set them down, filled their wineglasses, and withdrew.

"My mentor, Chris Heavers, called this morning."

"How's he doing?"

"He's well at the moment. They're trying an experimental regimen that seems to be helping."

"Had he heard about Saturday?"

"Yes," she said quietly. "He and my boss in Tucson have been very supportive. If I stay working in the network, I will never have to worry about working with Dan Partridge."

"Beth told me you've decided not to go after him."

"Yes, I want it behind me. Does that sound like the coward's way out?"

"No, but I hate to think of the bastard doing it to someone else."

Her face fell, and she lowered her eyes. "Yes, there is that."

"I didn't mean you should pursue it, Rose. Please know that I fully support your decision." He longed to reach over and touch her hand, but held back. *Let her come to you.*

Chapter 27

They decided against dessert. Both were pleasantly tipsy as they rose to leave. Sam insisted on paying.

"I asked you, remember?"

As they headed for the exit, Rose looked wistfully back at the beautiful private space and wished they could stay forever. Reading her mind, he whispered, "We can come back again soon. Promise." She nodded and took his arm, resting her head on his shoulder. Her touch was enough to send him into overdrive, but aside from leaning his head to touch hers, he made no moves. *Let her come to you!*

As they neared home, they skirted the town of Saguaro, and he said, "Ready to call it a night?"

"We didn't get dessert, did we?"

"You're the boss. What'd you in the mood for?"

"The Scoop's open till ten."

He grinned. "They'll never be the same when they see you in that dress."

Sam drove into town and parked just down the street from the Daily Scoop. Rose kicked off her sandals and walked barefoot to the shop. They ordered at the outside window, two small cones, his pistachio, hers peach. "Let's walk to the gorge. It's only five minutes, okay?" she said.

"Lead on, m'lady," he said, giving her a mock bow. "I can get used to this. Wanta run my office if I decide to set up alone?"

Her turn to laugh, she said, "You'd be sorry. I'm 'fraid I'd be terrible. I'm not very organized."

"I don't believe that for a second." As they walked, Sam marveled at her delicate chin, long neck, and peachy skin just waiting to be kissed. *If she gives you the go-ahead, you'll have to use every ounce of self-control to move slowly.*

They strolled past the town green. The park was deserted except for a dad and his son on the jungle gym. Sam eyed them, wondering if he'd ever have kids. He adored his niece and nephew and envied Ben and Maggie's happiness and their beautiful kids.

When they reached the grove, a smaller green space at the edge of town, they sat on a smooth boulder, licking their cones. Sam was amazed at how comfortable he felt sitting beside her, enjoying the stillness of the beautiful evening, not needing to talk.

The cones long gone, she finally spoke. "This is nice." Once again, she rested her head on his shoulder. "Even if I'm a trifle overdressed."

"You're perfect," he said, turning to meet her soft hazel eyes.

"Far from it," she said, her fingers tracing the line of his jaw. "Would it be okay if I kiss you?"

He grinned. "Are you kidding?"

In answer, she leaned in, her lips meeting his with a kiss that began lightly before her lips parted and her tongue sought his, teasing at first, then delving deeper. Afraid to spook her, Sam let her take the lead. He followed, exercising self-restraint he'd never have thought possible. "My sweet Rose, you are amazing," he said, breathless as she pulled away.

"Would you kiss me now?" she asked.

"My pleasure," he whispered, kissing her gently, then parting her lips, his tongue circling hers, teasing, caressing. "Okay?" he asked, his voice hoarse with desire.

"More than okay," she said, her arms circling his neck as she drew him close. "But I'm wondering if this is the best place for this? I'm afraid someone might happen along and tell us to get a room."

"You're the boss. Got any ideas?"

In answer, she stood and took his hand, leading him to the edge of a wooded area, where a trail led to a longer trail beyond. At the trailhead, there was a small path to the left, which they took. After a short walk, she led him into a grassy area, several flat boulders around the perimeter.

"Wow," he said. "Never knew this was back here."

"I love this place," she said. "When our mom brought us to town, Lang and I used to head back here to play. Hardly anyone knows about it."

"Someone must. Looks like the stones were placed here."

"Maybe," she said, drawing him close, her hands caressing his neck, moving to his chest. "Sam, I'm not sure I can do it, but I'd love to make love to you. Are you willing to try, even if I might freak out?"

"I thought you'd never ask. You tell me what you want, sweetheart. Take it as slow as you need, and yell stop if it's too much. Promise?"

She sat, then lay on the grass. "Please take me in your arms and kiss me," she said, drawing him closer.

"Can I touch you? Your breasts?"

"Yes."

"My beautiful darling," he said, kissing her deeply as his hands moved downward, gently slipping the bodice of the dress down to reveal her round, perfect breasts. He gently cupped each breast, fingers teasing her nipples until they were hard, ripe buds.

Rose moaned.

"Too much?"

"No, more, please," she said, kissing his neck, her hands caressing his hard, strong chest.

Sam lifted her and took one breast, then the other in his mouth, his tongue circling and driving her wild with desire. Rose pressed against him as his erection tickled her belly.

"Can I?" he asked as he moved his hand downward. Rose nodded, caressing his erection, slowly unzipping his pants.

Sam slipped her panties off and his hand moved to her moist, wet center. As his fingers slipped inside her, Rose cried out, and he stopped. "Still okay, sweetie?"

"Please, Sam. I want you inside me now. I can't endure another second apart." With those words, she released his penis from his pants, her fingers stroking him.

"I'm coming, my love" he said, slipping on a condom and lifting her. The flounces of the dress parted as he drew her nearer and plunged into her warm, wet depths.

They moved in tandem, thrust after thrust to a crashing climax. Rose's legs were wrapped around him, both of their bodies slick with sweat. Afraid he was crushing her, Sam moved to rest on their sides, still interlocked. "Okay?"

She nodded, but couldn't speak. When he touched her cheek, it was wet with tears. "Oh, God, Rose, have I hurt you?"

"No, I'm just…it's a lot."

"Want me to let you go?"

"No, please don't," she said. "It's just I didn't think I'd ever be able to. Thank you."

"No, sweetheart, it's I that should be thanking you. For giving me another chance and so much more."

She kissed his chest. "I love you," she said, softly.

"Hey! Is someone back here?" a voice called. Startled, they gazed up to see a flashlight flickering in the brush as someone approached. "I'm sick to death of you kids necking back here!"

Sam pulled them both behind the thicket long enough for them to pull themselves together. Rose's bodice was barely back in place when the beam of the flashlight caught them.

"Oh, my golly, is that one of the Morgan boys?"

The short, round form of Wilbur McGraw, owner of McGraw's Hardware, emerged from the darkness. Of course, Sam thought. This area backed up to Main

Street, and the McGraws lived in a cottage behind the store. This was probably their backyard.

"Hey, Wilbur, it's Sam Morgan. You caught us, sorry. Are we trespassing?"

"Sure are. Who's the pretty lady with you?"

Mortified, she waved. "It's me, Mr. McGraw. Rose Dillon."

"Don't you look pretty, honey. Sorry. Didn't mean to interrupt the neckin'. It's just that this spot has attracted a lot of rowdies lately. They wake me and the missus up at all hours. She's the one who spied you, headin' this way."

As they stood talking, McGraw shined the light on the ground between them. Dressed in overalls and a flannel shirt, his red hair stuck out at odd angles as if he'd been roused from sleep and had thrown on his clothes. *By tomorrow, everyone in the valley will know about this!* she thought, saying, "We're so sorry. I had no idea this was part of your yard. Lang and I used to play here as kids."

"No worries, darlin'. Everyone thinks it's town land, which has always been fine with us, but the middle-of-the-night shenanigans and the trash have been a real nuisance lately."

"Well, these shenanigans are over for tonight," Sam said. "Sorry to get you up."

"No problem. Here, follow me," he said, shining the light on the path.

Sam reached over and took her hand, and they followed the store owner back to the trailhead. "Thanks, Wilbur. We can find our way from here."

"You sure? Rosie there's barefooted. Wouldn't want you to meet a rattler."

"I'm fine, really," she said, gripping Sam's hand tighter. "Night!"

Sam and Rose hurried back down the trail and through the park. As they neared the car, they slowed down and he said, "Well, that's one way to let the valley know we're dating."

Rose groaned, and they burst out laughing as they walked arm in arm to the car. "I feel like I'm sixteen and have been caught necking behind the stadium," she said.

"Rose Dillon, I'm shocked. When did you neck behind the stadium?"

"Never, but you know what I mean."

"Sure do. You're a wanton woman."

"Stop it!" she said, poking him, laughing again.

When he pulled up to his brother's house, Rose sighed, not wanting the night to end. She collected her shoes and purse, and hopped out just as he reached her door to open it. "I had a good time," she said, hand caressing his cheek.

"Me, too," he said. "Okay if I kiss you goodnight?"

In answer, her arms circled his neck, and she drew him to her. The deep kiss undid her, and her knees grew wobbly. Rose sighed again, her tongue delving and dancing with his.

Sam felt himself grow hard and groaned. "Rose Dillon, if I don't say goodnight, I'm going to have to make love to you right under your brother's nose."

She snuggled against him, her lips against his neck. "Okay, then, I'll say goodnight, but I don't want to."

One last kiss and she stepped away. "Night," she said, waving as she turned.

"Night, my love," he whispered.

Sam watched her until she was safely inside, hoping Lang and Beth had gone to bed. Rose's beautiful dress was rumpled and covered with grass stains. *You never looked more beautiful, Rose Dillon.* As the door closed behind her, his heart ached with the loss of her warmth. Her sweet, peachy scent still lingered all around him.

Lang and Beth had left a light on in the living room but appeared to have gone to bed. Rose tiptoed upstairs and was halfway down the hallway when her brother emerged from their bedroom. "Hello," he said softly, blue eyes studying her from head to toe, a smile on his face. "Good time?"

"Yes, thank you," she said, smiling, her face beet-red. "Goodnight, brother dear." *Wait till he pops into McGraw Hardware for some nails!*

As Rose closed her eyes, she realized she didn't know when she would see Sam again. She ached for his touch, his hands gently loving her, not pushing, letting her lead. After the nightmare of the previous weekend, she'd never dreamed tonight would be possible. *What will Haley think? But more importantly, had Wilbur McGraw not happened along, would Sam have said he loved me?*

CHAPTER 28

Thursday morning, Sam dropped in to see Ben and Maggie just as Emma and her mother were heading toward the barn. "What's up?" he asked as his brother followed his wife and daughter, Ben the third on his hip.

"My wife has gone crazy, that's what," Ben said, jaw set, clearly angry.

"Em hasn't been riding in weeks, and we're taking an easy ride up the loop trail. We'll go as far as the Dillons' then turn back."

"I'm happy to take her, sweetheart. Please."

Maggie looked over at Sam and rolled her eyes. Then, when she turned to her husband, her lovely eyes were soft. "Listen, mother hen, I'm not an invalid. I want to go. Hey," she said, turning back to Sam with mischievous look. "Heard you guys had a fun evening."

"Wilbur McGraw's pipeline, I presume?"

"Hey, buddy," Ben said, "you should know you can't piss in this town and not have everyone talkin' about it. Necking in the McGraws' backyard—that's *big* news."

"What's necking?" Emma asked, leading her pony, Sunny, out of the barn. Her riding helmet was shoved down over her mass of brown curls, the straps dangling. Her father set the toddler down and stooped to fasten the straps and straighten the helmet. "Takin' a nice walk with a friend," her father said, kissing her cheek.

Her brother petted Sunny's leg. The gentle pony stood still, leaning down to nuzzle the child. "Sam, can you help watch 'em while I get Tabasco?"

"Mags, please. Maybe if you go down to the stables, Jeb or Nick would take Em for a ride?" Ben said.

Maggie gave him a backward wave and disappeared into the barn.

"I feel much better if you were on Dandy," he called after her.

Sam helped Emma into the saddle as Ben chased his son around the yard, one eye on the open barn door. A few minutes later Maggie emerged, leading her enormous horse, Tabasco. Part mustang, part draft horse, Tabasco had been part of the mustang rescue program. For the past several years, the ranch had been training wild horses for use by border patrol agents, but no agent would go near Tabasco. Eventually, the ranch gifted him to Maggie. Most people were scared to death of the huge horse, but he was gentle as a lamb with his mistress and the children.

"Sam, help me, man," his brother said, catching his son in his arms. "Talk some sense into my pig-headed wife."

Sam threw up his hands. "Leave me out of it," he said, watching Maggie swing effortlessly up into the saddle.

"We won't be long," she said, smiling at her husband and son, bending to give them each a kiss. "Bye, Sam. Can't wait to hear more about your date!"

"Bye, Mag. Bye, Emma. Have a good ride." Emma waved, then proudly led the way out of the yard, guiding Sunny toward the ranch loop trail. "That's my niece. Look how well she's riding."

"Yup," Ben said. "We're really proud of her. I just wish Maggie'd take it easy."

"She's an expert rider. I'm sure she'll be fine," Sam said, patting his brother's shoulder and ruffling his nephew's curls.

"Come on up to the house. Have some coffee and tell me all about your hot date?"

"Had enough coffee, and I gotta run. I just stopped by to see if you guys needed any help at the camp or stables. I'm trying to figure out next steps, but I have some free time, and if I don't stay away from the house, our mother'll henpeck me to death."

Ben laughed. "Come on. Bennie and I are headed down now. We'll check with Harley and the guys."

CHAPTER 29

Halfway to Lang and Beth's property, Maggie and Emma rode slowly. Whenever they reached a clearing, they paused, enjoying the beautiful day and the magnificent views of the valley and ranch.

They had just rounded the bend by Turtle Rock when Emma screamed. "Mommy, snake!"

Before Maggie could react, Tabasco shrieked and reared up, his front hooves thrashing at the enormous rattlesnake. In all the time she'd known him, the horse had never so much as lifted a front hoof from the ground, so the move caught Maggie off guard. Before she knew what was happening, she was flying through the air. She landed with a thud on the hard earth of the trail. When Tabasco reared again, his hooves crashed down and killed the snake. Emma jumped off her pony and ran to her mother's side. Maggie's eyes were closed, the wind knocked out of her.

She shook her mother's shoulders, eyes wild with terror. "Mommy, Mommy, Mommy!"

Maggie's eyes flickered open. "I'm okay, baby, just need a minute." But she was not okay. Excruciating pain ripped through her lower abdomen, and she felt a wetness between her legs, knowing without looking that it was blood. Not wanting to alarm Emma, she moved to her side, using her hat to cover herself.

"Listen, baby, I'll be okay, but I can't walk right now. You're going to have to go to Aunt Beth's and get help. If no one's home, use the phone and call Daddy, okay?"

"No, Mommy, I don't want to leave you here."

As the cramps worsened, Maggie feared she might pass out. She took a deep breath and grabbed hold of Emma's hand. "Baby, I need you to go now, and quickly. Do you understand?"

Emma nodded solemnly, kissing Maggie's cheek, then running to her pony. She led Sunny to the edge of Turtle Rock. Holding the reins, she scrambled up the rock until she was high enough to leap onto the pony's back. She had never mounted a horse or her pony by herself, but she made it in one try, holding on for dear life. Finally, settled in the saddle, she gazed back at her mother.

"I'll be back soon, Mommy." With one nudge, Sunny broke into a canter, then a gallop as they raced back along the dusty trail.

Her daughter out of sight, Maggie leaned back and lost consciousness. Tabasco stood still and silent by her side.

CHAPTER 30

Beth and Lang long gone, Rose was in the kitchen washing the breakfast dishes when she looked out and saw Emma and Sunny race into the yard. The child looked as if she'd seen a ghost. Dropping her dish towel, she ran outside. "Emma, sweetheart, what's wrong?"

"It's Mommy! There was a snake. She got thrown from her horse. She's hurt real bad!"

"Where is she?" Rose asked, helping the trembling child down.

"Near Turtle Rock. Come on, we've got to help her!"

Rose calculated the distance to be about a half mile. If Maggie was hurt, they would not want to bring her back on horseback. Like many of the ranchers, Lang and Beth kept an old golf cart in the barn to use as a motorized wheelbarrow. That would have to do, she decided, heading into the house and grabbing her medical bag and cell phone. "Come on, Em, we'll take the cart," she said, running toward the barn.

After several tries, the cart sputtered to life, and they headed off. As they sped out of the yard, Rose called 911 and asked for an ambulance to meet them at the house. She then called the stables and reached Harley.

"Hey, Rose, what's wrong?"

"Maggie's hurt. Thrown off her horse by Turtle Rock. Please find Ben and have him meet us at the house. We're heading out there now in the golf cart, and an ambulance is on its way. Probably best if he leaves the baby with you or his parents. Hurry!"

As she hung up with Harley, they made the last turn and spied Tabasco ahead, still guarding his mistress, who appeared to be unconscious. Rose gasped when she neared her friend and saw that her jeans were soaked with blood. She kneeled over and lifted Maggie's head. "Maggie, can you hear me?"

"What's wrong?" Emma wailed, standing over her.

Maggie's eyes fluttered open. "Hey, baby," she said, reaching up to her daughter. "You did it."

After a quick examination, Rose said, "If Emma and I help you, do you think you can make it to the cart?"

Weak and pale, Maggie nodded, reaching to circle Rose's shoulder on one side, Emma's on the other. They half carried, half dragged her to the cart and settled her in the open back. "Come on, Em, let's go," Rose said, indicating that the child should hop in.

"What about Tabasco?"

"We'll have to send someone out for him."

"No," Maggie cried, her voice weak.

"There's no time to argue," Rose said, gazing back at the enormous horse.

"I can ride him back," Emma said, her chin jutted out.

"No!" the two women said simultaneously.

"Let's see what he does," Rose said, hopping in, indicating the other seat for Emma. Sure enough, the horse followed them as they took off, cantering at a safe distance, his eyes never leaving his mistress.

As they drove into the yard, they spied the ambulance waiting. Just as Maggie was loaded onto a stretcher, Ben Morgan's Rover flew up the drive. "How is she?" he asked, his eyes wild as he leaped out of the jeep.

"No broken bones, but she's lost a lot of blood. It looks like the baby. Go with her. I'll take care of Emma and the horses. Go!"

Emma cried and begged to go in the ambulance, but Rose said they would get Tabasco and Sunny settled, then follow them to the hospital. "Come on, sweetie. Your Daddy'll take good care of you. Let's get these guys to the barn and then we'll head over there."

"I want Mommy," she said, sobbing now.

"I know sweetie," Rose said, folding her into her arms. "We'll see her real soon. You were a very brave girl today."

CHAPTER 31

Leonora Morgan phoned all of her children, then left the baby with Carmela as she and Ben Senior headed to the hospital. Rose and Emma arrived shortly after the elder Morgans, soon followed by Beth, Ruthie, and Lang. Ned Williams, Maggie's dad, was already in the waiting lounge, head in his hands.

"Oh, Ned," Leonora cried, going to hug their friend. Emma crawled in Ned's lap and started sobbing.

After helping Jeb and Nick Parker close up the stables for the day, Sam arrived. When Rose saw him, tears of relief sprang to her eyes. His strong, quiet presence comforted her.

"Hey," he said, patting Ned's shoulder, then coming to sit beside Rose, placing his arm around her.

Rose leaned into him, closing her eyes. "So glad you're here."

"How'd it happen?" Leonora asked, looking from Rose to her granddaughter.

"It was a snake, Nana. A huge rattler. Tabasco stomped it," Emma said, drying her eyes on her grandfather's sleeve.

"The horse spooked and reared," Rose said quietly. *She's damn lucky she wasn't killed.*

For what seemed like hours, the group kept vigil. Finally, Lang stood, announcing that he'd be happy to make a cafeteria run for drinks or food. As he began to take orders, Ben appeared looking weary and drawn, his shirt streaked with blood. His mother jumped up and ran to hug him. "How is she, sweetheart?"

"She'll be okay. Rosie was right. Nothing broken, some bruises. She lost the baby," he whispered, not wanting Emma to hear.

"Oh, sweetheart, I'm so sorry."

"What's wrong, Daddy?" the child cried. "I thought you said she was okay."

"Come here, baby," he said, opening his arms to lift his daughter. "Mommy's gonna be fine. She's just shaken up. Falling off old Tabasco is a big fall."

Emma nodded. "Then why did Nana say she was sorry?"

Ben looked around the room, then brought Emma to sit beside Ned. "Sometimes when people are pregnant like Mommy, a fall or a big bump can be too much for the baby. Do you understand what I mean?"

"Is the baby okay?"

"No, sweetie."

"Mommy's not gonna have a baby anymore?"

"Not right now, but maybe someday," he said, holding her tight, tears streaming down his face.

As the rest of them bowed their heads, Ned buried his face in his hands and wept. Finally, Ben Senior stood. "Come on, Nora. You, me, and Ned are gonna take Emma home. Ned, you ride with us. We'll take you back to the house and drive you home later. No one should be alone right now."

CHAPTER 32

The same evening as her fall, Maggie came home. Physically, she was fine, but very depressed. After all life had thrown at her as a single mom dealing with Emma's accident and surgery, this resilient, strong woman seemed to have given up. As days went by, she retreated into an impenetrable shell not even her adored husband and children could break into. Haley made regular visits, but even she couldn't seem to reach her.

As days went by, Sam and Rose saw little of one another, each involved in supporting Maggie and Ben in their own ways. Sam spent his days at the stables and Rose at the big house, Ned Williams' home, or Lang's, taking care of Emma and little Ben so that Ben could stay with his wife. Even though Maggie barely acknowledged his presence, he refused to leave her. It was the farm's busiest season, but Beth and Ruthie took turns helping out. Lang was also on call for stable work and to help with camp preparations.

In one of the rare moments when he dared leave home, Ben sat with his brother behind the barn. They both had beers in hand. "She blames herself. Keeps saying I must hate after what she's done."

"That's crazy."

"I know, but honestly, I'm not even sure she hears me when I talk to her."

Sam had never seen his older brother look so drawn and tired. "You know what this gathering at Mom and Dad's is about tonight?"

"If I had to guess, it's probably one of their interventions. I believe they cooked it up with Ned."

"Will Maggie come?"

"Are you kidding? She hasn't set foot out of the house in five days. I'll bring the kids with me."

CHAPTER 33

Rose, Beth, and Lang sat on their terrace, eating a quick meal before heading to the big house. They, too, had been summoned by Leonora.

"Poor Maggie," Beth said, looking from sister to brother. "She's been through so much, and now this."

"It takes time," Rose said quietly. "Her body's going through all the changes of not being pregnant on top of the loss and grief."

"How 'bout you, Rosie? We've all been going nonstop since Maggie's fall, but are you doing okay?"

"Much better."

"So, the Red Mesa night was a success?" Beth asked, smiling at her.

"Yes, we had a lovely time, even after Wilbur McGraw caught us. So embarrassing! It seems like a million years ago after the last five days." And it did. *A million years during which I haven't told Sam about Annapolis.*

"What's your plan about work and all?" Lang asked. "Not trying to get rid of you. We'd be happy if you stayed forever. Just wondering."

"Well, I'm going back next week. I have a full surgery schedule, but I had a call from Dr. Heavers. He wants me to apply for a position back east, at the clinic just outside of Annapolis."

They both stared at her.

"What did you say?" Lang asked.

"That I'd think about it. I had just emailed my application materials the morning of Maggie's fall. That doesn't mean I'll get the position, or that I'll take it if I do, but I wanted to keep my options open."

"We'd miss you, Rose," Beth said, reaching over to squeeze her hand.

"And I, you. I'd also feel really guilty being so far away with the situation with Dad."

"You know I don't want you to go, Rosie," he said, "but that situation should have no bearing on your decision. I'm here now. You shouldered the burden all these years. Maybe if you're back east, Mom can make lots of long visits to escape. They've got plenty of help over there."

"Please don't say anything. I haven't told anyone—not Mom, Dad, or even Sam. I was going to tell him the night we went to dinner, but after the episode with Wilbur McGraw, it went right out of my mind."

"Don't you worry," Beth said. "My siblings may be gabbers, but I am the quiet one."

"And the soul of discretion," Lang said, gazing at his wife with adoring eyes.

Rose was still amazed that her brother had found his match. He and Beth were so happy, and their joy about the baby was infectious. "I'm sure the competition is stiff, and I'm not sure I want to leave the clinic here anyway. I'll keep you posted."

The group assembled in the living room of the big house included Ben, Sam, Lang, Beth, Ruthie, Rose, Ned Williams, Harley, Jeb Barnes, Nick Parker, the elder Morgans, and Haley Alvarez. Emma and little Ben were playing in the backyard with Carmela and Raoul.

When everyone had a drink in hand, Leonora stood and motioned to her husband and Ned. "Thanks, everyone, for coming. I asked Harley, Jeb, and Nick because they are family. Spark and Amy wanted to be here, but they're in Portland settling things with the house. I'm going to turn things over to Ned, but I want my brood to know that your brothers are flying in tomorrow. It's coming into Robbie's busiest season, but he and Kyle both say they can stay for a week or so."

"I asked Mom to call them," Ben said quietly, "for Emma."

Emma adored all her aunts and uncles, but was particularly close to her Uncle Robbie, and no one could make her laugh like Uncle Kyle.

"So, Ned," Leonora said, "why don't you take over?"

The tall, lanky cowboy rose, looking every bit his fifty-eight years. "Thanks to Nora and Ben for gathering everyone. Sorry for the déjà vu, gang, but my baby is hurtin' again, and I suspect it's gonna take a group effect to bring her round. Ms. Alvarez is our expert, so I'm gonna turn things over to her. We've been talkin', and I think we have a plan."

Ned sat down and Haley stayed seated, clearing her throat. "This kind of loss hits people in many different ways, and it's actually quite common after a woman loses a child. Maggie's grieving, and she's in a major situational depression. This means that she's not ordinarily a depressed personality, but losing the baby has sent her spiraling downward. She has refused medication, which is her choice. Medication is not the only way to bring her back. It's going to take a lot of love and nurturing over next few months."

"Well, she's come to the right place for that," Harley said, gazing around.

"Yes, she has," Haley said. "It's also going to take a bit of tough love from time to time, because from what I know of Maggie, she has a stubborn streak."

"Pig-headed is more like it," Ben said. "I love her more than life itself, but when she's made up her mind, there's no moving her."

Sam watched his brother's eyes fill with tears and wondered if the couple would ever be the same. "The beautiful couple" is what townspeople called the eldest Morgan son and his gorgeous wife. It was said with affection since the pair's beauty was within as well as without. Their love for one another shone like a beacon of hope for anyone wishing to fall in love. *Ben's the only one who can bring her out of this.*

Echoing his thoughts, Haley continued. "I've had many conversations with Maggie since Wednesday and with some of you as well. It is my professional opinion that Ben is the only one who can pull her out of this, but he needs the help and support of all of you."

"We'll do anything," Ruthie said, eyes filling as she gazed at her oldest brother. Her father, who sat beside her, drew her closer, and kissed his youngest on the top of her head.

Rose happened to be looking at Harley when Ruthie spoke, and for one naked second, his love for the youngest Morgan was reflected in his deep green eyes. *When is he ever going to tell her how he feels?* Rose thought, then remembered that she hadn't heard a peep about love from Sam Morgan.

Haley smiled at Ruthie, then gazed around the room. "Yes, I believe this family will do anything for one another. Your job in this case, aside from helping out with all Ben's work, is to care for Emma and little Ben. Ned, Leonora, Mr. Morgan, and Carmela need help if this is to work. I know you've basically been doing this the past few days, but I'm suggesting that Ben take Maggie away for at least a few weeks, ideally a month or longer. The time away will help her to heal and bring them together. They desperately need it."

"Go for it," Sam said without hesitation. "I can fill in, albeit as a tenderfoot, at the stables and the Lodge. I'm willing to go on the next few pack trips, too, unless I'd be a liability?"

"I can step back in up at the Lodge," Ben Senior said. "I'd enjoy it and be happy to have you with me, Sammy."

"Jeb has already agreed to go with me on the two upcoming pack trips," Harley said. "We may need to tap Sam for the other one. We had already considered this earlier with Maggie not feelin' well. The college kids start tomorrow. Between all of us and Sam, we should be able to hold down the fort. The kids do the lion's share of the grunt work, Nick can give the lessons, and Sam can fill in as needed."

Ben looked from his best friend to his brother and nodded. "Thanks, guys. It's only for a few weeks. I'll try to get her to agree to a month, but we have to be back for the camp opening. Amy knows the routines there, as does Jeb. The staff are all coming back. We've gotten all the repairs and renovations completed, and the office staff will keep track of the campers before opening."

"Ruthie and I can take turns helping down there, too. Where will you go?" Beth asked.

"England, the Lakes. She's never been, and I'd love to go back. The reservations are all made, and her passport's up to date. Now I just have to convince her to go."

Rose opened her mouth, wanting to offer to talk with Maggie, but then closed it. This was a Morgan issue, and she felt she would be intruding. She was, therefore, startled when Ben turned to her.

"Rose, Haley has suggested that you might talk with Maggie. She trusts you, and right now, after you and my courageous daughter saved her life, your advice will carry a lot of weight. She'll listen to you. Please, Rose, would you be willing to give it a try?"

"Of course," she said quietly, glancing over at Sam. He gave her a crooked smile, his dark brown eyes shining with gratitude.

"So, let's all keep our fingers crossed that Rose and Ben are able to bring her around," Haley said. "Their flight is for six tomorrow night. I'll head out and let you all decide about the care of the children. I'm convinced that if this is to work, Ben must present Maggie with a clear, detailed plan for their care or she'll never agree to leave them."

They spent another hour making a month-long schedule for the children's care, and then the group broke up. As people dispersed, Sam caught up with Rose. Her familiar scent of peaches soothed his frayed nerves. "Hey, I've barely seen you since Wednesday night. You okay?"

"Yes," she replied, his nearness sending shivers down her spine. *There is so much to say.* "Sam, there's something I wanted to tell you."

"I have something I want to tell you, too. I can't remember what nights you're free on the babysitting schedule. Any chance of a dinner this week?"

She smiled, taking his hand. "I'm free tomorrow night, but then the kids are with us the rest of the week to give your parents and Ned a breather before I go back to work next Monday."

"Tomorrow, then. I've missed you." *Oh, God, how I've missed you!*

"I've missed you, too," she said, as her brother called from the car. "What time?"

"Pick you up at seven? Just casual, maybe the Bulldog?"

"Sounds perfect. See you then."

CHAPTER 34

The next day, Rose drove into Maggie and Ben's driveway just as Ben was loading the kids into his Rover. "Hey, Rose," he called, waving.

Emma was about to hop into the backseat beside her brother, but instead ran up to her. "Hi, Rose. Wanta come with us? We're going to the barn to help Uncle Sam and Harley."

"I'd love to, sweetie," Rose said, hugging her. "But I came to visit your mommy. Maybe I'll see you later?"

They walked hand in hand to the Rover, and Ben lifted her in. "Come, Peanut, or we'll be late."

Once he shut the door, he led Rose around to the back of the jeep. "Thanks for this, Rosie. She knows you're coming. She's in the kitchen. If you can pave the way, I'm gonna leave the kids with Harley and Sam, and I'll be back in an hour."

Rose placed her hand on his arm. "I'll do my best." She watched the Rover as it disappeared down the drive, then walked up the steps to the front porch. "Hi, it's me," she called as she stepped inside.

"I'm back here."

Maggie's jeans hung on her thin frame, as did a ranch tee shirt. Her long chestnut hair was pulled back in a loose ponytail. Still pale, she rose and came to hug her. "Good to see you, Rose. Want something to drink? A muffin?"

"Water's fine," Rose said, and started for the cupboard to retrieve a glass, then stopped, allowing Maggie to fill two glasses with ice and water. She brought them to the kitchen table and sat beside her.

"Is this okay, or would you rather go out on the porch?"

"This is fine," Rose said, smiling at her. "How're you doing?"

Maggie shrugged, a vacant look in her eyes. "I did want to thank you, though. If it hadn't been for you and Em, I wouldn't be sitting here."

"You have one courageous little girl."

"We do, and not only because of last week."

Rose nodded, meeting her friend's blue eyes. "Yes."

Maggie stared vacantly at her water glass. "I'm not sure I'm ever going to come out of this. And what's worse, I'm not sure I want to."

"It's been only a few days. Your body's all over the place hormone-wise, and you've been through a terrible shock. It's a miracle you don't have broken bones after a fall from that height."

"I should go see Carrie." She referred to Carrie Hale, a local chiropractor. "My body's got to be way out of alignment. Or maybe a spa massage? Trouble is, I don't have the energy for any of it."

"Those both sound like excellent ideas. Have you talked to Ben? He could drive you."

"Mr. Perfect? He's taken over everything—house, kids, my job at the stables, everything."

"He wants you to rest and recover."

"He wants me to feel as useless as possible after what I've done."

"Maggie, this is Ben we're talking about. He adores you and only wants to protect you till you're better."

"It's complicated, Rose. You should know. You used to have a thing for him, didn't you? It's not easy when you're married to someone who never makes mistakes, never makes a wrong decision."

"This is craziness, Maggie. I grew up with Ben. And yes, I had a crush on him, but once you came into his life, there's never been anyone else. I've never known any people as much in love as you two, and that's saying a lot, especially since I'm staying with my newlywed brother and the wife he adores."

"He told me not to go, Rose. He told me, and I hopped up on Tabasco and off I went. Emma could have been killed because of my recklessness."

"But she's fine, and so are you. Your children and husband need you, Maggie."

"I can't, Rose. I just can't." She collapsed, sobbing, head in hands on the table.

Rose put her arms around her shoulders. "Let it out, let it all out. Haley told me last week that tears are very cathartic. They help us heal, I'm told."

Maggie sniffed and gave her a wan smile. "She told me that, too, but I haven't been able to cry until now."

"Well, then, don't stop!" Rose said.

Despite the tears, both women laughed and held each other for a long time. Finally, Maggie's shoulders ceased to tremble, and her crying subsided. Rose stood and found a tissue box, handing it to her. "Would you like to take a walk or drive?"

"Thanks, Rose, but what I'd really like to do is talk to Ben. I've treated him like shit this week, and I want to tell him I'm sorry. I want to be here when he brings the kids back."

At that moment, the screen door slammed, and they turned to see who had come in. "If that's my mother-in-law," Maggie whispered, "please help me get rid of her. I love Leonora, but I'm not up to one of her pep talks just now."

Rose nodded as the kitchen door swung open and Ben stepped in. "Hey, ladies, am I interrupting?"

"Absolutely not," Rose said, standing. "I've got to be on my way." She stooped and gave Maggie a hug. "Take care and let's plan a walk soon, okay?" As she passed Ben, she gave him a conspiratorial smile.

"Thanks, Rose," Maggie said. "See you soon."

"See ya, Rosie," Ben said, sitting down beside his beloved wife.

***

Sam brought the kids to the big house for lunch, and they ran through to the backyard to find the farm dogs. Leonora gave him a thumbs-up. "She's agreed."

"Great news. Way to go, Rose and Ben."

"He's helping her pack, and they want the children back in an hour to tell them. Lang and Beth'll pick them up for the airport at three thirty."

"Thought you and Dad were doing it?"

"They offered, and since we have the kids tonight, we stepped back. You know they'll be with them the rest of this week. Poor Rose'll shoulder most of it, although your sisters are taking some time off. Robbie and Kyle'll be here, too."

"Is this bad timing for me to be going out for dinner tonight?"

"Absolutely not. Robbie's driving, and he won't be here till almost midnight. Lang and Beth are waiting in Tucson until Kyle's plane gets in at nine. You go have fun and make sure Rose has fun before her babysitting duties begin."

CHAPTER 35

Ben and Maggie got off smoothly in a whirlwind of packing and goodbyes. After helping with the children most of the day, Rose came back to the house to shower and change before her dinner with Sam. She rarely wore jeans as she favored more classic cotton or linen slacks, but she decided that a casual evening like this was the perfect time to try out one of the new pairs of jeans she had bought from Gabriela. She slipped them on and they fit like a second skin, as if they had been made for her slender frame. She selected low sandals and one of her new tops, its V-neck revealing a hint of cleavage, the pale coral bringing out the color in her cheeks, simple silver earrings and a bracelet her only adornment. She left her hair loose, falling round her shoulders. When she looked in the mirror, she barely recognized herself. Her bruises were fading and the stitches gone.

Sam pulled up a few minutes late and hopped out of the truck, spying her sitting on the porch. As he apologized for being late, she stood up. "Wow, you look sensational," he said, slack-jawed as she descended the steps.

"Thanks," she said, blushing. "It's not really my style."

"Well, it should be!"

She laughed. "I don't know if my budget can afford it." *You don't look bad yourself, Sam Morgan.* In fact, he looked gorgeous as always in jeans, running shoes, and what appeared to be a new ranch tee shirt in dark green.

"Looking at you in that outfit makes me think I should go home and change. They'll think you're with the hired help."

"Oh, no, is it too much?"

"I'm kidding, Rose. Let's go and give the Bulldog patrons something to talk about."

Owner Russ Keeler was behind the bar as they stepped into the saloon. Thanks to a new town ordinance, the bar was now smoke-free, its dark red walls covered with black-and-white rodeo photos punctuated with racks of antlers and a few stuffed heads. Russ waved. "Sit anywhere, folks. What can I bring you to drink?"

There were only a handful of customers at booths and tables and a few at the bar. They both ordered Desert Amber on tap, a popular beer from a local brewery, and headed to a back booth. Soon after they sat, Russ brought their beers and a basket of homemade chips and salsa.

"You folks gonna eat?"

"Yup, thanks, Russ."

"Just me and the kitchen staff till eight, so give a wave when you're ready to order, okay?"

Sam looked up at their host. "Why don't you give us a few minutes, then check back?"

"Will do," Russ said, disappearing.

They consulted their menus, then closed them. "So, I hear you saved the day this morning?" he said, smiling at her.

"No, but I am glad Ben was able to convince her to go."

"Me, too. Thanks, Rose. For all you've done and do for the Morgans." Just looking at her, Sam felt himself grow hard. What he wouldn't have given to carry her off and make wild, passionate love in the first secluded spot he could find.

She smiled at him, lost in his beautiful, dark eyes. "Morgans and Dillons are family."

"Yes, we are," he said, reaching across and gently taking her hands in his. "Are you really going to leave us next week?" She paled, and her hands trembled in his. "Sweetheart, what's wrong?"

She withdrew her hands and placed them in her lap. "I'm not sure. I can't explain it. There's just something about walking in there. I know he's gone, but the fear that he might… It's completely crazy. I know he won't come back, but I can't shake a feeling of dread, and thinking about going back to work's even worse."

"It's not crazy. It's perfectly understandable given the circumstances. Maybe it's too soon?"

"No, I've got to get back. They postponed three major surgeries, and the families have been waiting much too long. It's not fair to them."

Sam watched her shoulders tremble. Torture was too good for Dan Partridge. *If I ever set eyes on the bastard…*

"What'cha say, folks? Know what you want?" Russ Keeler appeared, pad and pencil in hand.

Sam looked at her. "Rose?"

"I'd love the Thai salad, please."

"You got it. What'll it be for you, buddy?"

"Bulldog Burger, medium rare. Thanks, Russ."

As the owner headed for the kitchen, she said, "I should have gotten a burger. They buy Dad's beef here."

"Want me to get him and change it?"

"No, I'm fine with the salad. Just sounded good. Despite growing up here, I'm not a big beef eater."

He laughed. "Me, neither. My poor father has Ben, the vegetarian, Maggie, too, and me, so-so about most meat. Fortunately, the rest of the clan shares his taste for red meat. At least here you know where it comes from and it's not pumped full of hormones and crap."

"And Enos Walker makes sure they are humanely slaughtered."

"Does he slaughter your dad's Angus?"

She nodded. "I watched once. It was still upsetting to see them grazing one minute and shot dead the next, but at least they were peaceful and death was quick."

"Thanks to Enos's expert marksmanship." Walker came to the farms for the slaughter and as the cattle grazed, he took aim from a distance so the animals never knew to be frightened. It was his sisters' least favorite day on the farm, but they prepared carefully and Enos took care of the rest.

They talked a while until Rose took a deep breath and said, "Sam, there's something I wanted to tell you last week when we had dinner, but there was never a good moment. Then everything got crazy, and—"

"Well, there you are, you naughty boy. I've been waiting for your call!"

As Rose turned to discover who was speaking, Sookie Fisher appeared, leaning on the table, revealing an alarming expanse of cleavage, which looked as if it might spill out of her lime-green Spandex top any minute.

Rose stared openmouthed at the woman, who looked vaguely familiar.

"Well, well, well," Sookie said. "I see you've found a lady friend. Oh, my, God, it's Rose Dillon. It's been ages!"

Flabbergasted, Rose found her voice. "Why, Sookie, how nice to see you." She extended her hand, which Sookie ignored, leaning over to peck her cheek instead.

"How's things? Did Sam tell you we used to be lab partners in chem class? Probably not, cause he and his buddies were always a little confused and thought we were in anatomy class, if you know what I mean?" she said. Winking, then batting her eyelashes, she plumped up her bodice.

"I heard from someone that you're working at Gabriela's?"

"Just part-time. I'm in nursing school, U of A."

"I just spent a fortune in the shop."

"Too bad I wasn't there to wait on ya. Not much in her shop that's my style, if you know what I mean, but Gabby's terrific. Lets me set my own hours."

"That's great," Rose said, wondering if Sam was ever planning to join the conversation.

"Aren't you some kind of doctor?"

"Yes, a pediatric neurologist."

"In Tucson?"

"Yes, at the Heavers Clinic."

"I've heard of that," Sookie said, smoothing the folds of her black spandex skirt that barely covered her sizable ass. "That a good place to work for a nurse?"

A voice from the other end of the bar called, "Sook, move it! We're goin'!"

"Oops, kids, gotta run. Gang's heading out to Pico Canyon for a bonfire. You wanta come along?"

"Thanks, Sookie," Sam said. "Maybe another time. I'd be careful with the fire, too. It's been unusually dry. They've got a ban on campfires on the ranch right now."

"Don't you worry, hon. Half the fire department's comin'. I'm sure they'll keep us safe. Night now. Rose, love to chat about your clinic. Sam, I'm still waitin' on that call." With a wink and a wave, she disappeared.

Rose grinned. "She's a force of nature, isn't she? Seems quite taken with you, too."

"According to Harley, she's quite taken with any male over the age of consent."

"I'd love to see her waiting on some of Gabriela's customers, like your mom or mine. Maybe she tones down her attire a bit when she's working?"

"Let's hope so," he said, smiling at her. "Now, back to what you wanted to tell me, if you can remember it after Cyclone Sookie."

Rose laughed, a lilting, genuine laugh that warmed his heart. *So beautiful*, he thought, watching her.

"Remember at the Red Mesa, I told you that my mentor, Chris Heavers, called me?"

"Yes, you said he was really supportive."

She nodded. "He always is. He also wants me to apply for a job back east, at a clinic near Annapolis, Maryland. It's part of the Heavers network. It would be a senior position and a big step up for me and my work."

Russ brought their meals, asked if they needed anything, then departed.

Sam's heart constricted as he watched her smile at the saloon owner, then turn back to him. Unlike her affect when talking about the Tucson clinic, her eyes sparkled and she looked happy, almost carefree, as if a huge weight had been lifted. *She has an out and she needs it more than anything right now.* "That's great, Rose. What did you say?"

"I said I didn't know. I said I'd have to think about it."

"And?"

"I applied, but it's highly competitive. I may be cut out after the first round."

"I doubt that with Dr. Heavers in your corner."

But what about you? Are you in my corner? Will you be sorry to see me go? "Maybe. Anyway, I had just faxed everything to them right before Maggie's accident."

"Have you heard anything?"

"Not yet."

Sam swallowed hard, trying not to choke on his burger. "I'm so happy for you, sweetheart. It sounds like the opportunity of a lifetime, and I'm sure you'll be their top choice." *And you will walk out of my life forever.*

Confused and hurt, Rose gazed downward, giving her attention to her salad. It was delicious, but after the first bite, she could have been eating sawdust. *It's almost as if he can't wait to get rid of me.* "Well, we'll see," she said, finally meeting his eyes. "What was it that you wanted to tell me?"

"It doesn't matter now, especially when we should be celebrating your news."

"Nothing to celebrate yet," she said quietly.

Sam watched her sadly, already missing her, the touch of her soft, peachy skin, her warm eyes, the feel of her breasts pressed against his chest, her scent that enveloped him and drew him closer until he was lost in her warm, sweet depths. Their bodies fit perfectly. Making love to any woman had never felt the way it did with her. In that split second, observing her eyes light up at the prospect of a new job and new surroundings thousands of miles from the memories of her attacker, he knew it would be wrong to tell her how he felt. He would not hold her here with professions of love. *I need to set her free.*

They both picked at their food and declined dessert. As they headed for the truck, he said, "Ice cream?"

"No, thanks, I should get back." Rose fought off tears that threatened to fall. *Once again, Sam Morgan has broken my heart. If he cared, he'd beg me to stay..*

"You okay?" he asked, taking her hand.

"Just tired, I guess."

They drove back in silence. When Sam pulled up, he spied Lang and Beth sitting together on the porch swing, mugs in hand. Lang waved. "Hey, guys, come join us."

Every fiber of his being wanted nothing more than to spirit her away, take her in his arms, and forget tonight had happened, but instead, Sam called, "Thanks, but I've gotta get going."

He took her hand as she stepped out of the truck and bent to kiss her cheek. "Night, Rose."

"Night," she said, turning away and walking quickly up the walk and into the house.

Beth and Lang observed the interaction, then looked at each other quizzically as her brother drove off. "Uh-oh, looks like trouble in paradise," he whispered.

"I wonder what my stupid brother's done now," she said, starting to rise.

"Leave her be, honey. It's their business. They'll tell us when they're ready."

CHAPTER 36

The next few days were a whirlwind of activity for Rose, caring for the children all day and helping with nighttime routines and awakenings, too. The baby missed his mother, especially at night, and his crying upset Emma, who soon joined in, wailing for both parents. Between the three of them, they managed to get through the nights, and by Sunday, the children seemed more comfortable. Their parents phoned every day. Sometimes the call led to a fresh bout of tears. At other times, the children were comforted by their conversations across the ocean.

Sunday morning, as the five of them sat at breakfast, Rose said, 'I'm gonna miss you guys."

"We're going to Grandpa's," Emma said. "You can visit us there."

"I certainly can, sweetheart. I have to go back to the hospital to work tomorrow, but I'll be back next weekend and, if needed, sooner. Uncle Robbie and Uncle Kyle'll keep you entertained."

"We going riding this afternoon," the child said, grinning from ear to ear. "I'm riding Dandy, Uncle Robbie's riding Royal, and Ben's riding Sunny with Uncle Kyle."

"Hmm," Beth said. "Did they get permission from your daddy for that?"

"Yup!"

"Relax, hon," Lang said. "They're using one of the camp saddles. He'll be perfectly safe." Lang's company had designed special saddles with backs and a secure strapping system to accommodate young handicapped riders, and, in this case, a wriggling toddler. This new product line had been put through rigorous safety testing, and the saddles were now one of the company's biggest sellers.

"I feel guilty bailing out," Rose said to her brother and sister-in-law.

"Don't," Beth said. "Ned has 'em for a few days. Then they'll be with Mom and Dad. Ruthie and I are going to switch off days and be there after Rob and Kyle depart. We'll be fine. What about you? Are you going to meet up with Sam today before you head back?"

"I doubt it," Rose said. "He's as busy as I am."

Beth exchanged looks with her husband, but said nothing.

***

Unused to manual labor, Sam nonetheless welcomed the diversion. He put his head down and worked hard all day, then cleaned up and went to the Lodge with his father for what they called "schmoozing." The Lodge was full, and guests expected to see their hosts. This also gave Sam and Spark time to chat daily about progress on the house.

One evening, Spark's daughter, Amy, joined Sam, his father, and Spark on the Lodge terrace, and they chatted about her upcoming wedding. She was engaged to Jeb Barnes, and they planned to be married at her dad's new house. Originally, the wedding date had been September, but construction delays and several other factors led to their changing to a winter celebration.

"I know I speak for my bride as well as myself in saying that if you'd rather stick with September, we'd be pleased and honored to host the wedding at the ranch," Ben Senior said.

"That's so kind, Ben," Amy said, her soft green eyes smiling at her father's dear friend.

The auburn- haired beauty was a physical therapist with a practice in Tucson, so Sam didn't run into her that often. *No wonder Jeb fell in love with her*, Sam thought morosely. *And he was smart enough to keep her.*

"Well, talk to your fiancé, then, and see what he says."

"We actually decided on a New Year's Eve wedding. Dad's house will be completed by then, and we're really excited to have the ceremony and reception in his beautiful new barn."

"First I've heard of it," Spark said, winking at Ben Senior. "But sounds good to me. Gonna celebrate my grandson's big day, too." Spark Foster had rarely denied his daughter anything and was crazy about Toby. He had fully supported Amy and Jeb's plans for adoption, and his attorneys were handling everything.

"When's Toby get back?" Sam asked.

"Jeb's parents have him now. Then he goes on a camping trip with Izzy Winkler, his social worker."

"Oh? Izzy's still in touch, then?"

Amy nodded. "Iz'll always be a part of Toby's life and ours. She's the person who kept him alive and loved his first few years. This'll be their third camping trip. He loves it and her."

As they continued to chat about wedding plans, Sam's mind drifted away, wondering what Rose was doing. *Letting her go is the right thing to do*, he thought for the hundredth time.

CHAPTER 37

Rose made sure there was still plenty of daylight when she arrived home and carried her bags into the condo. She had stopped for groceries, so she made several trips back and forth to the car, each time turning on more lights. She avoided the living room, put the groceries away and headed up to her bedroom. She had an early morning surgery, so she decided to turn in. As she lay in bed, she thought over the next few days. One of the first items was to call the local charity shop. With any luck, they could schedule a pickup for the living room sofa sometime this week or next. *Tomorrow I'll move anything I need from the living room to the den.*

As she closed her eyes, she saw Sam's beautiful eyes and stifled a sob. She missed him so much it hurt. Last time he had left her. This time, he was pushing her out the door. *Not sure which one is worse, but it sure hurts now.* Tears soaked her pillow as she finally drifted off.

The week was a blur. She saw patients in between four very long and delicate surgeries. Two nights she chose to bring a change of clothes and slept at the hospital. On Thursday, her landlady agreed to meet the charity shop truck, so the sofa was gone when she got home. She pushed two chairs together and partially filled the empty space, but the living room looked lonely and sad, a mirror of her feelings. As she prepared a simple salad for dinner, her cell phone rang. When she picked it up, she was surprised to see Sam on caller ID. Her brother and Beth called several times every day, but she had heard nothing from Sam all week. *Another hurt.*

"Hello?"

"Hey, Rose. How're you doing?"

"Okay. You?" *I am not going to cry. Please don't let me cry.*

"Exhausted. This city slicker is definitely not cut out for the cowboy life. Or, at least, I'm out of practice. Tryin' to keep up with the young guys is not easy. Harley's no slouch either."

"They're something, those cowboys," she said, thinking about her many years of pining away for Ben Morgan. *But he's not really my type. You are.*

Listening to her gentle voice, Sam ached for her. *If you love her, let her go.* He cleared his throat. "You comin' back this weekend?"

"I can't. I called Lang, and they said they have the kids covered. I'll try to get back the next weekend, but I've got a team meeting Saturday morning and a discharge that I'd like to handle myself."

His days were spoken for, but Sam knew he needed to see her. "Would you have time for dinner Saturday night? I could come down. Nothing fancy. I'd really like to see you."

Rose hesitated, not sure what to say. "Well, I don't know. I—"

"Please Rose, it's just dinner, promise."

Her resolve slipped away, and she heard her treacherous voice saying, "Okay, that'd be nice."

"Six okay?"

"Yes, that would be fine."

"I'll get directions from Lang. See you then?"

"Yes, goodnight."

Sam had made the call on his parents' front porch, and when he hung up, he shouted, "Yes!"

From inside, his mother called, "Sammy, is everything okay?"

"Leave the boy be, Nora," Ben Senior said quietly as Sam assured them he was fine.

Two days. I'll see her in two days, he thought, heading up to read a new novel he'd picked up at the library. *What the hell am I gonna do when she's all the way across the country?*

Rose hung up, wiping tears from her cheek. *This is a big mistake, Rose Dillon!* But she didn't care. *Maybe they won't want me in Annapolis*, she thought. *Maybe they've already filled the position? That doesn't change the fact that Sam Morgan was ready to send me on my way.*

Sam showered, pulled on a tee shirt and boxers, and was stretched out on the bed, reading, when his father knocked on the door. "Hey, son, okay if I come in?"

He sat up, patting the bed. "Of course, Dad. What's up?"

Ben Senior gazed around the room, smiling. While his wife had updated the furnishings, the pictures were the same as they'd been when Sam and Robbie had shared this room. Leonora had replaced the boys' twin beds with a queen, but it was the same style, rough-hewn log posts and a carved headboard. "Your mom has a good eye, doesn't she?" he said, patting the bed's striking patchwork quilt, also the product of a local artisan.

"That she does. Glad she redid the bathroom, although I do kind of miss the alphabet tiles."

His father chuckled. "Yup, they were something. How're you doing, Sammy? Harley workin' you too hard?"

"Nope," Sam said, regarding his beloved father. They had just had this conversation at the Lodge the previous afternoon during a cocktail party for the current full inn of guests. What was he really asking? "Dad, is something on your mind?"

"She's a sweet girl, your Rose."

"Yes, she is."

"You love her, don't you?"

"Yes."

"So, you two have gotten serious?"

Sam ran his fingers through his long hair. "Maybe. Yes. I don't know, Dad. Doesn't matter, cause more than likely, she's headed back east soon."

"I heard somethin' about that from Martha and Jaybo. Not definite, though."

"No, but I'd be really surprised if they didn't offer her the position. Her mentor, Dr. Heavers, wants it to happen, and he's pretty much in charge."

"What about you two?"

Sam shrugged. "It's a great opportunity for Rose. And she needs to get out of where she is now."

"Is that what she says?"

"Dad, I know you mean well, but I'm handling it. My track record with women is worse than Ben's, and that's saying a lot. I acted like a complete jerk to Rose last year. I won't do that again."

"So pushing her out the door is handling it?"

"I'm not pushing her anywhere. I'm being happy for her."

"Is that what she thinks?"

"I don't know, Dad. Reading women has never been one of my strong points. All I know is I'm not going to beg her to stay on my account. This is what's best for her. Period."

Ben Senior patted him on the shoulder, standing up. "You owe it to that girl to tell her how you feel. That's all I'm sayin'. Night, son."

"Night, Dad." His father meant well, but Sam knew with certainty that if he told Rose how he felt, she'd waver. *It just isn't fair. Period.*

CHAPTER 38

Friday afternoon, Rose was in the on-call room, gathering her things, when her boss, Richard Pruit, popped his head in. "Got a minute, Rose?"

"Of course. Can I clean up and come to your office in five minutes?"

"You bet." He closed the door behind him.

A few minutes later, they sat in Pruit's office, each with ice water in hand. Richard Pruit was six-three with a receding hairline, long, lanky legs, and patrician good looks, and he knew it. He slouched back in his chair, regarding her.

He offered her a drink, but Rose declined. She trusted her happily married superior, but with the exception of Chris Heavers and Dan, she made it a rule not to drink with colleagues. After several minutes of companionable silence, she asked, "Is everything okay?"

"Yes and no. As I'm sure you know, you were Chris's first choice for my job?"

"I'm not sure what you mean?" *And I'm not about to have this conversation with you.* She respected her boss, but found him a bit arrogant and self-important. The last thing she wanted was to get into a pissing contest with him.

"Okay, if you want to play coy, we won't go there. You've been through a lot, and I don't want to upset you."

"Rich, this is making me uncomfortable. I'm not sure what's on your mind, but please say what it is that you want to say."

"Okay, sure. Here's the thing. I've applied for the position in Annapolis. I want it. I deserve it. I'm the most qualified for it."

"I'm sorry. Are you referring to the senior director position at Heavers East?"

"Yes, we're rivals."

"I'm surprised. I thought the applicant pool was confidential. How did you—"

"I have a friend on the inside, just as you do. I'm surprised Chris hasn't given you the list."

"He would never do that, and I wouldn't ask him."

Pruit shrugged, leaning back in his chair. "Here's the thing, Rose. I want the job. Your place is here. I'm asking you to withdraw."

"Excuse me?"

"You're my strongest competition. The rest are not qualified. If you drop out, the position's mine, and I'll recommend that you succeed me here, permanently."

"Rich, I'm sorry. I cannot have this conversation with you. First, it borders on unethical, and second, I'm unlikely to get to the finalist stage."

"You have."

"Excuse me?"

He threw a long envelope on the table between them. "Came today. Relax, relax," he said, throwing up his hands in mock distress. "I didn't open it, but I got one just like it."

Rose picked up the envelope and placed it in her lap.

"Aren't you going to open it?"

She shook her head. "I'd rather wait until I'm alone. Now, if there's nothing else, I should get going."

"Wait. I don't want you to go away mad. I was trying to make things simpler for everyone."

"Thanks for your consideration," she said, trying without complete success to keep sarcasm from her voice. "See you tomorrow?"

"Nope. I'm flying east. My interview's Monday morning. I've alerted the team. Call me if any problems develop. And good luck with that," he added, pointing to the unopened envelope.

"Have a good weekend, Rich."

Rose tucked the envelope into her jacket and hurried out to the parking lot. Once in the car with the air conditioning on full blast, she opened the letter from the search committee inviting her to come for the day the following Tuesday. They gave her an alternate day of Thursday should she not be able to come on such short notice. An open-ended ticket had been booked for her, and hotel accommodations made. If she had any questions over the weekend, she was directed to call Sandra Haskell. Sandra's cell was listed along with Dr. Heavers's home and cell numbers. *Chris, what kind of hornet's nest have you gotten me into?*

By the time she unlocked the door to her condo, Rose had decided she would go on Tuesday, the better of the two days, as she had only a few appointments and one surgery, which would be easy to reschedule. She phoned her assistant, Sadie, and asked her to reschedule her Tuesday and Wednesday appointments. *Might as well see what it's all about. Certainly nothing to keep me here.* And the prospect of continuing to work for Richard Pruit was not a happy one.

It was too late to call people on the East Coast, but she would make a note to call Sandra and Dr. Heavers in the morning. She called home to check on her mom and listened to messages from Lang and Beth, then made an omelet and toast. *What a topsy-turvy few weeks it has been,* she mused as she headed into the den to find something escapist on television.

CHAPTER 39

After an unusually long Saturday, Rose showered, changed, and was just reading the mail when her doorbell rang. Sam. She had completely lost track of time!

She opened the door and there he was, the love of her life, who had discarded her like an old dishrag.

"Hi. Come in. I'm afraid this place is in transition. Redecorating."

Sam stepped in, giving her a peck on the cheek, his hand lingering on her waist for a few seconds before she stepped away. He noticed the empty space where the sofa had been and his anger rose, wishing he could thrash the bastard who had hurt her so deeply. *Then there's you, buddy, and you're not much better.*

"You look lovely, as always," he said.

She wore khaki linen slacks, flat shoes, and a loose, pale green linen top that obscured her curves and figure, giving only a hint of the luscious body beneath.

"Thanks. You, too," she said. *No man has the right to look that great in jeans and a tee shirt.* "Would you like a drink?"

"Your choice. I'm easy."

"Let's go, then. I'll just get my jacket."

As they walked to the truck, he turned to her. "I haven't spent much time in Tucson since high school, so I'm not familiar with the hot spots. Have you got an idea for dinner?"

She smiled. "Yes, there's a place right around the corner. Kind of a bistro-pub. Food's good. Doesn't usually get too crowded until later."

"Sounds great," he said, opening the cab door, his hand grazing her back as she slipped in.

Despite the unspoken undercurrent, they had a relaxed dinner and shared highlights of their week. He had many tales from life at the stables as well as babysitting stories. "Robbie and Kyle have been like the cavalry. Just the reinforcements the troops needed. We'll all be reeling when they leave next week, especially the kids. Kyle's trying to extend another week or two, but Robbie has to get back to Sedona by Wednesday."

"I'm all set to come the following weekend."

"That's the last thing you need after your brutal week."

"Pure joy," she said, placing her fork down. "Sam, I wanted to tell you something else that's happened."

Dreading her next words, he sat up, waiting.

"I'm a finalist for the position back east."

"That's great news, sweetie."

"I'm flying out on Monday for all-day interviews Tuesday. I'll be back Wednesday, though."

"Wow, that was quick." *Too quick.* "Does that mean if you get the job you'll be leaving soon?"

"No, I'd want to give the clinic here at least a month's notice, longer if possible. I had a very strange and unsettling conversation with my boss yesterday."

"Oh?" he said, not wanting to pry.

She needed to tell someone, so Rose related the details of the meeting with Richard Pruit. Sam listened with furrowed brow. When she finished, he said, "Watch out for that one. He sounds like a sleazebag."

"I wouldn't have thought it, but I don't know. I didn't say anything when I spoke with Chris Heavers this morning. Do you think I should have?"

"Absolutely. Whoever his mole is, you can be certain he or she will be working behind the scenes to screw you and promote this Pruit jerk."

Rose sighed. "You're right, I'm sure."

"What do you say? Want dessert or a drink?"

"Let's go back to my place. I have stuff there," she said, taking his hand. *If I'm going to move three thousand miles away from you, Sam Morgan, I'm entitled to one last fling.*

Her touch sent him into overdrive, and Sam felt himself grow hard. He paid the check, and as he rose, he kept his jacket draped in front of him. *Not sure how this is gonna work, buddy, but if she just gave you the signal I think she did, this is gonna be one hell of a night!*

CHAPTER 40

"I prefer going in the back door," she said, leading him around to the side of her building.

Sam longed to take her in his arms and kiss away the memories of the awful night of the attack, but he nodded and followed, deciding that this was another one of those times he should let her take the lead.

Rose led him upstairs to her bedroom, then turned to him. "I don't know what's going to happen with you, me, or us, but would you please make love to me, Sam Morgan?"

"You know I will, sweetheart," he said softly. His hands reached down and slipped her blouse over her head. She wore a white lacy bra, her perfect round breasts visible through the gauzy fabric. He cupped both breasts as he leaned forward, capturing her mouth, tongue delving deeply. Rose sighed and gave herself to him, her arms circling his neck, fingers running through his hair.

The bra soon followed the blouse to the floor, and he took one, then the other breast in his mouth, teasing her nipples to hardness, before his lips moved to her neck. "Come here," he whispered, leading her to the bed, slipping off her slacks and panties, laying her naked on the bed. After long, deep kiss, he stood and undressed, his eyes never leaving hers. "I'm going to make love all over you, my darling Rose. Will that be okay?"

She nodded. "Yes, please."

He kissed her forehead, then the tip of her nose, before finding her lips. "You are so beautiful. You know that, don't you?" he said huskily, kissing her, his tongue playing everywhere. Rose responded, arching her back, wanting him beyond all reason. He moved down to her neck, whisper kisses driving her crazy with desire before he moved to her breasts and belly.

"Please, Sam, please," she begged, blind with wanting him.

"I'm coming, sweetie, don't you worry," he said as his fingers moved between her legs, lips and tongue following into her warm, sweet depths.

"Oh, oh, oh," Rose screamed as another crashing climax washed over her.

Sam smiled, trailing kisses along the soft skin of her thighs, all the way to her toes. He now knelt at the end of the bed and reached to his side. His erection felt harder and more substantial than he'd ever experienced. He was astounded that he'd been able to hold on so long. *She's worth it. That's why.*

He rose up, gazing down at her with soft eyes. "You ready, darling?"

"Sam Morgan, if you aren't inside me soon, I'm going to die!"

"Well, we wouldn't want that," he said, smiling as he slipped on a condom and entered her, his thrust taking her breath away.

"Oh, Sam, I've missed you so much!"

"Me, too," he whispered. "More than you'll ever know."

They came together again and again, reaching higher and higher till a blinding climax left them limp and sated, their bodies deeply entwined. With one sweet kiss, they slept.

At four, Sam's phone alarm went off, and he groaned. Moving away from her was torture as he slipped out of bed and dressed. Rose slept on, so he found paper and wrote a note.

"Dearest Rose, Hate to go, but have to be at the stables by six. I'll call, my love. Last night was amazing, Sam."

CHAPTER 41

Sandra Haskell met Rose at the Baltimore airport and drove her to her hotel near the clinic. Exhausted, Rose declined Sandra's offer of a bite to eat and decided room service and an early night were what she needed. When she switched on her cell, she had three texts from Sam and a missed call. Now, in the quiet of her room, she read the texts.

"Thinking of you."

"Hope flight was smooth."

"Call if you're not too tired."

He had not left a message when he called. It was six in Maryland so only three in Arizona. Sam would be at the stables. She decided to text instead of call. *"I'm here, safe and tired. Don't work too hard."*

She hadn't invited him to call. Why? Was it self-protection? Three little words—*I love you*—and the fact that he had not said them spoke volumes, especially after she had expressed her love for him. *You are right to be careful, Rose, very careful,* she thought, grabbing the room service menu.

***

Sam, Harley, and Jeb spent the afternoon going over supplies and preparation for the upcoming five-day pack trip. Jeb had a school conflict, so they had decided that this was the trip on which Sam would go, leaving Nick, Jeb, when he could, and the college kids to take care of things at the stables. Jeb made numerous trips to town for food and other supplies while Harley and Sam planned each day's ride.

"These are the only first-timers we've had all year," Harley said as they sat in the shade with a beer at the end of the day. "Figures, your brother skips town when we need him the most. Get ready for the moaning and groaning. It'll commence after the first day and won't let up till they're back at the Lodge in their Jacuzzis."

Sam laughed. "I was talking with a couple of the ladies last night."

Harley grinned. "I'll bet you were. Remember, they're all married and you're spoken for, buddy, whether you realize it or not."

"Yeah, right," Sam muttered, shaking his head.

There were six in the party, three couples. The trip was a tenth anniversary gift to one of the couples. All were in their early forties, fit, and athletic, but only two had ever been on a horse before. The Lodge personnel had tried to steer them toward a ranch retreat, which included daily trail rides and a full week of spa treatments, but they were determined to have the whole experience.

"Yes, two of the ladies are married, but I don't think that's ever stopped them. They were all over Dad and me, especially Dabby and that real estate woman. The agent's a piece of work. She was actually handing out her business cards to everyone up at the Lodge."

"I'll bet your dad loved every minute."

"He did, even though he agreed that the business cards were a bit tacky. *Kingdom's Crossing* is one of his favorite TV shows. Apparently Dabby's had a few cameos on hubby's show." He referred to a wildly popular fantasy show in which Whit Foreman, Dabby's husband starred.

Harley laughed, nodding to Jeb, who joined them, cracking open a beer. "So the old man has dreams of knighthood, heh?"

Sam laughed. "Who knows? He loves reading about King Arthur, and my mother thinks *Camelot* was the greatest movie ever made."

"What's *Camelot*?" Jeb asked.

"Before your time, lad," Harley said, throwing Sam another beer. "Think *Kingdom's Crossing* with a bunch of goofy singing and silly outfits."

"How'd this crew find out about the ranch?" Jeb asked. "Little I've seen of them, they don't seem like the type. I mean, I like *Kingdom* as much as the next guy, but the Valley's hardly Middle Earth."

"I learned that last night from the ladies," Sam said. "One of Dabby Taylor's best friends is Julie Bliss." Bliss, a top-grossing actress, had booked a family pack trip a few years ago and now came back yearly. After a less than successful trail experience, Bliss and family now booked weeklong Lodge and spa retreats. The parents did a few daily rides and arranged for shorter two- or three-night pack trips for their teenagers.

"Christ, don't mention that woman's name," Harley said, pushing his hat back. "I'm gonna arrange my vacation for the week she comes this summer so I don't have to babysit her and hubby. Even day trips are torture. Let's hook her up with Parker. He's her type, I reckon. What d'ya think?"

"Poor Nick," Jeb said. "You guys all set? Toby's with my folks and this is Amy's first free night, so I'd like to take off."

Harley grinned. "Git, Romeo. We're fine."

Jeb tossed his empty bottle into a nearby recycling barrel and disappeared into the barn.

The wrangler turned to Sam. "Heard Rose went back east?"

Sam nodded. "Job interview."

Harley regarded the other man. While Ben Morgan was his best friend, he barely knew his younger brothers, particularly this one, who'd been away for many years. Not his place to pry, but the man had been moping around the barn all day. "So, she's movin' back east?"

"Maybe."

"I thought you two had something goin' on?"

"It's complicated. I was a royal shit to her last year, and it's her turn to leave. Besides, she needs to get out of Tucson. Don't want to hold her back."

"I see," Harley said.

"I gotta get going, Harl. See you in the morning."

"Sure thing, buddy. Take care."

Instead of turning up the hill toward his parents' house, Sam drove the truck down the camp road and parked in the deserted parking lot. It was close to five thirty, so eighty thirty her time. Not too late to call.

Rose answered on the first ring. "Hi, Sam," she said shyly.

"You made it." *I miss you so much, my beautiful Rose.*

"Yes, smooth, easy flight." *Except that it took me two thousand miles away from you.*

"You ready for tomorrow?"

"Ready as I'll ever be. It's an all-day interview with a number of people, individuals and groups."

"Sounds like fun."

"How's everything back there?"

"Same old, same old. We're all set for the Hollywood pack trip tomorrow. Harley's dreading it. I hope I'll be helpful and not a liability."

"Speaking of liability, those are major stars."

"If you like cheesy fantasy shows."

She laughed. "Well, good luck. Have you packed plenty of Gatorade and extra-large panty hose?"

"Yup, and all the special foods our prima donnas have requested."

"Hmm, should be interesting."

"I miss you, Rose. The other night was incredible."

"I miss you too."

"You sound tired."

"I am, a little."

"I'll let you go, then. Just wanted to hear your voice. Good luck tomorrow. I'm sure you're shoo-in."

There it is again, pushing me away, hoping I'll get a job that takes me so far away. "I doubt it, but goodnight."

"Night." He wanted to say more, but heard her click off. *Probably best,* he thought and started up the truck.

CHAPTER 42

After a blur of interviews and many conversations, Rose sat with Chris Heavers in his sunporch, Chesapeake Bay visible from three sides of the room. Her mentor was much thinner than the last time they had met, but his cheeks had color, and he was clearly more energetic.

"So good to have you here, my dear."

"What a place."

"Property's been in my family for generations, but it was just a shack until last year, when I bought my siblings out and renovated it."

"It's beautiful. You must hate to leave it to go to work."

He smiled. "I often don't. That's one good thing about cancer. You have a ready excuse if you want to play hooky and go fishing."

Leave it to Chris to find the positive with his incurable diagnosis. "I'm glad you play hooky. You've earned it."

"Of course, you've been at the clinic before, but we've made lots of changes. What are your impressions?"

"It's incredible, Chris. And an amazing opportunity for the right person."

"And that means?"

She smiled, sipping her wine. "It means that I came here on a lark. I never expected to be a finalist, and also couldn't imagine being so far from home. After this whirlwind day, I can honestly say I would love the position, even if it's a long shot."

"That's what I wanted to hear. No ties back in Arizona? I know your father's been unwell?"

"My brother's moved back. He and his wife are nearby."

Heavers refrained from asking about inconvenient boyfriends, assuming after the episode with Dan Partridge that she didn't have one. "Good. Time you had help shouldering that burden."

"Yes," she said, nodding, eyes gazing out the window.

"Is everything alright, my dear? You seem distracted."

"Yes. No. It will be."

"Anything I can help with?"

She smiled, gazing into his warm blue eyes. "There's a man, someone from my past. We've been seeing each other, that's all. He's been great after the nightmare of Dan Partridge. I will regret leaving him behind, even though he's been encouraging me to go. But then, I doubt I'll get the position, so it's a moot point." She threw up her hands. "Me and men. I don't seem to have much luck."

"Then they're idiots and not half-worthy of you."

"Who knows? Enough about my travails. Tell me about you! You look so well."

They spent a pleasant few hours talking over dinner. Not once did the subject of Richard Pruit arise, except for the brief time they spent talking about the clinic in Tucson. Sandra Haskell magically appeared at nine to drive Rose back to her hotel. As she hugged her friend, he said, "We'll be in touch. Couple more candidates coming in, but the committee wants to make a decision by Friday. Safe flight, my dear."

"Thanks and take care," she said, waving as she headed for the car.

"He's remarkable," Rose said as she and Sandra neared the hotel. "Every time I see him, I wonder if it will be the last, and now look at him."

"Yes," the other woman said, her voice grave.

"He's not as well as he looks, is he?"

Sandra pulled up and parked, turning to her. "No, he isn't."

"Oh, dear. What's happened?"

"They've given him three to six months. He's been so excited about you coming that the adrenaline's taken over, along with lots of pain meds, but the cancer's everywhere. There's no way to stop it or treat it anymore." Haskell dabbed tears from her cheek.

"Oh, Sandra, I'm so sorry," she said, tearing up as well.

"We all are. They've told him he may have a month or two when he feels pretty good. Then everything will start to go. After that, it will be relatively quick."

"I wish I'd known."

"He doesn't want you to know, especially not until they announce who will be offered the position."

"Of course. Will you keep in touch no matter what?" she said, handing Sandra a business card.

"Of course."

The two women hugged, and Rose headed up to her room. As she gathered her things together in preparation for her early flight, she felt lonely and sad. Five days without hearing Sam's voice seemed like an eternity.

CHAPTER 43

"Julie neglected to mention all the gross, disgusting bugs we'd be plagued with when she went on and on about this place." Dabby Taylor snapped, swatting a mosquito from her impossibly skinny leg. "The least you could've done is bring citronella torches, for Christ's sake!" She spoke to no one in particular, and her companions appeared to be ignoring her.

Sam and Harley stood in the shadows, allowing the six guests space around the blazing campfire. Harley leaned over, voice low. "This is only the beginning, buddy. Wait till day four. I'm surprised the mosquito can find anything in that bony leg. Wouldn't be getting bit if she'd kept her jeans on."

"That is one skinny woman," Sam whispered. "She doesn't look as anorexic on TV."

"Hey, guys," Whit Foreman called. "Do you have anything stronger than this for Dab?" He held up a pink bottle.

Harley rummaged around in his pack and produced the ranch's brand of insect repellant. "Here you go. They make it at the spa. It works better than anything I've ever tried. You should've gotten one in your travel kit they brought to your room."

Dabby waved her hand dismissively. "I never use anything but my own products."

Harley shrugged, handing the spray bottle to Foreman.

"Just try it, Dab."

She snatched it out of his hand and rolled her eyes at the two other women. "Whatever."

Nan Stevens, the real estate agent, stood on shaky legs and stretched. She, at least, had the sense to wear jeans, Sam thought, observing her preening, which was lost on her husband. Lon was chatting with Gray Malone, boyfriend of Dabby's sister, Punky. Malone had bankrolled the trip, an anniversary present to his sister and brother-in-law. Whit sat back down stiffly. Apparently, the day's ride was more than he was used to on the *Kingdom's Crossing* set. Earlier, as the group unpacked for the night, he had quietly accepted the extra-large panty hose Harley had offered him. In fact, five of them were now in possession of panty hose to wear under their jeans. Dabby insisted that her special Spanks longs would be much more effective, "thank you very much." Punky had been the only one smart enough to wear them today, so while she was stiff, her inner thighs were not chafed and red like her companions'.

Sam sat on a boulder at the edge of the clearing and gazed up at a clear, starry sky, a sliver of moon rising. Where was Rose? he wondered, missing her voice. She was a whole different species than the women sitting round the fire. In fact, truth be told, most Valley women were. He pictured his sisters, strong, beautiful, and resilient, and Maggie Morgan. Even his mother. They were all amazing women. To be fair, Punky was fairly normal, but Nan and Dabby? Different universe. *Dabby and Punky—what kind of names are those?*

The campfire group slowly dispersed into their respective tents, with groans and grousing. The women complained bitterly about the lack of bathrooms and the strict guidelines Harley had outlined about toileting on the trail. Each guest had bags and instructions, and each had had to sign an agreement to follow the instructions to the letter or the trip would be cancelled with no refund.

Harley gave Sam a pat on the shoulder. "It's gonna be a long week. Better get some rest."

The two were sleeping under the stars, their bed rolls at the edge of the clearing. It had been a while since Sam had slept out, and he was pretty sure he'd have his own share of aches and pains in the morning. He was already saddle sore, despite the panty hose and liniment he'd applied liberally before they set out. After taking care of business and cleaning up a bit, the men laid out their rolls side by side and were soon asleep. Sam's last thoughts before he drifted off were of Rose and her impossibly soft skin, the way her nose turned up slightly, her scent of peach blossoms and lemon.

CHAPTER 44

Rose flew into Tucson and took a cab to her condo. She had a full two days at the clinic and did not get to Saguaro until late Saturday afternoon. Lang and Beth were up at the big house, helping with the kids, so she threw her bags on her bed and headed back out. She found a lively group on the terrace. Ben Senior and Ruthie were playing with Emma and the farm dogs, games only they knew. Ben was crawling around the grass with Beth keeping a watchful eye. Lang manned the grill with Raoul, moving back and forth from bar to grill as needed. "Hey, Rosie," he called, coming to embrace her. "Good to have you home."

"Good to be here," she said. "How are the kids doing?"

"Great. Their parents phone once or twice a day, and things seem to be going well. They've been hiking and sightseeing all over the Lakes, and they plan to spend their last week in London."

"I'm so glad," Rose said, patting his arm. "When are they due back?"

"'Bout two weeks, I think. Beth knows the date. What can I get you to drink?"

"I can't believe I'm saying this, but if you've got any margaritas mixed, I'd love one."

"Comin' right up."

"Hi, sweetie," Leonora said, hugging Rose. "I asked your folks tonight, but Mom thought it best to stay put."

Rose looked from Leonora to Lang. "Same old crap," he said. "Dad's fine, just refusing to move, and you know she doesn't like to leave him."

"I worry about her," Leonora said, "But Martha knows what she wants. I keep trying to get her to go on a short trip or an adventure, but so far, she won't leave him."

"If Rose gets the job back east, she'll have an excuse to get away," he said.

"That's right, darlin'. I forgot about that. How'd it go?"

"Great," Rose said. "It was wonderful spending time with Dr. Heavers, and the job is really interesting. I doubt I'll even get considered, but it was nice to be asked."

Lang and Leonora exchanged glances. "They'd be crazy not to hire you, darlin'," she said, winking at her son-in-law.

At that moment, Emma ran onto the terrace. "Hi, Rose!" she said, racing into her outstretched arms. "Can we have a sleepover tonight?"

"Absolutely sweetie, if it's okay with your grandparents?"

"Perfectly fine," Leonora said, grabbing Ben as he toddled toward the grill. "Ruthie, come get your nephew! I want to help Carmela with dinner."

Ruthie grabbed the child and came to stand beside Rose and Lang. "Hey, Rose. How was your trip?"

"Quick."

"Sounds like life around here."

"Have you heard from the pack trip?"

Ruthie laughed. "Harley called Daddy today. I'd pay big money to see Harley dealing with Whit and the gang. Day three's when the saddle sores are the worst. They've already had three falls, and a couple of the stars refuse to eat anything. Oh, and Dabby left her stash of power bars somewhere, and an animal got into it and ate every one last night."

"Uh-oh," Rose said. "How's your brother holding up? He's not exactly saddle-ready himself."

"Won't be able to sit down for a week. If he knows what's good for him, he'll head straight to the spa for a whirlpool and a massage or two. Like my other macho brothers, he'll probably pretend everything's hunky-dory and only moan and groan in private. Speak of the devils."

Rose followed her gaze and spied Robbie and Kyle Morgan stepping onto the terrace. Like the rest of their family, they were rugged, handsome men. Robbie, the fourth child, was fair-haired like his mother, with dark green eyes and the Morgan killer smile. Although shorter than Ben or Sam, Kyle, the fifth sibling, was a dark-haired clone of the other two, always with a mischievous twinkle in his dark brown eyes.

"Hey, Rose," Kyle said, embracing her as Robbie scooped Emma up in his arms.

"Hi, Kyle, Robbie. Wonderful to see you both."

"Same here, Rosie," Robbie said. He gave her a quick peck on the cheek before carrying Emma off to the grass to join his dad.

Ben Senior sat at the edge of the grass on the terrace steps, petting one of the dogs, smiling as he watched the melee. Nothing gave him greater pleasure than his family coming together.

"So, what's new?" Kyle said, smiling at her. "I hear you and Sammy boy have been seeing a bit of each other."

"Some," she answered.

Lang watched his sister's face turn crimson and decided a diversion was needed. "So, we're keeping you a while longer, I hear," he said to Kyle.

"At least another week. I'm trying to stretch out long enough to see Ben and Mag before I go back, but I'm in the middle of my large animal rotation, and if I miss too much, they'll make me do it again." Kyle was in his third year of veterinary school at Montana State Veterinary, after transferring from Tufts.

"Too bad you couldn't do some work here," Lang said. "They can sure use vets. Ned Williams is always swamped."

Kyle laughed. "Wouldn't that be cool? I'd love it, but you forget, I'm kind of busy this visit," he said, taking the toddler from Ruthie. "Me and Ben got our routines, don't we, bud?"

Ben wriggled down, and Ruthie ran after him as he headed for the grass, his sister, and Robbie. Rose watched as he grabbed his uncle's leg, then turned back to Kyle. "How is life in Bozeman?"

"I love it, but I'm still thinking of applying to go back to Tufts for my residency. I want to live back east, see if I like it, then decide if I wanta stay or come back this way."

"It's tough to leave the Valley," she said softly, catching her brother's eye.

At that moment, Leonora stepped out on the terrace and called, "Dinner is served! Come and get it!"

The table was lined with salads, bowls of guacamole, and platters of red and green enchiladas. As they made their way to a seat, Lang whispered, "Follow your dream, sweetie. We'll always be here."

CHAPTER 45

Their final day on the pack trip, Sam was daydreaming about Rose. He was the last rider on the narrow, winding trail. Nan Stevens was just ahead of him, the others a fair distance in front. She had been complaining since she woke up, and Sam noticed that Lon, her husband, had elected to ride at the front of the line with his *Kingdom's Crossing* costar. The men rode just behind Harley, the others following. *Smart guy,* he thought, watching Stevens fidget. Her long red hair was pulled back in a scraggly ponytail under her wide-brimmed sunhat. Her jeans were caked with mud from a fall the day before. *Please make her stay in the saddle,* he thought, wishing it was Rose riding ahead of him. He'd spied any number of spots during the morning's ride that would make perfect places to spread a blanket, take her into his arms, and make love to her. *That is, if my body could even manage it. Spirit willing, but not sure about the flesh.*

Suddenly, Stevens slid off Misty. Standing in the middle of the dusty trail, she glared back at him, arms akimbo. "I can't go any further! You'll have to send a jeep."

Sam hopped off Rowdy and steadied himself, mentally counting to ten. His own legs screamed in pain as he approached her. "Look around you, Ms. Stevens. There's no way to get a vehicle up here. We have only five hours to go. Then you can sink into the whirlpool."

"You bet your ass I will. What about a helicopter?"

"Excuse me?"

"They could get a helicopter in here."

"That would be only in case of an emergency," he said patiently, watching the others as they disappeared around a bend in the trail. They were descending a ridge, but would be climbing again soon as they made their way south to the Valley. The open trails ahead of them would be scorching by midday. They needed to move.

"What the fuck do you call this, honey? Where's my goddamn husband? Figures he'd leave me in the dust."

Sam wanted nothing more than to hurl the woman over the next cliff, but he forced a smile and extended his hand. "Nan, let me help get you back on your horse. We don't want to get too far behind the others."

"I'll ride with you. That's the only way I'm continuing. We can pull this nag along behind us."

"That's not possible."

"Why the fuck not?" Nan's language, which has started out prim and proper, had deteriorated with each day to vernacular that would make a longshoreman blush.

"Because—"

"You can't think of an excuse, can you?" she said, stepping closer, playing with his collar. "You're a slippery one, Sam Morgan. If I wasn't so goddamn sore, I'd pull you into the bushes and fuck your brains out."

For an instant, Nan Stevens and Meryl Wainwright merged into one, and Sam had to work hard to control his anger. "Let's get you back on Misty, okay?" he said softly.

In answer, she drew him closer and kissed him, all tongue and lips. Instantly, Sam pushed back. "Hey, lady, this is not gonna happen."

She laughed, shrugging. "Get me some fucking water, cowboy."

As Sam turned to get the water, he spied Harley heading toward them and breathed a sigh of relief.

Dusty like the rest of them, Harley was clearly in his element astride his magnificent Appaloosa stallion, Pepper. As the women had proclaimed all week, he was a quintessential cowboy, handsome, rugged, and fit. "Hey, what's going on?"

Behind Nan Stevens' back, Sam threw up his hands.

"I'm not going on, that's what's going on. You may be the twin of the fucking Marlboro man, but I'm not going an inch further unless I ride with someone."

"Lady, that's not gonna happen."

"What did you call me? Don't you take that tone with me, cowboy."

Harley dismounted and patted Pepper's flank, handing the reins to Sam. The Appaloosa had a mind of its own and had already run off several times over the past few days. "Look, Ms. Stevens, out here, I'm in charge, and at this point, I'll take any tone I need to get us movin'. The others are way ahead, waitin' on you, and we're not gonna stand around while you have a temper tantrum."

"Why, of all the nerve!"

"Come on," he said more gently as he whistled for Misty. Leonora Morgan's gentle white stallion came to his side, nuzzling Harley's shoulder. "Up you go."

"I said, I'm riding with him, and that's fucking final."

"No, you are not."

"Why the fuck not?"

"Because it's too hard on the horse in this terrain." *Furthermore, Sam Morgan is not an experienced enough rider to handle that, and I'm sure as hell not taking you.* "Let's go, Ms. Stevens. The others are waitin' and it's gettin' hot."

She took a long, slow drink of water, then threw the canteen at Sam. It dropped at his feet. As she struggled to get her left foot into the stirrup, Harley grabbed hold of her waist and threw her up, then circled the horse, making sure she was settled. Sam watched the set of his jaw and realized that the other man was furious and struggling mightily to control it. *Please let us get back in one piece,* he thought as Harley took Pepper's reins from him.

"You still okay back here, buddy?"

"Yup."

As Sam mounted, Harley led Pepper a short distance ahead and leaped up into the saddle. With a backward wave, he was gone.

"The man may be gorgeous," she said as the horses followed Pepper, "but he's one of the rudest people I've ever met!"

Pot calling the kettle black, Sam thought, following her.

CHAPTER 46

As Beth, Lang, and Rose sat with the children having breakfast, the back door opened and Ruthie popped in. "How'd you guys sleep?" She plopped down and grabbed a piece of toast, which she slathered with farm honey.

"Great," Beth said. "Bennie was with us, and he didn't make a peep until almost seven."

"If you don't count the midnight run," Lang said, ruffling the toddler's curls.

"And I had a sleepover with Rose," Emma said proudly.

"And of course, she was as good as gold," Rose said, smiling at the child. Emma reflected her mother's delicate beauty, but was also the spitting image of her dad.

"I just stopped by to see if anyone wanted to come meet the pack trip with me," Ruthie said. "Jeb's busy with the camp and Nick's swamped, so they need bodies to help transport the touristas back to the Lodge and get all the horses settled down. I'm out at the farm this morning, but I'm swinging back after lunch. They're expected back around three."

"I can't," Beth said. "As you know, we've got three trucks coming for large orders this afternoon, and one of us has to stay."

"I'll help," Lang said.

Rose raised her hand. "Me, too. Ned's coming for the kids in a little while."

"I wanta come and help, please," Emma said, looking from one to the other.

"Well," Beth said. "That's up to Rose and your grandpa."

"I'm happy to have her with me," Rose said, "as long as it's okay with Ned."

Midafternoon, Rose and Emma drove down to the stables in Lang and Beth's golf cart. Lang met them there, and a ranch van was already parked in the lot. Two of the staff, stood in the shade, each playing on their cell phones. Rose waved to the two men, whom she knew vaguely, and followed Emma into the barn.

"I love it here." Emma sighed as they passed the clean, empty stalls. Every horse was either on the trip or grazing in one of the corrals. Nick Parker was just finishing a lesson with a local woman who boarded her horse at the ranch. They sat in the shade and watched the woman dismount and lead her beautiful Arabian toward the barn. "Thanks, Nick," she called, waving at the handsome trainer, her body language screaming, *Take me.*

Lang laughed. "Parker's the newest in a long line of stable darlings, isn't he?"

Rose poked her brother in the ribs as Parker approached, tipping his hat. "No sign of 'em yet, but they should be here soon. Hey, Em, wanta help me bring in the horses?"

A half-hour later, a dust cloud heralded the group's approach. Emma, who had been walking Ruthie's pinto around the east corral, spotted them first. "Here they come!" she called, leading Jadie toward the barn.

As they drew near, Rose made out Harley in the lead, two men close behind him, followed by two women.

A short distance further back, Gray Malone rode, tall and straight in the saddle, a grimace on his angular face.

"That Punky chick looks pretty good," Parker said, leaning against the corral fence, "but the Taylor broad looks like she's fixin' to keel over."

Jeb Barnes came around the barn from the drive and called to him. "Get ready, Nick. They're all gonna need help gettin' down except Harley."

Lang and Ruthie came forward, Rose following. As the horses reached the yard, Harley jumped down and helped Lon Stevens off his horse as Jeb assisted Whit Taylor. While both men looked wobbly, they managed to walk to the shade as

Ruthie grabbed the horses and Rose offered them a drink. "What's this, a welcome home party?" Dabby said as she gazed down at Lang standing ready to assist her.

"Dabby, hush," her sister said, grinning as Nick Parker took hold of her waist and lifted her down.

"Can I help you down, Ms. Taylor?" Lang said, patiently waiting beside her.

"What do you think?" Dabby said, slipping into his arms, not even bothering to stand. "Take me to that green chair and get me a drink, now!" Her arms circled Lang's neck as he carried her across the yard.

After he deposited her in the shade, Lang took her horse and Pepper into the barn as Gray Malone neared them. Jeb came forward to see if he needed help, but Malone waved him away and dismounted stiffly. "Thanks," he said as Jeb took his horse.

"Where are the others?" Rose asked, looking back along the trail. No one else was in sight.

"Oh, they'll be here shortly," Harley said. "Sam gets the combat medal for this trip, that's for sure."

The others knew enough not to ask, but simply stood waiting. A few minutes later, two more riders came in view. The woman was in the front and seemed to be almost lying on Misty. Behind her, Sam and Rowdy kept their distance, watching her every move. As Rose caught sight of him, her heart skipped. *He looks tired.*

When they reached the corral area, Sam gazed over, giving her a weary smile. He then slipped off Rowdy and handed the reins to Lang, moving to Misty's side. "Okay, Ms. Stevens, we're home."

"Huh?" she said, lifting her head, gazing around at the group. "Whoop–de-doo, I'm in cowboy heaven," she mumbled, sliding into Sam's arms. "Take me to the Jacuzzi, sugar. I'd be happy to have you join me there. Bathing suits optional."

"Here's your husband, Ms. Stevens," he said, plunking her down on the bench beside Lon Stevens, who looked none too happy to see her. Lon handed her a water bottle, which she applied to her forehead.

"The vans are out back," Harley said. "They'll take you up to the Lodge whenever you're ready."

As the group dispersed, Harley, Jeb, and Nick headed into the barn to tend to the horses, Emma at their heels. After telling Rose they could leave the golf cart there until the morning, Lang said he'd be back to collect her and Emma after assisting with unloading at the Lodge. He disappeared, leaving Rose and Sam alone in the shade of the barn.

"Good to see you," Sam said, finishing his beer and tossing the bottle into the recycling barrel.

"You, too. How was it?"

"Let's just say I won't be changing careers anytime soon. I don't know how my brother and Harley do it."

She laughed. "Practice, maybe?"

"Maybe. And another thing—I've never been a fan, but I will never watch another episode of *Kingdom's Crossing*. I mean, Whit and Lon were okay, most of the trip, but their wives. There're no words."

"You looked pretty cozy with Nan Stevens," she said, her eyes teasing.

"Yeah, just what I needed. Another cougar breathing down my neck. How's your week been?"

"Busy."

"I'd say let's grab dinner, but I'm not sure I could sit up straight for an entire meal."

"No worries. I've got to head back home in an hour or so. I've got a really busy day tomorrow."

"Have you heard anything about the job?"

She shook her head. "No, but I'm assuming they've offered it to someone else. Chris—Dr. Heavers—said they planned to make their decision by last Friday."

"You never know. When can I see you?"

"I'll try to get home next weekend. Your brother and Maggie come back Sunday."

"A little earlier than expected?"

"They miss the kids, and Ben told your parents that Maggie's doing great."

Lang's Rover drove in, and he called to Emma and Rose.

Sam reached over and took her hand. "I'm filthy, sweetheart, so I won't attempt to hug and kiss you, but I really would like to get together. Can I call you and we'll make a plan?"

"Of course," she said, standing, then leaning over to kiss his parched lips. *I'd be happy for you to hug and kiss me, Sam Morgan, trail dust, sweat, and all.*

Despite the fact that he was bone-tired and practically comatose, Rose's kiss was electrifying, and he felt every fiber of his being rise to attention. He longed to pull her close, but spied her brother at the barn door with Emma on his shoulders. "You ready, Rosie?"

"Yup."

"Can we give you a ride, Sam?"

"Thanks, but I'm all set," Sam said. "I'll wait for Harley to get back and catch a ride with him. Night."

CHAPTER 47

On rounds Tuesday afternoon, Rose had just stepped out of a patient's room when she heard Sadie's voice paging her. *Something's happened with Dad*, she thought, taking the stairs to her office. Sadie looked up as she entered.

"What's up?" she asked her assistant.

Sadie smiled, tearing a pink slip of paper from her message pad. "Dr. Heavers asked me to page you. He'd like you to call him at this number as soon as possible."

Rose took the paper and headed in to her desk. "Thanks, Sade."

Chris answered on the first ring. "Ah, perfect, my dear. Glad I caught you. Sorry this has taken a little longer than necessary. As you know, we had hoped to reach our decision last week."

"Yes," she said, quietly waiting. Her mentor could be incredibly long-winded when he chose. *Her hand shook as she held the phone. Please just tell me, Chris!*

"I was pleasantly surprised, to tell you the truth. We had a very strong applicant pool, stronger than I expected." Heavers paused for a few seconds.

Rose realized she had been holding her breath, and she let it out. *He's trying to let me down gently.* "I'm not surprised. It's an amazing opportunity, and I am honored even to have been considered."

"Yes, it is an amazing opportunity for the right person. And we need the right person, my dear. I hope you understand?"

"Of course." She struggled to keep from crying. "Listen, Chris, I'm grateful for the call, but I—"

"Just a moment, then I'll let you go. I know this is a busy day for you. As I was saying, with my declining health and the clinic's expansion, we need the right person, which is why *you* are the committee's unanimous choice. We cannot envision anyone else filling the role."

"Excuse me?" she sputtered, afraid she had misheard him.

"I know what you'll say. You're too young, but that's malarkey. Alan Roth is a very capable director. He'll manage that side of things, but we need a surgeon to run the team, and *you* are the best pediatric neurosurgeon surgeon I know."

"Chris, I-I don't know what to say. I never dreamed I would be…I can't believe it."

He chuckled. "What I'd like you to say is yes, my dear. We'd also like you to come east again soon—tomorrow, if possible. I know you need time to decide."

"Yes, I do. What about my position here? My patients? I'd be leaving them midtreatment, and the clinic incredibly short-staffed."

"I have someone in mind. I'm not going to say anything to Rich Pruit until I hear from you, but I can get her out there as your replacement within a week or two. She wants the position and wants to relocate to Arizona to be near family."

"How long do I have to decide?"

"A week or two. While you're deliberating, I'd like to get you back here to talk things through and have you meet the whole team. Any chance you could get out here again?"

Are you crazy! It's too soon! "Not this week. I'm swamped and also committed to help out at home this coming weekend. I could fly out Sunday night for a day or two and take the red-eye back Tuesday. Would that work?"

"I'll have Sandra make the arrangements."

That is, unless I decide not to take the job, Rose thought, thanking him and hanging up.

"Good news?" Sadie asked as she headed back for rounds. She knew all about the job offer and had been waiting with bated breath to hear. Unbeknownst to Rose, Chris Heavers had been in touch with her assistant at home Saturday. Rose's mentor was an extraordinary listener, and he remembered that Sadie and her husband, a successful copywriter, had grown up on Maryland's Eastern Shore. Wanting adventure, Sadie had come to Arizona with him, but it was no secret that she wanted to return to the East Coast to raise her children. Her husband, could work anywhere and would follow his beloved wife to the ends of the earth if she asked him.

Heavers had already queried Sadie about moving with her boss should Rose be offered the position, and Sadie had not had to think twice. He had thanked her and asked that she keep it quiet until the committee made their decision, and Rose hers. If Rose decided not to take the job, he promised Sadie that he would begin looking for other positions should she still wish to relocate.

"I got it, Sadie. They've offered me the position."

Sadie leaped from behind her desk and came to embrace her. "Congratulations!"

"Thanks, I think," Rose said, still in shock.

"What did you say?"

"That I'd have to think about it. They've given me time, but Chris wants me to come east while I'm deciding. I can't go this week, but Sandra is making arrangements for me to fly out Sunday and return Tuesday. My Monday and Tuesday are light next week, but you'll have to reschedule a bunch of appointments. I should be back and able to put in long days Wednesday through Friday, so why don't you extend my appointment hours until seven thirty those days?"

"Will do," Sadie said, grinning. "So happy for you."

"Thanks. I'm kind of in shock, and I cannot imagine not working with you."

"Take your time, boss. You'll figure it out."

"Don't suppose you'd like to go home?"

Sadie smiled, determined to keep her promise. "That's for Dr. Heavers to decide."

"Yes, I suppose so. I'd better get cracking. I'm incredibly behind!"

CHAPTER 48

When Sam got back from the stables Tuesday evening, Martha and Jaybo Dillon were sitting with his parents and Spark Foster on the terrace. He'd forgotten they were coming to dinner and was thankful he'd made plans with the guys. He liked Rose's mother very much, but her brooding, alcoholic father gave him the creeps. Leonora always said were it not for Martha, they would probably have cut Jaybo out of their lives long ago, even though Sam knew his dad would never completely sever ties. The Dillons were their closest neighbors and old friends. You didn't cut ties with family, Ben Senior always said, even if they'd hit a bad patch.

Before heading up for a shower, he poked his head in to say hello.

"There's my hotshot," Spark called, raising his glass in a toast.

"Hey, Sammy," his mother said. "Your sister's gone out with friends, but we'd love for you to join us."

"Thanks, Mom, but I'm meeting the guys at the Bulldog."

"Good, then you can keep an eye on her. Ruthie's friends are a bit on the wild side," she said, addressing their friends.

"Now, Nora, they're good kids, all of 'em. Got time for a beer with the old geezers?" his dad said.

"I'm really grungy, Dad."

"Nonsense. You can sit on the wall," Leonora said. "Raoul, please bring Sam a beer."

Sam nodded to Raoul, who was grilling steaks and a large rack of vegetables. He came to sit on the wall near Spark and Jaybo, greeting Rose's father, who looked better than he had the last time he's seen him.

"We were just talking about Rose's big news," Martha Dillon said. "I think she wants to keep it quiet until she decides, but we're all family."

"Oh?" he said, knowing with certainty what was to come.

Jaybo took a huge gulp of what appeared to be straight bourbon. "She's going east, to Maryland."

"Now, Papa, we don't know that yet. She hasn't decided."

"So, she got the job?" Sam said, trying without complete success to appear nonchalant.

As the conversation continued about Rose's skills and her brilliant rise to a position ordinarily held by a much more experienced physician, Ben Senior's eyes were trained on his son.

Sam drained his beer and excused himself, despite protests from the group to have another. *You thought your life was over before, buddy, but now it's official. The woman you love is moving two thousand miles away and there's not a goddamn thing you can do about it!*

Showered and changed, he was just heading out when his father caught him in the front hall. "Hey, son, you okay?"

"Sure, Dad. What's up?"

"Looks like you hadn't heard Rose's news?"

"No, but that's okay. We're not…I mean…we're not committed or anything."

"What're you gonna do about it?"

"Be happy for her. It's a huge promotion. She deserves it."

Ben Senior held his gaze, blue eyes full of concern. With the authority that had made him the most successful rancher in the Valley, he said, "Don't let her go without tellin' her how you feel, son. You'll regret it for the rest of your life."

"It's done, Dad. Not everyone has you and Mom's happy ending. I've gotta go."

He met Harley, Nick, Robbie, and Kyle at the Bulldog. They sat at the bar, and Sam ordered a shot of tequila and a large draft.

"Gonna be that kind of a night, is it?" Harley said, wondering what had gotten into his best friend's brother. *Problems with Rose Dillon, I'll wager.*

About an hour later, Ruthie and several girlfriends came by. After flirting shamelessly with Nick Parker, Ruthie looked over at her brother. "Better watch it, Sammy. You're not the drinker these guys are."

Sam pointed at her. "I'm s'posed to be keepin' an eye on you." His speech was already slurred.

"I'm guessing this is a response to Rose's news?" Ruthie said, gazing over at Harley.

Sam downed his sixth shot, followed by most of his beer chaser.

"We'll make sure the lad gets home," Harley said, winking at Ruthie.

"Thanks, guys." She leaned over Parker and ignored Harley. "See ya. Come on, ladies."

Sam staggered up to his room and flopped into bed fully clothed. He gazed at his cell phone. *No calls. Screw her,* he thought, kicking off his boots and passing out.

Rose wanted to call Sam but didn't know what to say. She hadn't heard from him since the weekend, so after a busy day, she had decided against calling. *It's for the best. Let it go until you decide,* she thought as she drifted off. *Nothing left for me here now. Might as well say yes.*

CHAPTER 49

The week flew by. Heart heavy, Rose barely had a minute of down time between two long surgeries and many rescheduled appointments. The greatest source of pride in her work had always been the relationships she built with the families of children contemplating serious, life-threatening surgeries. Thus, she felt guilty pushing them off when every minute pre- and postsurgery was traumatic and stressful. Now, added to that guilt was the realization that if she took the job back east, most of the patients with whom she was now consulting would be assigned to a surgical team that did not include her.

Her mother called Friday evening and asked if she would stay with them Saturday night rather than at Lang and Beth's, and she agreed. She knew they had a million questions about the job and what she was going to do. While she would rather have avoided such conversation until she'd made up her mind, for her mother's sake, she would go home.

She arrived midday and was sitting with her mom on the back terrace when she spied Sam's truck coming up the drive. "That'll be your brother, honey. Sam gave him a lift cause Beth and her mom took the Rover to Phoenix to pick up Maggie and Ben."

"That's right! They're due back today," she said, stating the obvious. "Can't wait to see them." She stiffened, wondering what she would say to Sam, when the front door slammed and they spied the truck headed back down the drive.

"Hey, ladies," Lang said, smiling broadly as he gave them each a peck on the cheek. "Where's Dad?"

"Napping," Martha said, fingers to her lips. "Let's hope it's a long one. He's been out of sorts today. How are you, baby?"

"Great. I'm pretty free," he said. "Ned and Dad have both kids, or should I say Carmela has the kids and the grandfathers are supervising, and the guys've got the stables covered. They're scrambling around like crazy trying to get everything cleaned up before Maggie's return."

"What about you?" Rose asked. "You're probably so far behind at Rambler West."

"Au contraire, sister dear. When you have great staff, a business practically runs itself. And I do have great staff."

Rose smiled at her handsome sibling, knowing that he was lying through his teeth. Not about the staff, as he did have good people, but she knew with certainty that he was way behind on almost every aspect of the business. *He doesn't want Mom to worry,* she thought, patting his arm. "Want an iced tea?" she asked, rising.

"Thanks, but I'm gonna grab one of the winery jeeps and head into town. We gonna see you tonight, right?"

Their mother shook her head. "I regretted, sweetie. Your dad's not in the right frame of mind, and I figured Rose would be tired. Besides, it's a Morgan family gathering, of which you are a part, but not us."

"That's baloney and you know it, Ma, but you know best." He gazed over at Rose and added, "I know one Morgan who'll be sorry not to see you."

Rose blushed, and he disappeared.

"Everything okay, honey?" Martha asked.

"Yes, why?"

"I mean between you and Sam?"

"We're friends, Mama. That's all."

"Okay, if you say so. Anyway, I'm so pleased to have you all to myself tonight! I almost hope your daddy doesn't feel like coming down to supper," she whispered.

Sam had seen Rose's car, but had no excuse to come in. He also didn't know what he'd say to her if he did. He knew his mother had invited the Dillons. *Maybe tonight I can pull her aside and make a plan,* he thought as he pulled up behind the big house to rejoin the melee. It would be good to have the couple home. Harley might be the head wrangler, but everyone knew that Maggie was the boss and had been the boss long before she married Ben Morgan.

CHAPTER 50

Everyone cheered when Maggie and Ben stepped onto the terrace, each with a child in their arms. Emma's rested her head against her father's shoulder, grinning from ear to ear. "She looks terrific," Beth whispered to Sam as the siblings stood side by side. Kyle was manning the grill with Raoul, but dropped his spatula and came forward to greet the couple. He then tickled Emma as he hugged her daddy.

"Yes, she does." Sam nodded, waiting until the crowd dispersed to greet the couple.

"Too bad the Dillons couldn't come," Beth said, "but it's kind of nice, just us and Ned. Jaybo is such a downer." She gazed up to see her brother's face drop, his disappointment clear. "You still haven't talked to her, have you?"

"What's the point? She's going."

"From what I hear, she hasn't made up her mind."

"Which is why I'm steering clear. She certainly doesn't need me begging her to give up the opportunity of a lifetime to hang out with me."

"Is that what you call it, hanging out?" Beth eyed him, eyebrow raised.

"You know what I mean. I'm not going to stop her."

"You know what? You're my brother and I love you, but right now you are one of the stupidest people I know. You also have a bigger ego than I thought. What makes you think you have the power to stop her? She's not some weepy little nobody. She's a world-class surgeon who most definitely knows her own mind."

Sam stared at his sister, who rarely said more than a few words to anyone. She was right, of course.

Ben approached and handed Emma to Kyle. "Hey Sammy. Good to see you!"

"Welcome home, brother," he said, hugging him. "You both look great. How was the trip?"

"Better than our honeymoon," Ben whispered, patting him on the back. "Thanks for all your help. Sounds like you went above and beyond."

"Happy to help."

"Well, you're officially off duty, man. Time to get on with your life and work. How's that going?"

"Slowly, although Kevin and his crew are making great progress out at Spark's."

"On schedule, then?"

"Pretty close. Should be completed by mid-December, in plenty of time for the wedding."

"Excellent news. Come on, let's get a drink to celebrate!"

Sunday morning, Sam woke with a headache after too many margaritas and beers with his brothers. He had volunteered to take Kyle to the airport, so after breakfast, they headed out. As they parted company in Tucson, Kyle said, "Thanks, Sammy. Hope things work out with Rose. It's clear she's the one."

"Excuse me?"

"Buddy, I may be an animal doctor, but I can still read you like a book. I've never seen you like this over a woman. Tell her you love her, man, and get on with it, before it's too late."

"Get on the goddamn plane," Sam said, smiling at his brother. "And come back soon!"

"Christmas for sure. See ya!"

As he drove out of the airport, Sam made a decision. He called Rose's cell, but it went straight to voice mail, her home phone too. He then called the Dillons, and Martha answered. "Hi, darlin'. No, Rose is gone."

"So, she's headed home?"

"No, she's on a plane to Maryland. Be there for a couple of days."

Sam thanked her and clicked off. *It's now or never,* he thought as he headed back to the ranch.

CHAPTER 51

After a whirlwind day, Rose met Sandra Haskell in the clinic lobby. "Chris wanted to be here, but he's having a rough day."

"I was afraid of that. Is he at home?"

"Yes, and he's waiting for your call. Can I take you to dinner?" Heavers's thirty-eight-year-old assistant was dressed more casually today in a pencil skirt, flats, and a crisp white blouse, her shoulder-length blond hair pulled back by a tortoise shell band.

"Thanks, but I'm beat. I'd also like a little time to think about the day before I call Chris in the morning."

"Can I at least give you a lift?"

"Thanks, but I think I'll walk."

"Of course. Take care, and I'll see you in the morning."

The day's heat had let up as she began the four-block walk back to her hotel. A park across the street beckoned, its shady paths inviting, so she crossed the street and decided the longer walk would do her good. It had been an amazing day, meeting many of her future colleagues, should she come to Heavers East to what was definitely a dream job. She'd be a fool not to take it.

Forty-five minutes later, she was still wandering in the park and realized she had lost track of time. She gazed around and spied the roof of her hotel, orienting herself. As she headed in that direction, she spied an empty bench near the pond and came to sit in the shade. She had reached her decision. *I cannot accept it, not now. I haven't a clue what's happening with Sam Morgan, but I know I cannot be two thousand miles away from him.*

Tears dampened her cheeks, and Rose sat silently weeping for a long while before rising. At peace, she still wondered how she would ever tell Chris Heavers. Lost in thought, she entered the hotel lobby, eyes on the floor, so she was startled by his voice.

"Hey, Rose."

"Sam? What are you doing? How did you find me? Why are you here?"

"Are you free for dinner?"

"Yes. How did you know I was here?"

"Dr. Heavers was really helpful."

"But why? Why are you here? You couldn't wait to get rid of me last week."

"I didn't want to hold you back, sweetheart. This is your dream job. You deserve it."

"I've decided not to accept it."

"What?"

"I could not imagine being so far away from you, at least until you ride off into the sunset again."

"Well, that's not *ever* gonna happen." He led her to an enclosed garden patio room, which he had reserved and was now set with a table for two.

"How did you arrange all this?"

"That's my secret, darling. Come over here, please," he said, leading her to a stone bench. After she was seated, he knelt in front of her, pulling a tiny box from his pocket. "I love you, Rose Dillon, more than anything in the whole world. I cannot imagine another day of life without you in it. I will do anything to keep you in my life. Will you marry me?" He opened the box to reveal a beautiful sapphire in an antique setting, surrounded by diamonds.

"Oh, Sam, it's so beautiful," she said softly, her hand caressing his cheek. "I love you, too."

"Is that a yes?"

"Yes."

He slipped the ring onto her finger, a perfect fit. He then drew her into his arms, kissing her deeply. Rose melted into his embrace, trembling with tears of joy.

"And you're going to call Dr. Heavers tonight and accept the job."

"And have a bicoastal relationship? I don't want that."

"Neither do I, which is why I've been in serious negotiations with West-cott Associates, an up-and-coming architectural group here in Annapolis. They want me."

"Oh, Sam, I can't believe it." She wrapped her arms around his shoulders and kissed him.

He sat beside her, drawing her closer. "Well, believe it, my darling, cause we're going to be together no matter where. Sadie's ready to move and help us house hunt whenever we're ready."

"Sadie?"

"Blame your boss for that. He's been plotting with her all week."

"I feel like I'm in a dream. A beautiful dream from which I hope I never wake up."

"Then don't, my darling. Let's live the dream for the rest of our lives."

She nodded, head resting against his strong chest. "Do we have to eat dinner down here?"

"You wicked woman," he whispered, nuzzling her neck. "I thought you'd never ask."

Please read on for chapters from Hestor's Way!

ABOUT THE AUTHOR

M. Lee Prescott is the author of dozens of works of fiction for adults, young adults, and children, among them **Prepped to Kill, Gadfly, Lost in Spindle City (Ricky Steele Mysteries), A Friend of Silence, In the Name of Silence and The Silence of Memory (Roger and Bess Mysteries), Jigsaw, Song of the Spirit**, and her newest contemporary romance series, **Morgan's Run,** of which **Rose's Choice** is the fourth! Three of her nonfiction titles have been published by Heinemann, and she has published numerous articles in the field of literacy education. Lee is a professor of education at a small New England liberal arts college, where she teaches reading and writing pedagogy. Her current research focuses on mindfulness and connections to reading and writing. She regularly teaches abroad, most recently in Singapore.

Lee has lived in southern California (loved those Laguna nights!), Chapel Hill, North Carolina, and various spots in Massachusetts and Rhode Island. Currently she resides in Massachusetts on a beautiful river, where she canoes, swims, and watches an incredible variety of wildlife pass by. She is the mother of two grown sons and spends lots of time with them, their beautiful wives, and her amazing grandchildren. When not teaching or writing, Lee's passions revolve around family, yoga (Kripalu is a second home), swimming, sharing mindfulness with children and adults, and walking.

Lee loves to hear from readers. Email her at mleeprescott@gmail.com, and visit her website to hear the latest and sign up for her newsletters!

A Note from the Author

I am thrilled to bring you Rose and Sam's story, the fourth of *many* **Morgan's Run** books still to come! Thank you so much for reading it. These beloved characters will be around as the series continues to grow. The Morgan's Run books are set in the gorgeous American Southwest, an area of the country that is dear to my heart because it is home to my youngest son and family, but also because its beauty is so extraordinary and so startlingly different from that of my New England home. What a backdrop for romance and adventure!

If you like **Rose's Choice** and would be willing to write an Amazon review, I would be very grateful. If you would like to sign up for future book releases and occasional notices about my books, please visit my Author Website and sign up for my newsletter. I promise I will not share your address, nor will I flood you with emails. Do visit my site to read more about my books and to hear what's next.

Finally, this book has been revised, proofed, and edited many, many times, but my intrepid assistants and I are human, so if you spot a typo, please email me at mleeprescott@gmail.com and I will fix it. If you'd like to know more about my other books, please scroll ahead to the next section, which is followed by sample chapters of **Hestor's Way,** a sexy romance in my **Well-Loved Series.**

Warm wishes,

M. Lee

Contemporary romances and mysteries by M. Lee Prescott include:

The Ricky Steele Mysteries
Book 1: Prepped to Kill
Book 2: Gadfly
Book 3: Lost in Spindle City

Also featuring Ricky Steele:
Jigsaw

Roger and Bess Mysteries
Book 1: A Friend of Silence
Book 2: In the Name of Silence
Book 3: The Silence of Memory

Contemporary Romances

Well-Loved Romances
Widow's Island
Hestor's Way

Morgan's Run Romances
Book 1: Emma's Dream
Book 2: Lang's Return
Book 3: Jeb's Promise
Book 4: Rose's Choice

Young Adult Historical Romance
Song of the Spirit

Hestor's Way

Love is the last thing on gifted artist Beth Hadley's mind as she prepares for a one-woman show while enjoying a bittersweet summer before her son, Kit, leaves for college. Then, out of the blue, an unexpected secret love blossoms with Jack Talbot, Kit's best friend. The two begin a passionate affair that could destroy her world, tear her family apart, and shatter the peace of her close-knit community. As Beth struggles with guilt and remorse over the relationship with Jack, an old love returns, and with him, a chance for deep, abiding eternal love. Is it too late for her?

Sneak Peek of Hestor's Way Chapter 1

The studio's screen door banged behind her, and Beth headed through the gardens toward the house. Passing through the grape arbor at the path's end, she spied her son, Kit, as he raced across the terrace.

"Hi, Mom! Gotta go. See you this afternoon?"

Her eighteen-year-old jumped over the terrace wall and waved as he headed for the driveway and his beat-up Volvo, his father's gift of safe, reliable transportation for the summer.

She marveled at the change in her only son. Where was the round-faced, chubby boy? He had disappeared, and now there stood a six-foot-tall man in his place! Of her three children, Kit looked the least like his sandy-haired father. Dark curls framed his slender face—"the young Shelley," Beth's friend Clarice called him. Although tall, he was slight, almost delicate on first glance, until one noticed the powerful legs from years spent on the soccer field. Kit would be playing soccer at Bowdoin in the fall.

"Kit, remember to ask your boss about tomorrow night. It's Nanny's birthday," she said, referring to her youngest.

"Mom, don't worry. We're only workin' a half day, then coming back here to work in the barn. We'll probably head to the beach after that, but I'll be home in plenty of time to get the grill going."

"Kit," she called as the Volvo's door creaked open. "I forgot to tell you, Dad's coming. He…well, he asked and I said fine. You know how he is about the grill."

"Well, tough shit. It isn't his house or his grill anymore."

She came to stand beside him, eyes soft and pleading. "Kit, please, it's a little thing, and it's Nanny's night."

"It's not a little thing to me. Who does he think he is? We've been doin' fine without him. Now he thinks he can waltz back in whenever he wants and take over. God, and you just let him, every single time!"

"Honey, I know it's hard, but it's only one night. I'd never have made it through the last three years without you. We can do this. Have a birthday party for Nanny and be together. You're right about the grill, though. I'll have a word with Dad. You should do the cooking. But, Kit, do try to be civil, okay?" She rubbed his shoulder.

Shrugging from her touch, he dropped into the car seat, muttering.

Beth's heart ached, watching him and remembering the shy, introverted fifteen-year-old who'd so desperately tried to take his father's place three years earlier.

"It's okay, Mom. I'll be home around five, but don't expect me to be jolly. Is she coming?"

"No Chloe." She closed the car door. "You'll be civil, for Nanny's sake?"

She noticed a glimmer of a smile as he pulled away. "Stinker!" she called as the Volvo tires crunched down the drive.

Turning toward the house, she glanced down at her watch. Nearly nine. Kit was late for work again.

When she entered the kitchen, Kat, her oldest, stood at the kitchen counter, barefoot, in the long tee shirt she used as a nightshirt. Kit, short for Kittredge, and Kat, short for Katherine, had been Alan's ideas.

"Hi, Mom." She turned and gave her a sleepy smile as a dollop of strawberry jam dropped from her knife to the floor. Tall and slender like her mother, Kat also had long, straight hair, lighter than Beth's chestnut color. Auburn tendrils framed her sleepy face as she smiled sheepishly, stooping to wipe up the jam. "Oops."

Beth flicked on the burner under the teapot. "Late night, huh?"

"Kinda. You didn't wait up, did you?"

"I heard you come in, if that's what you mean, but I was only semiconscious. So?"

"So, Rob took me to Newport and we went clubbing."

"Clubbing? Kat, you're only nineteen."

"Mom, it's not that kind of clubbing. We didn't drink, not even Rob."

Rob had just turned twenty-one, and the difference in their ages worried Beth. He and Kat had been dating since her freshman year at Dartmouth. Rob would be a senior this fall, Kat a sophomore. His parents lived in New Jersey, but Rob had found a job painting houses with a local contractor in Windy Harbor for the summer. He shared a house with four other guys who had already thrown several raucous parties.

"Kat, you know I trust you, but I'd rather you stayed closer to home."

"There's nothing to do here. If the Harbor wasn't so dead, we'd stay home, but it is. You worry too much. Anyway, we'll be taking a break next week when Rob goes to training."

A nationally ranked collegiate soccer player, Rob had hopes of a professional career, and it looked as though he might have a shot at it.

"Kat," she began, her voice tentative as she embarked on a touchy subject. "I know we've discussed this before, but I wanted to check that you and Rob are taking precautions."

"Mom!"

"I'm serious. I'm not implying that you're sexually active, and I don't mean to pry."

"We are, on both counts," Kat replied. "Mom, we've been sleeping together for over a year, but it's okay. Rob uses condoms every time. Want to know what brand?"

"Very funny."

"Don't worry. We're careful." Kat put her arms round Beth's shoulders and hugged her.

She returned the embrace, then turned away, not letting her daughter see the tears in her eyes. "Fine. That's all I need to know."

"Mom, we had this conversation six months ago."

Beth blushed. "Did we? I'm sorry." Relieved and embarrassed, she rushed to add, "Maybe you and I can snatch some time together in the next few days? I feel like I've barely seen you since you got home." Beth played with a lock of her daughter's hair. Even in a ripped tee shirt, with sleep-drenched eyes and tousled hair, what a beautiful woman her eldest had grown into.

"Sure, love it. Let's plan something for my day off. Shopping, a movie?"

"Or a canoe trip up the river or a day at the beach?"

"Yeah, sure, sounds good. This jam you made is great. A little runny, but I love it. Can you save a couple of jars for me to take back to school?"

"Of course. Your brother's already put three aside."

"The pig. He doesn't even like your jams."

"Stop it and don't be greedy. You'll have to leave a jar or two for Nanny and me. We like it too, you know."

"Speaking of Nan," Kat whispered, sitting down next to her mother at the long wooden table. "I haven't gotten her anything yet. What's she want for her birthday? I thought I'd ride up to the Mill shops after work today and get her something."

Beth laughed. "You know Nanny; she likes almost anything, especially coming from her older sister. Just surprise her. You always do."

"Dad's coming, isn't he?"

"How'd you know?"

"Nanny told me, plus we ran into him last night and he mentioned it."

"Ran into him where?"

"Thames Street, can you believe it? We go down to Newport to get away from Windy Harbor for a few hours and who's the first person I see after Rob parks the car, but Dad? Chloe was draggin' him around to every shop on Thames. He looked real happy, as you can imagine. You know how much he loves to shop."

Beth laughed, almost pitying her ex-husband. "Chloe must have strong arms."

"What an airhead. What he sees in her is beyond me."

Youth, Beth thought, but added charitably, "Chloe is far from an airhead. She's a gifted artist, and you know how much that means to Dad."

"Yeah, if you like nihilistic heavy metal."

Her daughter was referring to Chloe's massive metal sculptures, welded together with a blowtorch. Beth smiled, brushing a lock of hair from Kat's forehead. "Now, now. Anyway, your father's coming tomorrow around six, and I thought we'd eat and then have presents. Supper around seven? What do you think? That way we'll be finished in time for the fireworks."

"Rob is taking me."

"Why don't you have Rob and the kids come to the house to watch them? We can all sit out on the porch and…"

"Thanks, Mom, but we really like to be up close and personal, right underneath 'em."

"Uh-huh."

"We're meeting a bunch of kids in the Commons at nine," Kat continued. "Kit's friends will be there too."

"Suit yourself, but remember, Fourth of July or not, Nanny comes first. Just family till eight-thirty."

"Course, Mom. What do you think?"

Her children treasured the rituals and traditions that accompanied birthday celebrations. The previous September, Kat had been despondent when Dartmouth's preseason field hockey schedule had taken her away on her birthday. To make it up to her, Beth and Alan, on one of the rare occasions when she'd agreed to go anywhere with him, had packed the other two into the car, along with a birthday cake, dinner, and presents, and traveled to New Hampshire. They found a campground nearby where they could grill shrimp—Kat's favorite meal—and have cake and presents on the cool September afternoon, sharing a few precious moments together. When they walked onto the practice field, Kat's face had made every minute of the three-hour drive with Alan worth it.

CHAPTER 2

The light was perfect, or nearly so. A faint mist in the air sprayed the canvas, running the colors slightly, but Beth didn't mind. Not with early morning light like this, clean, soft, and pure, filtering through the trees at the edge of the pond, bathing every inch of the grassy woods with warmth. The trees mirrored in the pond's glassy surface stretched their branches from sky to the middle of Echo Lake, their reflections an impressionistic extension of reality.

She was working on a commissioned piece for the Wanamakers, who owned the stone cottage at the far edge of the pond. Together they had scouted every inch of the far bank on which she now sat until they fixed on the very spot where her easel rested, a spot Herb Wanamaker had marked with a white stake. After a week of mornings spent in the shady spot, Beth had nearly completed the picture of the turn-of-the-century cottage dwarfed by the towering elms and firs that surrounded it. Some last touches and the painting could go to the framer.

Beth enjoyed working outdoors but had had little time for it the past six months. Her agent was pressing her to show, and she needed at least thirty paintings for a one-woman exhibit. A prestigious local art gallery granted three solo shows a year and chose its artists carefully. Every exhibit at the Lynch Gallery attracted national attention, drawing critics from New York, Boston, and California. Rick Gould, Beth's agent, had been negotiating with Margot Lynch for six months on his client's behalf, but so far the gallery owner showed no signs of capitulating.

Beth had tried, unsuccessfully, to tell herself that it didn't matter. Fueled by the influx of summer people, the local market for her work remained strong. She usually sold fifteen or twenty paintings a year, and several gift shops carried her prints, postcards, and notepaper depicting local scenes, all consistent sellers.

It wasn't that she needed the money. Alan had been very generous in the divorce and had cheerfully divided his considerable assets in half, signing the house completely over to her. "Guilt money," Beth's attorney called it. It wasn't money she needed from her work, but something else, less tangible and much more important. Maybe it was recognition, or perhaps the opportunity finally to emerge from Alan's formidable shadow.

Satisfied with the painting, she packed up her things and called to Jasper. Jasper had been Alan's dog, an old springer spaniel, left behind when his adored master had walked out. Chloe was allergic to dogs. Jasper usually went to work with Kit, but this morning he had trailed along with Beth instead.

The route home took her through the village, where she stopped for tea and muffins at Begley's. Upon leaving the café, she spied Ed Talbot and waved. Ed was a lobsterman and father of her son's close friend Jack. Windy Harbor was just as its name implied, a town built around a harbor. Main Street ran north to south, the southern end running smack dab into the water, its long piers stretching for almost a quarter mile into the bay. In keeping with an old whaling village, the narrow streets were lined with all manner of Cape Cod architecture. A few larger homes were sandwiched in between Capes and colonials, some with porches trimmed with lacy gingerbread. Widow walks crowned a number of the larger homes' mansard roofs.

Beth and her family did not live in the village proper, but in an outlying area known to the locals as Hen and Chicks. So named because of its peculiar topography—a large knoll, the Hen, surrounded by many smaller hills, the Chicks—the area had originally been part of a three-hundred-acre estate. When the original landowner sold off the rolling woods and fields, he had divided the property into five- and ten-acre lots. Most of those original boundaries remained today.

Soon after their son's marriage, Alan's parents had purchased a five-acre lot for the young couple, and the newlyweds built their home together. Both Rhode Island School of Design graduates, they had definite ideas about the house's design. Their collaboration had produced a comfortable, light-filled home, a sort of adapted saltbox with a few extra interesting angles.

As the family expanded from two to five, they added on several times, but each addition succeeded in retaining the shingled charm of the original structure. No longer boxy, the house now crawled out both east and west, hugging the landscape that surrounded it. Like the brambles and beach roses growing in wild profusion around the property, the additions appeared to have sprouted from the sandy soil, fed by the passage of time and pruned by the winds.

To the north, a freestanding barn served as a two-car garage and woodshop. Alan's summer project their third year in the house, the barn had been built entirely of salvaged wood taken from several city demolition sites. Alan's one request in the divorce settlement had been to have access to the woodshop. While his furniture workshop was attached to his new home, he still kept machinery and an enormous collection of tools in the barn.

The rear of the house faced south toward open fields dotted with fruit trees. Beyond the fields, woods stretched for miles. It was common land held jointly by all owners of Hens and Chicks property. The common land would always remain a wilderness populated by deer, foxes, coyotes, and smaller mammals as well as countless species of birds. Situated along the Atlantic Flyway, Windy Harbor played host to thousands of migrating birds with the changing of the seasons. The small pond at the back of their property had afforded them hours of bird watching over the years.

Beyond the pond, in the southeast corner of the property, Beth's studio stood alone, surrounded by fields of Queen Anne's lace and goldenrod. Built by Alan as a present on their tenth wedding anniversary, its exterior was weathered shingles like the house. The large, airy one-room studio welcomed light through floor-to-ceiling windows on all four sides; its north wall was one huge expanse of glass. Whitewashed barn boards covered the interior walls. There were a small bathroom, a refrigerator, a hot plate, and a black slate sink for washing up, but few other amenities.

A dilapidated couch and chairs were arranged around an enormous, threadbare Oriental rug that had belonged to Beth's grandmother. Dominated by shades of burgundy and dark blues and yellows, the carpet ran to the very edges of the wide pine floors. The only other furnishings were two bookcases and a massive white Hoosier cupboard housing her paints and supplies. Two easels supported works in progress at opposite ends of the room. Warm in the winter and breezy in the summer, the studio was Beth's spiritual home. It was here where her soul resided, at peace, while she worked.

A driveway stretched around to the back of the studio so she could bring in supplies by car, but generally she walked from home to the studio along the gravel path through her gardens. A profusion of perennials lined the path—hollyhocks, delphinium, asters, baby's breath, statice, yarrow, coreopsis, foxgloves, and many varieties of flowering bushes. Every year she added a few new plantings, and her labors rewarded her with riotous color from early spring to late fall.

As she pulled the car to a stop alongside the house, she heard laughter and shouting coming from the barn. "Fuck you, too, Hadley!" he called, emerging from the side door covered in sawdust.

"Jack? Is that you under all those shavings?"

"Mrs. H., hi," he said, grinning sheepishly as he spotted her. "Sorry about that—the yelling, I mean. We're almost through in there, and we were foolin' around. We'll clean everything up."

"Where are you, Talbot? You chicken shit!" Kit called, crashing through the door. "Uh-oh, Mom, hey."

"Hey yourself. Taking a little break, are you?"

"Sort of…well. Really, we're finished, aren't we, Jack?"

"Yup." The other smiled a beautiful, open smile that Beth returned.

Jack and Kit were on the same construction crew, and they spent nearly every waking moment together.

It was an unusual friendship. Jack was fifteen years older, one of the harbor boys who had never grown up. On off-moments, Jack and Kit worked for Beth. Their current project involved cleaning out the barn loft, hauling junk to the dump to clear storage space. In a year or two, she and her sister planned on selling their mother's cottage, Hestor's Way. At that time, she would need the room to store everything from the cottage. Lanie would have no use for it in her Boston apartment, but Beth was certain her sister would not allow Beth to dispose of or sell one stick of furniture, one piece of chipped crockery, one moldy, moth-eaten blanket, or one spineless, dog-eared Agatha Christie novel, at least not right away.

Jack had filled out the past few months. Looking at him, Beth experienced the same sensation as when she regarded her son. With his sandy hair covered with sawdust, broad shoulders straining the fabric of his faded blue work shirt, he was a handsome man indeed.

"How 'bout some lunch, you two?"

"Great, sure, Mom. Just let us clean up this mess and we'll be in."

They joined her several minutes later, still talking and laughing. Both had changed into tee shirts and swim trunks.

"We gonna head out after lunch, if it's okay. Go out on Pete's boat, fishing or diving."

"Lucky you. What can I fix you? I've got turkey, cheese, avocados, lettuce, tomatoes, tuna fish?"

"What about veggie burgers?" Kit asked, rummaging in the freezer.

Beth watched him, wondering what or who had turned him into a vegetarian overnight. "You might find a package in the downstairs freezer. Run down and check. That what you want, Jack?"

"I'd take a turkey sandwich, if you have enough," he said, coming to stand beside her. "I can make it, though."

"Okay, I've got pita bread here, and there's whole wheat in the freezer. White and Italian, too." Stepping aside, she continued to assemble ingredients for her own lunch, a pita pocket stuffed with slices of avocado, lettuce, tomatoes, and alfalfa sprouts. As she worked, she popped wedges of luscious, ripe tomato into her mouth. Kit finally appeared, proudly displaying a package of soy burgers in hand. "Anyone want a slice of tomato? These early ones are from Wilson's stand, and they're incredible."

Kit wrinkled his nose, making a face. "No thanks, Mom."

For reasons Beth could never fathom, all of her children disliked fresh tomatoes. Much as they loved Italian cooking and tomato-based sauces, none would willingly eat an uncooked, "raw tomatoes," as Nanny called them.

"I'll take one," Jack said, both hands occupied as he constructed a monstrous turkey club sandwich.

Laughing, Beth popped a thick tomato wedge into his mouth. "Here, I'll slice a few more for your sandwich."

"Thanks, Mrs. H.," he mumbled, tomato juice trickling from the corner of his mouth.

"Not too much of a slob, are you, Talbot?" Kit elbowed him as he reached over to pop his soy burger into the microwave.

"People who do not appreciate the sensual pleasure of a fresh, ripe tomato should not call people slobs."

"There you go again, always taking his side! You'd think *he* was the favorite son." Kit threw up his hands in mock dismay.

"No, but he is a guest."

Her lunch assembled, Beth poured three tall glasses of iced tea and retreated to the terrace. To her surprise, the boys joined her. Pleased at the unexpected company, she rose and made room for Jack at the end of the chaise longue.

"So, I just saw your dad in town. How's the rest of the Talbot family?"

"Great. Dick and Perry are away at camp for two weeks, in New Hampshire, and Caitlin's working at the marina, in the bait shop."

"How old is she now?"

"Nineteen."

"Amazing. It seems like only yesterday your mom was pushing her in the stroller."

"Mom, you're doing it again. You promised, no more living in the way-distant past."

"Oops, sorry, you're right."

She turned away, hiding unexpected tears. The summer had been a roller-coaster ride of ups and downs as she anticipated losing yet another of her children. He was right. She had been reminiscing about the past lately, with too many references to her babies, and she knew it was wearing thin with Kit. Despite his mother's protests, her son felt guilty abandoning his household obligations and worried constantly about who would take his place when he left in September.

Sensing the tension between mother and son, Jack intervened as he always did, lightening the mood. "So, what project do you have for us next, Mrs. H.?"

"The basement," she replied, turning back to her sandwich. "It needs the same going over as the barn. And there are a bunch of boxes you guys can take over to Mr. Hadley's. Old books, college notebooks, sketchbooks and things. I'll see what he says, but if I know Alan, he'll want them all."

"I doubt they'll fit with Chloe's décor," Kit muttered, taking a last bite of veggie burger.

It was on the tip of her tongue to ask how he knew so much about Chloe's décor when he had supposedly never set foot in his father's new home, but she stayed silent, not wishing to provoke an argument in front of Jack.

CHAPTER 3

"No, Rick," she said for the tenth time. "I'm taking Nanny and her friends to the beach. Period."

"Beth, be reasonable. If I can set something up with Margot this afternoon, it might be the break we need, *you* need. Sweetheart, I'm serious. She'll be making her decision about the gallery's fall schedule soon. They've gotta print programs, get the right people here."

"It's Nanny's birthday. We're having a beach picnic, then a family dinner, and that's enough. It's a perfect beach day, by the way. Wanta join us?"

"Just what I need, a bunch of teenage girls screaming in my ear. Thanks, but no thanks. I'll just sit here and weep over missed opportunities. Not to mention all the precious hours you're wasting away from your easel."

"Don't sound so despondent, dear agent of mine. You can always meet with Margot by yourself. You have the portfolio. I trust you. Besides, you'll do better without me. You always do."

"Bullshit. Margot likes to bond with her artists, not their underpaid, unappreciated agents."

Giving up, she sighed, the futility of further argument clear. "Rick's a bulldog," Alan had told her five years earlier when he had recommended that Beth hire him. Alan had been right. "Alright, you win, dearest. Go ahead and set something up with Margot for another day this week. Any day but Friday is fine with me."

"Hmm, I'll see what I can do. I am going into the city tomorrow. Maybe Margot and I can muddle through today alone."

"That's the spirit. And remember, we'd still love to have you stop at the beach for a piece of birthday cake."

"Gritty butter icing—now, isn't that tempting?"

"Bring Gary along. It'll be fun."

"Get real, girl. Gary, sand, water? No way. He's working, and besides, he'd spoil the party with all his complaining. Been in a filthy mood lately. Impossible to live with."

The two men had moved in together a year after Beth and Alan's marriage, and the occasional separation notwithstanding, their relationship had endured.

"Good luck with Margot," she said, hanging up.

He really has gone crazy over this Lynch Gallery show, she decided as she keyed in her friend Clarice's number. It was not the end of the world if Margot Lynch turned her down. A disappointment, yes, but there would be other shows.

"Hey, Clary."

"Who the hell's been talking on your phone?"

Clarice never bothered with hellos.

"I've been calling for hours."

She was a shameless exaggerator.

"Sorry, Rick's been haranguing me about the Lynch show."

"Time for you to invest in call waiting, dearie, or keep your cell phone charged and on. With three teenagers, you need to be reachable at all times. What's the story with Miz Margot? You're a shoo-in for that show. The gallery would be lucky to get you, for Christ's sake. Besides, I have it on good authority that Miz Margot no longer makes the decisions."

"Oh?" Beth sat back, waiting for the gossip that was sure to follow. Clarice despised Margot Lynch. The two strong-minded women had served on too many committees together, usually taking opposing sides on whatever issue arose. There was no love lost between them.

Beth and Clarice had been roommates at the Rhode Island School of Design and had stayed in touch over the years. After years in the Midwest, Clarice and Ben had moved back east to Providence, Rhode Island, where Ben had grown up and where they'd both gone to college.

They had rented a small apartment in Providence, an hour's drive from Windy Harbor, but six months later they packed up again. Like Beth and Alan, they had wanted to start a family. Clarice, a very successful freelance silversmith, whose studio was at home, convinced Ben that a move to Windy Harbor "was best for the children," so Ben commuted to his graphic arts studio in a converted mill building in the south end of Providence.

"Yup," Clary continued. "Margot the Magnanimous has ceded all decision-making to the prodigal son, returned from the wilds of Chicago."

"You mean Graham?"

"None other. I'm surprised Rick didn't mention it. Surely he knows? Maybe not. I know cause we ran into him the other night. Better call Rick, hon, or he'll waste a lot of time sucking up to the wrong person."

She laughed. "I'll let him find out himself. At least he'll be off my back for a while. Graham, you say? I had no idea he was back. Why, it's been years since I've…"

"He's still gorgeous, by the way. We saw him at the Butlers' last night. Salt-and-pepper, but otherwise he looks the same. It's been how many years since he was back in the area?"

"Well, Nanny's fourteen, so that's it—fourteen, at least, as far as I know."

Several weeks after Nanny's birth, Graham Lynch had come to see Alan. Her body hidden under a shapeless muumuu, Beth had excused herself immediately and left the two men to catch up. Graham had been Alan's best man, but as the years passed, the two friends had drifted apart. That had been just fine with Beth because, from the moment she met the shy, slightly awkward friend of Alan's youth, she was inexplicably drawn to him. Despite the fact that she and Alan were wildly in love, the unreasonable, surprising attraction persisted, and she never completely trusted herself to be alone with Graham. Some years later, she had greeted the news of his marriage to a high-powered Chicago attorney with a mixture of relief and jealousy, glad at least that they would be living halfway across the country.

"From all the reports, he's home for good," Clarice continued. "So you're a sure bet for the show no matter what Mommy Dearest says. You guys go back a long way, don't you?"

"I'm sure that will have no bearing on his decision. After all, the Lynch is not the Guild."

She referred to the Harbor Arts Guild founded by herself and eight other local artists. The group had pooled their resources and purchased a small garage in the village center, which they had converted into a small gallery where they could exhibit and sell their artwork. Alan was not a member of the Guild. His furniture, too pricey for Windy Harbor, went directly to a gallery in New York City. Even so, Alan had provided much of the capital and completed the lion's share of carpentry work for the building's restoration.

"That's right. It's not as cool or prestigious as the Guild!"

"Very funny. The Lynch has a national reputation. They can't be handing out favors to old friends."

"Beth, get real. Who are they gonna get who's more talented than you?"

"Thousands of people. Almost anyone. Let's drop this, okay? I've got a lot to do, and I'm calling about Carrie. Want us to swing by for her on our way to the beach?"

"That'd be great. I'm swamped here. Probably won't make it down to the beach after all. I'm sorry."

"That's okay," Beth said, secretly glad. Once the girls were fed, they would run off and leave her with her book for an hour or so. "I'll catch up on all your news tomorrow night. Hope it's good weather. We're all looking forward to our first beach cookout of the summer."

"Ben's dragging me over there tonight to watch the fireworks. Just the two of us, because the kids are going in four different directions."

"Mmm, romantic."

"Yeah, the two of us and several hundred horny teenagers."

Beth laughed. "You'll fit right in. If I know Ben, he'll find a secluded spot."

After thirty years of marriage, Ben and Clarice were still honeymooners.

"Ha. See you in a few minutes, then." The change in the voice she knew so well told Beth her friend was blushing.

Two hours later, Beth was serving chicken salad rolls and sodas to Nanny and four friends under the shade of an enormous blue-and-white-striped umbrella. She had brought china, a linen tablecloth, and napkins, and they were sipping soda from Beth's best crystal. Nanny had requested an "elegant beach picnic," and she was getting it.

"Thanks," Chrissie Moniz mumbled through a mouthful of chicken salad.

Dark-skinned, raven-haired, Chrissie's voluptuous body stretched her tiny lime-green bikini to its limits. Her dark eyes twinkled as she added, "This is the best, Mrs. Hadley. Nanny is so lucky."

"Mom's gonna be pissed she missed this," Carrie Rollins added, smiling at Beth.

She had her mother's enormous blue eyes, but otherwise Carrie was the image of her father. Her easy smile a mirror of his own, her complexion, while not the deep chocolate-brown of Ben's, was still a far cry from her fair-skinned mother's. She, too, wore a bikini, hers looser, less well-defined, on her flat-chested, boyish frame. Her long, reddish hair cascaded in ringlets to her waist and was tied back in a loose ponytail with a twist tie she had borrowed from Beth.

"I'll catch up with her tomorrow night, but I don't think I'll bring these wineglasses across the way." Beth referred to the beach across the harbor's channel, reachable only by boat, where they went for summer cookouts.

After the sandwiches, a tiny marble cake appeared, which the girls devoured down to the last crumb. Then, hopping up, they declared themselves ready for a walk. As Carrie and Crissie headed off, Nanny lingered behind.

"Thanks, Mom. It was great!"

Beth smiled. "Having a good day so far?"

"The best!"

"There's more coming."

"I know. Thanks for having Dad. I know you'd rather not."

"Nonsense. I'll enjoy every minute of your party. Tonight's focus is on a certain fourteen-year-old, I believe, not on a couple of old divorcés."

"It still hurts, doesn't it?"

The question startled Beth, and she peered into the blue eyes, wondering at the reason for her daughter's question. Nanny had never wanted to talk about the divorce, and Beth and Alan hadn't pressed her. Three years ago, the two older children had had endless questions, demanding almost continual updates, but Nanny had said little, seeming to accept the divorce like she did everything, with an easygoing affability. An almost innate sense of security seemed to carry Nanny through the crisis; however, recently she had had her first boyfriend and subsequently her first heartbreak.

Beth brushed errant strands of sandy hair from her daughter's cheek. "Yes, it does sometimes, but not like three years ago. It's much smoother sailing now."

"You'd still rather not see him. I know that."

"Sweetheart, this is different," she replied, cupping the smooth, soft chin in her hand. "This is your birthday. Remember Kat's last fall? We had a great time, didn't we?"

"Yeah, except you looked like you were gonna throw up all the way up and back in the car."

Laughing at the idea of vomiting all over Alan, Beth said, "Don't worry. We're not traveling by car tonight, and I'm going to have a great time at your party. Honest. Dad, too."

"Not Kit."

"Of course he is. You know Kit. He's still angry with Dad."

"Hates him. He does, Mom, so don't even try to deny it. Chloe too, especially Chloe."

"Nanny, your brother doesn't hate Dad. He's just going through a rough time. He's about to leave for college, and he's worried about us and who'll take his place. He's tried so hard the last three years to fill Dad's shoes."

"I'll say. Thinks he can boss me around worse than Dad ever did."

Leaning over to hug her, Beth said, "Well, don't worry. He'll be fine tonight. He's just tired out from his job, and you know when Kit gets tired he gets a little testy."

"Plus he stays out till dawn with Jack and the guys."

"You'd better scoot off and catch up to the girls. Remember, this is your party. We'll have a great time tonight. Don't worry."

If Dad behaves, she thought, watching Nanny run down to the beach after the others, her compact, sturdy frame in sharp contrast to her taller companions. All except Nanny wore bikinis. Except for Carrie's, they left little to the imagination, especially from the rear. Nanny, who declared bikinis to be uncomfortable and silly, wore a navy racing tank. She swam two miles every day of the summer.

Yes, Beth thought again, pulling out her book and leaning back in her beach chair. *If Dad behaves, we'll have a lovely time. Miracles can happen.*

And Alan did behave, through most of the evening, at least.